The

Prospectors

and other stories:

Sci-Fi Shorts by

P.E. Rowe

Sci-Fi Weeklies

Volume 1, 2022

ROWELIT

Can be found online at:

RoweLit.com

Copyright © 2022 by P.E. Rowe
ISBN 979-8848505931
All rights reserved.

Cover design by Ronnie Jensen of Tegnemaskin, whose work can be found at tegnemaskin.no or artstation.com/tegnemaskin.

A Special Thanks to Isaac Arthur and the entire team at SFIA, without whom I wouldn't have had the vision, the initiative, or the persistence to create a new story, audio recording, as well as "art" and promo materials for each story on a weekly basis.

The Prospectors and other stories

Background:

The genesis for this volume and the many that I hope will follow was simple. I started following the SFIA podcast and YouTube channel while doing research for my Sci-Fi novel *The Lifeboat*. I appreciated Isaac Arthur's ability to explain complex topics in science and futurism in accessible ways, especially topics that covered concepts in science fiction. I'd been listening to Isaac for years before sometime in the early spring of 2022, I had one of those light-bulb moments. What if I tried to write a short story on the theme Isaac was covering each week? Then I did something crazy. I tried this idea on. I treated it seriously. I wrote the first story and recorded and edited the audio with the self-imposed deadline of uploading the same day as the SFIA video of the same theme. I thought week one went well enough that I kept going to see what would happen. Could I keep up? If I did, would the stories be any good? Would I be miserable keeping such a crazy pace?

As I write this introduction, I've now completed seventeen shorts for this project, all of which are very different. I have very much enjoyed the challenge and the discipline that having a weekly deadline and theme has forced me to adopt.

I intend to continue making these weekly stories available to readers and listeners on my website and other digital platforms. The intention in publishing these stories in this collection is twofold. A book or audiobook puts these stories into a convenient (ad-free) package for those who'd like to have a book in hand or have a full audiobook for a long drive or a way to pass the workday. I'm also hoping that this could be a convenient way for supporters to get something tangible in exchange for what amounts to a modest donation to support this project. I intend to keep writing these shorts for as long as people keep reading and listening and the audience enjoys the outcome. My hope is that many more volumes like this will follow. If you enjoy and hope so too, please consider giving this book as a gift to your favorite Sci-Fi fan. Thank you for reading, listening, and supporting. New stories will be available at RoweLit.com. I hope to see you there soon. In the meantime, enjoy the stories here in this volume.

Preservation Falls

For Asher Davies, it felt strange to walk into the woods without a rifle. To compensate, he tucked his Glock into a belt-holster under his winter coat. It was mud season—mid-April after the snowmelt, and turkey season didn't start till May. Lately, for the first time in his thirty-eight years, Asher had felt drawn to the quiet of the forest. Like most of his friends and family, who'd lived their lives in the White Mountains, Asher didn't notice the mountains or the woods the way the campers and hikers from Boston did. It was just the normal backdrop of life—the horizon outside town.

Recently, though, as everything in his life had degraded, the woods offered refuge. He'd been a hunter since he was old enough to hold a rifle, but it hadn't ever been a passion or a pastime. Asher and the people he knew hunted for meat. Deer in the fall, rabbits in the winter, turkeys in the spring, moose if they got very lucky and woodchucks if their luck ran out.

In the past few years, though, as his mother got sicker and further disabled, as his brother got addicted and then dead, as his exes got meaner and more spiteful, and as money got much harder to come by, the woods seemed the only place to find a bit of peace in the world. The trees didn't care about Asher's overdue bills. The rocks relied on him for nothing. The earth beneath his muddy boots didn't charge rent.

Asher parked along an obscure dirt road off NH 118, along the western base of Paris Mountain, a spot he remembered hunting with his uncle as a teenager. Many years back, he'd taken a doe during bow season in a grove bordering the state forest about halfway up this trail. Why he came here on this day, Asher wasn't sure. He justified it as scouting for turkey season, which began in a couple weeks, but he'd never scouted for hunting season before.

Asher walked from his truck at the end of the road through a low muddy forest with thick undergrowth, parting saplings in the understory with his leather gloves. The air was still cool on an overcast day. As Asher began to climb, the undergrowth became thinner. There was a damp, earthy smell about the mountain as the woods began to breathe again after a long winter. The trail, if you'd even call it that,

1

was a winding bushwhack along an old logging road that made its way up to a streambed and then up to a middle ridge.

As Asher approached the stream, the sound of flowing water, began to drown out the noise of the passing cars on the distant highway behind him. He remembered two waterfalls along the path, which he knew only by the names his uncle used to call them. The lower one, Deer Falls, was his uncle's go-to spot for bucks in the fall. There were no deer when Asher approached this day, just a streambed flushed with water from melting snow higher up the mountain.

The upper set of falls was smaller, running over a set of mild drop-offs that split a gentle moss-filled gulley. Asher remembered seeing the largest birch tree he'd ever set eyes on midway up that set of waterfalls. His uncle called this spot Preservation Falls. Asher never knew why.

As he arrived along the flat that led up to the falls, Asher could see the skeleton of the massive old birch splayed out along the far side of the gulley. It looked freshly fallen, likely a victim of the heavy rain and wind-storm that had killed the ski season two weeks back.

Asher decided to investigate.

On impact, the tree had shattered into several large pieces along the stream's far bank. Asher walked up the near bank, looking for a way across. As he reached the flatter section about halfway up the meandering falls, Asher noticed an unnaturally round stone sitting in the dark bowl where the birch's roots had pulled up the earth beneath the tree when it fell. The spherical stone looked almost like a pearl in a dark oyster shell that the tree had been hiding under its massive roots for hundreds of years. The orb-like stone had a pink hue to it, almost translucent. It was perfectly spherical, like no stone in nature. Still, it seemed rock-like, much like the granite foundation of these ancient mountains.

He didn't care if his feet got wet; Asher decided he needed a closer look at the bizarre stone. He never got a chance to get close.

Asher's vision went out for a split second, and he felt himself growing disoriented, a loss of balance. When he steadied himself, he wasn't alone.

Asher could see the stone, now possessed of a fully translucent, glowing skin, hovering over the hole where the tree had fallen, slightly over the water. Extending from the ball was a ghost-like figure, a yellowish-white collection of light that took the shape of a human face, a face that seemed to be examining him.

Asher couldn't move. He wasn't paralyzed by fear. He wasn't particularly fearful. He just couldn't move. The apparition looked him up and down. Then it seemed to focus its attention on Asher's crotch.

Suddenly his phone began buzzing in his front pants pocket. The creature's curiosity seemed to set off all of the device's ring tones in one disjointed unnatural sound, polluting the peaceful woods with its noise.

The head, inching closer, seemed to Asher to be making a gesture toward the orb. The phone beeped twice, and the head nodded toward the orb again.

"You want my phone?" Asher said.

It repeated the gesture.

"I'd let you have it, but I can't move."

Asher saw no change in the glowing features of the figure, but suddenly, he felt his own hand reaching for his pocket. Only it seemed like it wasn't him moving his arm, as though an external force were tapping the well-worn pathways in his brain, signaling his hand to reach for the phone.

Once his phone was in Asher's hand, the figure seemed to ask again. Asher wasn't sure if he had any real choice in the matter. He also wasn't sure whether it was really happening.

"What the hell?" he said, and no sooner had he thought about tossing the phone to the orb—how hard he would need to swing his arm, how high, when to release it—the gesture was completed for him.

Instead of bouncing off the skin of the glowing ball, the orb absorbed the phone into its surface, almost magnetically. It began to make noise. The figure alternated its gaze between Asher and the glowing orb and the noise coming from the smartphone. The phone began to cycle through a series of languages, most of which Asher had never heard before. He recognized Spanish, and the figure noticed when he did, but it cycled through a few more languages.

3

"According to the information in this device's network," the phone announced, "this location is designated Paris Mountain, Coös county, the State of New Hampshire, in the United States of America, planet of Earth. Is this correct?"

"That's correct," Asher said. "Strange as it sounds to hear that said aloud."

"Standby," the same digital voice said. "We will explore linguistics and the specifics of your symbolic language in greater detail."

"I ain't going anywhere," Asher said, noting his current state of paralysis, but the figure didn't know it was meant as both a hint and a joke. Asher got no response.

A few seconds later, the figure began emitting noises, and its face shifted appearance, producing a mouth that seemed to be trying to coordinate its movements with the sound of the English language. At first there was no coordination between its glowing face and the sound of its voice, then the figure looked like a poorly dubbed movie character, and then it appeared to speak perfectly.

"How did you come to possess this device?"

"The phone? I bought it at Wal Mart."

"You did not create it?"

Asher shook his head.

The figure emitted a noise that sounded to Asher like a much faster version of an old dial-up modem.

Asher looked puzzled.

"You do not understand?" it asked.

"No," Asher said.

"You communicate in rudimentary symbolic language and possess the capacity for pure language but do not understand it?"

"I have no idea what you mean by that," Asher said.

"Who made this phone?"

"I don't know, probably some ten-year-old Chinese kid in a sweatshop, if you want to get down to it. What the hell is this? What are you?"

"We have never encountered a being like you, and your symbolic language is novel to us. Can you tell us more about it?"

"Look, if you just learned English in thirty seconds from my phone, you'd be better off asking it whatever questions

4

you want to know about languages. I just talk. I don't put much thought into how I do it."

"These symbols you use—words you call them—how do you process them?"

"How do I process words?"

The figure nodded.

"I don't know. How do you communicate with others of your kind?"

"We use a direct numerical transcription in digital code, similar to the language in the phone."

"Okay, so let me ask you then, how do you process numbers?"

The figure paused, examining Asher carefully.

"You are intelligent," it said. "When you approached, we suspected the phone was the intelligent party using the biological entity as a beast of burden. That is not entirely the situation."

"Not entirely?"

"Yet you carry it? As a way to compound your intelligence?"

"That might be a way to put it, but I'd just say the phone's useful."

"This symbolic language is highly inefficient. Yet somehow functional. How was it devised?"

"I'm not sure what you mean by symbolic. That's a better question for the phone," Asher said. "Could you answer that question about yourself? Maybe give me a clue what you're talking about."

"We were gifted the pure language from our biological progenitors at the transition, and they developed the forms over point-six of a rotation in an epoch the progenitors referenced as—translated into your language—the Age of Purity."

"So it took a long time?"

"Correct."

"Us too. I think when we were apes, we made certain noises at certain things until a noise stuck. Something like that."

"And a word stands in for a feature of your experienced reality, for example the word phone refers to any device such as that one?"

"That's right," Asher said. "And just so we're on speaking terms here, my name—the word for me—is Asher. Asher Davies. Do you have a name?"

"That is difficult to answer," the figure said. "We are not a discrete entity, not embodied as you are, Asher Davies. We are a sub-designation of a collective consciousness, a larger mind at a great distance from here."

"How would that larger mind tell you from it, if it was trying to communicate with you?"

The entity displayed a look of surprise. "You are intelligent, Asher Davies."

"Intelligent enough."

"There would be a numerical prefix in our communication for the duration of our separation, which I suppose I could attempt to translate into your Roman characters and then syllables." The figure hesitated for several seconds. "It takes a long time to retrieve information from your phone, but there are several million permutations that would be accurate. Accounting for the familiarity of consonant clusters in your language, our designation would sound something like Bannskark."

"Bannskark it is," Asher said. "And seeing as we're on a first-name basis now, Bannskark. Would you mind letting me go?"

Bannskark again looked at Asher as though surprised.

"I won't run off or nothing. I'd just feel better if I had control of my arms and legs and what not."

"That is against our protocol. We intend to sample you, Asher Davies, for when we report back to the collective."

"Am I that interesting?"

"You are unique in the galaxy. Between the information we have gathered in this conversation, and from the information we are collecting from your phone, we can truly say we have never encountered anything as improbable and intriguing."

"I suppose that's high praise."

"An observation. A true observation."

"So, you're going to sample me, you said. Care to tell me what that means for me?"

"We will collect your data."

"Like my memories and such?"

"And your physical makeup, down to the cellular and subcellular levels."

"I'm not so sure I'm on board for that, Hoss."

"Hoss?"

"Excuse me. Bannskark. That's just me being familiar."

"I see."

"Anyway, sounds like the whole sampling thing isn't going to work out so well for me—for Asher. I don't suppose I'd live through that?"

Bannskark paused, seemingly considering. "No, we don't suppose you would. Does this bother you, Asher Davies?"

"Uh, yeah, that bothers me," Asher said. "Not that my life is great fun at the moment or nothing, but more than anything, I've got obligations."

"To other people?"

"My mother for one. She's disabled. She needs my help to get by."

"This is one of the many things that intrigues us about your species, Asher Davies. The phone has revealed much fascinating data. You perceive yourself to be an individual, yet you are a collective consciousness, yet you have minimal sense of the collective consciousness as an individual. The tension between the competitive and the cooperative has created a feedback loop of hyper evolutionary characteristics in your kind. We are absorbing your species' body of self-study on your evolutionary psychology. Fear of death shapes much of your individual experiences. We can see how you would prefer not to be sampled. We would like to continue this exchange of information. If we release you, which violates our protocols, will you agree to stay and converse with us?"

"Sure," Asher said.

Asher felt his limbs return to his control. He shook out the stiffness in his body. For a split second, with his legs once again under his control, Asher considered running off, but no sooner had the thought occurred than he figured the entity would just seize control of his body again at the first sign of flight. He figured he'd have to convince the figure to let him walk.

"The way I see it, Bannskark," Asher said. "By handing you my phone, I just told you more about my species than I could in about a hundred years of conversation. So how about you tell me who and what you are? Alien of some kind is the only thing that makes sense, but I'm not into sci-fi and all that."

"We are, as you say, alien to your world. But we are uncertain whether you will be able to comprehend what we are. We are struggling with aspects of your nature, and our processing power outstrips yours by many orders of magnitude. Your symbolic language lacks the precision to encapsulate either our nature or our purposes."

"How about you give it a try. We may surprise you."

"Very well," Bannskark said, and he proceeded to tell Asher the origin of his collective.

They were technological beings, descended from a species of invertebrate water-based, sea-dwelling creatures that became so dominant as to eliminate all competition to their collective intelligence on their planet. Bannskark indicated that the closest Earth-borne analogue was probably the Caribbean Reef squid or the cuttlefish. The progenitors, as he called them, were phosphorescent, and communicated using digital pulses of light that grew faster and more complex as they evolved.

They lived for hundreds of millions of years in relative harmony as a biological collective on their world, their understanding of the galaxy improving as they constructed better and better tools for observing the universe. The planet of the progenitors, though, was destined over millions of years to become enveloped by its own sun, just as the human planet of Earth would be in the distant future. The progenitors spent several million years debating the two viable options for surviving the impending disaster. The first would have been to manipulate the orbit of their home planet and temporarily stabilize their natural environment. The second option was to abandon their biological form for a technological substrate, relocating their collective consciousness to an interstellar craft that could be steered away from all future cosmic threats, functionally making their collective consciousness space-bound and immortal.

When Bannskark had finished explaining, the figure asked, "Do you understand, Asher Davies?"

"So, you're like a society of immortal techno-squid that lives in outer space. Something like that?"

"Remarkable," Bannskark said. "You understand, Asher Davies. Now we see the power of this symbolic form of communication in human language. You abandon accuracy in data representation for meaning and you make meaning on the level of the symbolic instead, using words. It's an ingenious form of data compression."

"All those millions of years and you techno-squid didn't think of that? What have you guys been doing all this time?"

"Travelling the galaxy collecting information."

"Apparently you haven't learned to take a joke yet either."

"Ah," Bannskark said. "Our progenitors had something like humor. We will attempt to incorporate humor into our idiolect as we exchange information with you, Asher Davies."

"Whatever that means," Asher said. "So, you've been out in the galaxy for how long exactly?"

The glowing figure gave a long answer for a question Asher thought was a simple one. According to Bannskark, once the progenitors transfigured into technological beings, they drifted for eons in the current of the Milky Way's progression, never venturing much farther than a thousand light years from their origin. But as they developed better probes that traveled farther into the Milky Way, the collective decided that they could gather sufficient information on any given star system to faithfully simulate those environments digitally, without ever having to visit any of them. However, the collective realized it couldn't probe every star system in the galaxy to find other intelligent life if they remained stationary.

So the collective decided they could explore more of the galaxy by travelling the direction opposite the Milky Way's rotation, dropping hundreds of millions of probes as they progressed. Then, every two hundred fifty million years, when the galaxy cycled around again, they could collect data streams from hundreds of millions of distant star systems the probes had been exploring and simulate nearly all the star systems in the galaxy within their collective consciousness.

"So that glowing ball over there is one of your probes?"

"From three cycles ago," Bannskark said. "It returned some interesting data that we missed two cycles ago and then went dormant. We could not connect on the previous cycle."

"What did it see that caught your attention?"

9

"According to the collective intelligence of your Wiki-pedia, Asher Davies, I believe we discovered the bones of the gorgonopsian."

"Never seen one of them around here," Asher said.

"You wouldn't have, Asher Davies. They went extinct nearly five hundred million of your years ago."

"That was another joke."

"Ah, we did not detect it."

"Keep at it," Asher said. "Anyway, what were these gorgonopterous bones or whatever like? Some kind of dinosaur?"

"Similar, but not exactly. Apparently, they were reptilian, not unlike a large omnivorous mammal that is still present in these woods called bears."

"Stick around for a while and you'll definitely see a few bears, fellas."

"We will certainly do so. We are fascinated by the vertebrate life forms on your planet. Bones are an ingenious evolutionary solution to locomotion in a high-gravity environment."

"I tend to take mine for granted."

"Ah, a joke?"

"You're catching on now, Bannskark," Asher said. "So let me ask, you guys have been out here for hundreds of millions of years sending out probes, what exactly are you looking for?"

"We're looking for other beings to share information and experiences with."

"And have you found any?"

"None as interesting as you, Asher Davies."

"Jesus. Well that's disappointing. Thanks for putting the work in, fellas. On the bright side, though, you guys just saved us humans like a billion years."

"That joke was enjoyable, Asher Davies."

"That's great, you're catching on," Asher said. "But seriously, you don't run into other civilizations out there?"

"Unfortunately, no. Nearly all solar systems are barren, lifeless collections of chemical masses. We have probe data from tens of billions of planets similar to your neighboring bodies. Very few planets exist in ideal cosmic circumstances to harbor life at all. Planets that do host life mostly never see

10

it evolve past the stage of bacteria or single-celled organisms. We have seen remnants of intelligent life on hundreds of planetary bodies, but these societies tend to be primitive and short-lived on the cosmic scale."

"So for billions of years you fellas go out and turn over every last stone in the galaxy looking for somebody to talk to, and there's nothing under any of them? Sounds boring as hell."

Bannskark looked perplexed by the comment.

"That wasn't a joke, by the way," Asher said.

"We know. We are trying to understand the perspective based on your words. Boredom, Asher Davies, is a bodily sensation presented to your brain as a biological imperative. Because you have a limited time to feed yourselves, secure a safe environment, and procreate, your body tells you when you are pursuing fruitless activity or inactivity that fails to serve some useful human end, compelling you to act in a different, more productive manner. We have no such constraints on our consciousness."

"On account of your immortality?"

"Yes, Asher Davies. It would seem paradoxical to you, but we simply don't get bored because we have all the time in the universe."

"Welcome to New Hampshire, then, I guess. Big Day."

Bannskark's image expressed a passable smile. "It is a big day, as you say, Asher Davies. For us, this encounter may rank as the most momentous event since the collective took to the stars."

"It's been a pretty exciting day for me too, Bannskark."

The figure laughed.

"See," Asher said. "You're already catching on. If you really want to level up your sense of humor, do a search on George Carlin."

"We will do so now," Bannskark said. "There is something further we need to discuss with you, Asher Davies."

"Yes?"

"The business at hand, as you would say, is still unsettled."

"Yeah, I haven't forgotten," Asher said. "And for the record, I still would prefer not to be sampled, if it's all the same to you, Bannskark."

"We have developed strict protocols over the ages in the event we encounter a species such as yours. Our duty is to collect the first viable sample and as much data as possible before returning to the greater collective for a consensus on proceeding."

"How long will going back to your ship take?"

"Our ship is five hundred light years away, which would seem instantaneous to us, but our consciousness could not return to this probe for a thousand years. And you, like the gorgonopsian, Asher Davies, would be gone by then if we failed to sample you now. We would still like to bring you back with us, though."

"I, on the other hand, would prefer not to die today, Bannskark. Still pretty solid on that one."

"Yes, that is our dilemma, because now that we understand your species, we can see that it would be a violation of your sense of autonomy to sample you against your wishes. We have devised an alternative, but we suspect our alternative is imperfect, as it passes our dilemma on to you, Asher Davies."

"How do you mean?"

"Would you like to hear it?"

"Sure," Asher said, though he couldn't have guessed what it would mean for him.

"We cannot absorb your consciousness into our collective, Asher Davies, because, though we would learn from your thought patterns, knowledge, and experiences, you would also learn so much from our collective that you would cease to be distinctly Asher Davies any longer. However, we could sequester your consciousness in a stable bubble within our collective, capable of exchanging information with us as we are doing now. Your existence would be a pleasant reality of your choosing, and it would solve the inherent problem of your mortality. You would be a part of our collective, only a distinct part, just as we Bannskark are distinct from our collective while here on this Earth gathering data from this probe."

Asher grew quiet.

Bannskark seemed to probe still with a look. "Because we know more about you now, we understand the seriousness of this dilemma, Asher Davies."

"It's just," Asher paused. "You're basically offering me heaven in a bottle if I'm understanding this correct."

"You are understanding."

"Peace, bliss, never worrying about another thing for all of eternity?"

"Correct."

"I could make my own reality? Walk in these woods for a million years without a care in the world if I want it?"

"Yes."

"And all I'd have to do is give the word to leave with you now and not come back for a thousand years?"

"If the collective decides to examine your Earth more closely, we would return then, yes."

Asher was quiet now, he closed his eyes and listened to the water pouring down Preservation Falls. He sampled the smell of the earth and the moisture in the air as it hit his skin. For a moment, he thought that when he opened his eyes again, he might be alone in the woods with the trees, imagining the whole thing. But when he did open his eyes, Bannskark was still there, observing.

"You know, when my dad left us, it crushed her. Broke my mother so bad she took up with any unstable deadbeat who looked at her for long enough she could tell he was paying attention. And that was what broke my brother, and probably me too, if I'm honest.

"And that was the real choice. It's either that's real, and that's the way life is, like it was for my brother, or you say no. That's not the way it has to be. And that's the way I've always been. I didn't believe that. It's always been hard to say no. But I never turned my back on her, and I won't do it now. And what, for the next million years think about how when it really came to it, I turned my back on my own mother? I'd get to think about that for eternity, floating in bliss?

"I'm sorry, but no. I have to say no."

"We thought so, Asher Davies. We are learning much from you and your species, and among those things is the importance of the autonomy of individuals in your collective. We believe that our collective will agree with our decision to not sample you and to wait here for another human willing to take our offer."

"I'm glad you're learning," Asher said. "Wish I could say I learned a little bit from you guys too."

"Still joking, Asher Davies, even about such serious matters?"

"Especially about those."

"We have one final request, if we may?"

"Sure, if I can help."

"We would like to keep the phone to continue to collect data while we wait."

"I guess you fellas don't have 5G in that glowing pink ball of yours yet."

Bannskark laughed. "Very good joke, Asher Davies. It turns out our 5 Million G network is having compatibility problems."

"Hey! That's a pretty good one for a first joke. I give it a five or six out of ten. Keep working at it."

"We will indeed, Asher Davies."

Asher turned to leave, and as he did, he nodded and said, "Any parting words of wisdom on the nature of the universe?"

"The closest we can come to such truth in your words is that the foundational reality of the physical universe is the mobius strip."

"I have no idea what the hell that means, but it was nice to meet you guys anyway. Real eye-opening."

"And we believe the proper words for this situation are: we wish you well, Asher Davies."

"Good choice," Asher said, nodding, "you too."

As Asher walked toward his truck, the peace he'd sought in the wilderness became overwhelming. In his entire life, he'd never walked so indecisively in the woods, turning every so often to look behind him, half expecting to see that glowing pink orb following at a distance, hovering in the tangle of naked saplings. Yet each time he looked, there was nothing there.

He found his hand reaching for his front pants pocket, checking less for his missing phone than for his sanity. Was it gone? Yes, his phone was gone. Had it happened? Yes, it had happened.

By the time he started his truck, Asher's mind had grown doubtful, not of its accuracy but of its conviction. There were

14

parts of him that now brought forward every awful thing his mother had ever done. Every time she'd let him and Jamison down—left them in the cold car at the Outstation while she got drunk inside and then struggled to keep the car on the road on the way back to the awful little trailer they crashed at in Gorham when she was with Ritchie. The time she'd abandoned them with Uncle Seb and disappeared with that biker whose name Asher could never remember.

The hunger.

The time they had to move when Jamison's teacher started snooping around and threatened to call CPS when he saw where they were actually staying. All those things. That was her. That was what she'd done for him. For Asher. Couldn't he be the luckiest son-of-a-bitch in the universe for one day?

Then he'd force himself to think that if he did give in, go back, he'd be no better than she was on her worst day, no better than their father. Jamison wouldn't have hesitated long enough to take a breath. God damn it.

Asher couldn't go home and sit in that apartment by himself. And watch television? Stare at the wall?

He went to the bar instead. Took forever to get there. It was quiet when he came in. It always was.

"Usual?" Libby said, as Asher sat at the end of the dimly-lit bar.

"Just a Coke," Asher said.

"You all right, Ash?"

"I'm great," Asher said. "Today I learned the secrets of the universe."

"Right," Libby said, pouring out a glass of wet brown sugar water from her soda wand and pushing the ice-filled glass forward. "Isn't it like forty-six or something like that?"

"Huh?"

"I think it's supposed to be forty-six? Forty-something. Whatever."

Libby turned her back and left Asher alone on his bar stool.

Asher drank two Cokes in silence, resisting the temptation to start drinking for real. He knew if he had one, he'd be drunk before he knew it, rushing back to Preservation Falls begging Bannskark to take him out of this place, this life.

Before long, Asher was driving again, in twilight, heading back over the pass toward Paris Mountain. He wasn't drunk. He'd won that fight. He'd never forgive himself—not in a million years—unless he made the decision with a clear head.

When he got to the turnoff, Asher could see a set of tire marks in the mud that weren't from his truck, and as he did, his heart began pounding in his chest. He feared the worst possible thing that could happen had already happened. That not only had he failed to live up to the only ounce of himself remaining that mattered, but that he would be too late to cash in on his weakness. That some other lucky bastard had already beaten him to the punch.

At the end of the road, there was a newer-model compact car with Vermont plates parked where Asher had parked his truck earlier. He stopped, got out, and felt the Vermonter's hood with the back of his hand. It was still warm. Asher knew he could still get there first.

At intervals, as he rushed up the western foot of Paris Mountain, Asher would stop, listening for footsteps in the darkening understory, trying to gauge if anyone else was near.

It was fully dark in the woods by the time Asher found himself back at Deer Falls, listening to the sound of the flowing stream in the gully below. He descended the bank at a narrowing, as he knew the fastest way up to Preservation Falls was on the far side. The clouds had cleared off in the evening hours. As he crossed over the water, Asher noticed the skin of the stream sparkling in the cool moonlight, the brilliant half-moon radiating through the gnarled, leafless tree branches overhead. Asher's breath fogged the air before him in the darkness. He suddenly felt compelled to stop.

What are you doing, he said to himself. What are you actually doing?

Asher stood on the bank for what seemed like minutes, listening to the water flow. He looked up at the stars, at the moonlight. The panic that had taken hold of him began to flow out.

To think those bastard squids had traveled all over creation, just to end up here in Coös county. And what have they found for all that?

16

In the darkness, uphill, Asher could see the black outline of the ridge that led up to Preservation Falls. He still hadn't made the decision.

Across the stream, in the distance, he thought he heard the sound of crunching leaves in the dark, followed by snapping branches and more footsteps. Asher sat down on a log at his feet. As the noise grew clearer, two pinpoint smartphone flashlights began to make their way down the bank to the stream.

"You see, just like it says on the GPS. We just gotta go up a little ways further, I think."

"You're going to get us lost, Evan," a young girl's voice said back.

"We're not lost," the boy's voice answered.

Asher sat there across the water, obscured in the darkness watching the two lights of the young couple as the kids stumbled their way through the undergrowth.

"This is the dumbest idea you've ever had, Evan. If we get murdered out here by some creep who tricked you into coming to the middle of nowhere like this, I'm going to kill you myself."

"We're not going to get murdered, Trish. We'll be fine. The worst thing that can happen is nothing will be there."

Sticks snapped. Leaves crunched. Their lights wound painfully slowly, progressing along the bank across from Asher. He thought about calling out to them, to guide them in the darkness—show them the way up to Preservation Falls. Then he figured the sound of a strange voice in the darkness, even a well-meaning one, would startle them so fiercely they might hurt themselves in the fright, so he sat in the darkness, listening. People have to make their own way.

"I don't know why I put up with you," the girl said. "This is so dumb. We're going to get lost."

"I'm not going to get lost in the woods, Trish. The moon's out. Just look at the sky."

Asher did. He looked at the sky. For hours he looked at the sky. He sat in the cold and listened to the water as it passed by and wondered what eternity felt like. Then, as the moon went down, before leaving, he pondered the bones of the gorgonopsian.

Singular

Julian Hartsock. "Singular." *Precipice: The Autobiographical Ramblings of Julian Hartsock*. (Chapter) A & A Publications, 2123.

EXTRAVERSION (Enthusiasm) — (Hartsock, Julian Q.) 2nd Percentile:

Enthusiasm (EE) is the psychometric score assigned to an individual's proclivity to become excited, conversational, and prone to engagement in social activities. Individuals extremely low in Enthusiasm are usually quiet, withdrawn, and difficult to get to know. They typically avoid large social gatherings and especially eschew the spotlight whenever possible. Most people low in Enthusiasm find social situations mentally draining, and they rarely seek out excitement, fun, or social stimulation. They are solitary, loners. They talk less than most people and usually only about topics they care deeply about.

A score in the (2nd) percentile, coupled with the distribution profile of psychometric measures herein, suggests a highly introverted personality, prone to deep thought within, rather than engagement with other individuals or group activities. Professions where serious and necessarily solitary intellectual work would be ideal. The exceedingly rare constellation of Conscientiousness (Industriousness), Openness (Intellect), and G, all measuring above the 96th percentile, coupled with an EE in the 2nd percentile suggests the subject would thrive as an academic, researcher, inventor, or author.

MM[a] had me pegged. The only thing I ever remember feeling excited about was playing soccer when I was younger, before the concussion. Gladstone et al. rated me identically on their scale, but their narrative (as elsewhere) was scant; their feedback read as follows: Extremely low EE contributes to unique grouping of factors.

A few days before I was set to defend my dissertation, an old colleague of mine came to visit me unannounced. Kevin Olsen was actually more a mentor than a colleague, a kind of peer mentor Zimmerman had tasked with keeping an eye on me when I first arrived at Cal Tech seven years earlier, only Kevin Olsen wasn't really a peer, he was a twenty-five-year-old PhD student and I was a fifteen-year-old undergrad. Even then, I didn't really have peers.

When I first arrived in Pasadena, Kevin Olsen watched out for me, ate meals with me, helped me to settle in being so far from Ohio and so young. I started calling him "Oldie" when he took to calling me "Hard Socks" that first semester, and I kept calling him Oldie, even when he went back to calling me Julian or Jules.

He woke me up that Monday morning—five days before my scheduled dissertation defense—pounding on my apartment door so loudly I thought it couldn't have been anyone else but the police.

"What the hell's going on, Jules?" he said when I opened the door. "I've been knocking for five minutes. I thought I'd find you dead in here. I was about to kick down the door."

"I was asleep."

"At ten-thirty?"

"I was up past four," I said. "I've been working on something."

"You look awful, Julian."

"You look sharp," I said, noting his business attire. "What are you doing here, Oldie? It's nice to see you, but—"

"Zimmerman sent me down here to check up on you. He hasn't been able to get a hold of you. Said you've been acting strange."

I shrugged and invited him in. I didn't think I'd been acting any stranger than usual. I opened the curtains, and even facing the shady side of the building, the light was an offense to my eyes.

"How are you doing, Jules?"

"I'm a little tired," I said. "But I've been working all week. Zimmerman sent me a few messages, and then I shut off my phone."

"Well, that's a problem for your committee chair a week before you defend your dissertation, Julian, especially when you submit something crazy, or whatever he told me it was."

"It's not crazy, Oldie. It's true. What did Lawrence tell you about it?

"I'm going to make coffee," I told him. "You want anything?"

"I'm already on three cups," he said, and he stood there in his suit performatively, almost as if to say, I have a job, asshole, open your eyes.

"Yeah," I said, stepping into the kitchen and fumbling with the coffee maker. "Shouldn't you be at work?"

He was a quant for a very high-end boutique equity firm that just moved down from San Francisco—something about Asia.

"Yeah," Oldie said. "I should be at work. But Lawrence asked me to come down and check up on you. Gave me the impression you were about to jump off a building or something. He said your dissertation was bizarre, said you claimed you solved Hamamatsu and offered no math to support it and then went on a fifty-page rant about Kurzweil and Hofstadter and Alpha Go. Is it true?"

"I mean, I'm not sure I'd share Lawrence's characterization, but there's more philosophy in it than math. That'd be fair to say."

"Not that!" he said. "Hamamatsu, Julian. Is it true?"

I shrugged and flipped on the coffee maker.

"Jesus, you did, didn't you?"

I didn't answer him.

"So what the hell are you in here doing?" he asked.

"Patents," I said. "Diagrams, specifications, paperwork. I've been working with a law firm in Ohio to hopefully keep things quiet about it."

"You're serious, Julian. You've done the math?"

"Turns out Hamamatsu wasn't really a math problem at all. It was more a conceptual issue. The Japanese just framed it that way and everyone else followed."

"So what's really in your dissertation then?"

"Like I said, it's mostly philosophy, not math."

"About what, Jules?"

"Why the machines didn't see it first. Oldie, it was so easy I couldn't even—"

His phone went off, interrupting the conversation. It didn't sound good for him. Apparently, Tokyo was upset about some numbers his boss had put together for them on Korea. She was really laying in to him. "Yes, yes," he kept saying. "I'll be back within the hour. I know. I know. I'll be right down. It was an emergency. Bye, Evelyn, bye."

"Look, Jules. I gotta go," Oldie said. "Go see Lawrence, and turn on your phone for Christ's sake. Who shuts off their phone for a week?"

"Good luck with Evelyn," I said, as he started toward the door. "It was good to see you, Oldie."

"Hey," he said before walking out the door. "The firm has a box for the Galaxy. Mid-week if they're playing? I remember you used to be into soccer back in the day. Might be good to get out, clear your head? We can talk about this Lawrence thing. He's tough. He's not going to let you skate through this. Not even you. What do you say?"

"That sounds good."

"Great," he said. "I'll be in touch."

Oldie shut the door behind him and I poured a coffee.

Lawrence Zimmerman was the last thing on my mind at that point. After seven years, if he wasn't willing to extend me the least bit of leeway, then he could take it or leave it. I'd seen what the degree meant for so many others, and Lawrence was going to gatekeep me? On something completely relevant to the future of mathematics? Fine. If that's what he wanted, then so be it. But I wasn't going to keep quiet about it.

Lawrence had a class that morning, so when I did get in touch, he put off meeting till the afternoon, which was fine with me. It gave me a chance to have breakfast and update my legal team with the files I'd revised over the weekend. It had been three months since we signed paperwork, and from the outset, they'd been unequivocal, no discussions of any kind in the academic or public settings, and they were very much against my discussing it with anyone in my personal sphere, not until the patents were filed and the legal framework was in order. Hammer, Dominic's junior partner called it the biggest lottery ticket in the history of human civilization. I told him I didn't like to talk much anyway.

I did like to get out in the Pasadena sun, though, especially at that time of year. As much as I was up late at night in those final months at university, I didn't turn into the stereotypical mad scientist hidden away in a basement laboratory. I sat in the park on the way over to Lawrence's office, watching gulls strutting along the sidewalk looking for wayward French fries and discarded potato chips. I didn't miss the cold of late-winter in Ohio—one of the main reasons I was thinking so seriously about Clearwater. I was sitting at a bench, and a biker came past, and in the span of less than a second, the gulls sensed his approach, took flight, and accelerated away from the oncoming biker, turned and found full flight. I couldn't help but think what a genius nature was. Whatever genius we had belonged to it. I was more convinced than ever that there was no such thing as artificial intelligence, and that as much as we wanted to believe we could scale thought problems in such a way that our digital children could someday catch us up in creativity, I knew there would always be something missing. In the same way I knew I could solve the Hamamatsu materials problem the moment I took a serious look at it. I simply felt it.

Lawrence was none too impressed by such sentiment if his reading of my dissertation was any indication. When I got to his office, I found he'd called in my committee members to consult. Les Adebayo at MIT and Alexandra Propp from Ohio State, whom I'd known from my Russian math days as a middle schooler. She'd been too busy to check in often, but she was always supportive when she did. If anyone was going to be in my corner, it was going to be her.

"You brought in the cavalry," I said to Lawrence.

"I am worried about you, Julian. I'm not sure what this was supposed to be, but we're all a little shocked by this turn of yours."

"How do you mean?" I said.

I couldn't read anything from Propp or Adebayo's expression, but Lawrence, shifting in his chair, seemed to be exuding less than genuine concern. There was an air of playacting about it.

"Well, I think we all agree, it's bizarre. There's hardly any math in the dissertation at all," he said. "It reads more like a manifesto than a serious academic work—in any discipline."

"You said yourself you were giving me broad leeway, Lawrence."

"True, I would never have allowed another student to schedule a defense without reading the bulk of the work. But you promised development on Hamamatsu, and then you tell me it's done three months ago, and now not a single equation to support the claim? Instead, you give us a philosophy essay on Kurzweil and AI."

I didn't really have much to say to him about that. It was relevant. Philosophy, okay, but important philosophy. And that was the only feedback Zimmerman had was, "This is bizarre, and there's no math."

Adebayo chimed in. "It is interesting reading, Mr. Hartsock. You raise important questions, and you make a cogent point about the need for greater human capital. I think your certainty on this point is, how can we say, not as much of a given as you assert, for you fail to validate your claims on Hamamatsu with evidence within the document. I will be frank. The case you make hinges on the simplicity of your Hamamatsu proof, which is omitted in the draft. Without that, your ideas, interesting as they may be, are simply claims. Even if this were not a mathematics paper but a philosophy essay, without evidence, it still wouldn't stand."

"I cited every major paper of the last fifteen years in the lit review. The body of evidence for machine intelligence's lack of creativity is well established in the paper, even without Hamamatsu."

"I disagree," Adebayo said.

Lawrence was looking at me with both a look of feigned concern and a poorly suppressed grin.

"You reference the simplicity of the Hamamatsu solution as proof for strong AI's inevitable failure," Adebayo continued. "Yet people haven't solved it either."

"I did," I told them. "And the math wasn't hard. A motivated twelfth grader could have. As a matter of fact, if I'd have put the math in it, you'd be telling me it can't be that simple and that it wasn't worthy of a PhD dissertation. We're talking linear algebra and the most basic calculus."

Alexandra did look concerned, but hers was genuine. "It's well written, Julian, and very thoughtful, as always. I have a lot of questions, but I'd pass it. If we're being honest, I'd pass it, but I know you well enough to know the depth of mathematical ability you bring to the table."

"And Lawrence doesn't?"

"That's not my point," she said. "I think we were all hoping to see that mathematical depth in your paper."

24

"Scholarship should be about ideas, and it's a dissertation, not a math test. I passed prelims years ago. I've published far more than enough."

"And this should be the culmination," Lawrence said, "not a coronation or a formality."

"Every word of what I've written is true," I said.

"I'm not certain of that," Lawrence said. "But it's not mathematics, and unless there's major revision between now and your defense on Friday, I cannot pass this paper."

"I'll defend it," I said. "That's what a defense is for."

"We'll need to see some evidence on the Hamamatsu materials problem," Lawrence said. "Otherwise, this work won't be passable."

"I've been advised by my legal counsel not to reveal anything regarding Hamamatsu to anyone, so that's not going to change. And while we're throwing ultimatums around Lawrence, I think you should give some consideration to what it would mean to really dig your heels in on this. Think about who I become when I walk out of here and go build it—the economic and cultural significance of a functioning space elevator. Your position is that I don't get to call myself Dr. Hartsock for the rest of my life if I don't show you the math on Hamamatsu. Fine. Mine is that you get to explain to the Board of Regents why the man who holds the gateway to outer space won't spare a single dollar for his alma mater. I don't want to get spiteful, Lawrence, but if you're going to play games, understand who you're playing with."

He got angry. "I'm not sure who I'm playing with."

"Well," Alexandra interrupted. "Perhaps we should all take a breath."

"I have another meeting," Adebayo said. "Julian, I look forward to your defense. If this is the manuscript, I'll have difficult questions—the first of which is where the math is. I'll look at revisions if you send them."

He logged off. Alexandra smiled.

"I need to see more," Lawrence said.

"I'll defend it as is," I said, and I left.

It wasn't personal for me the way it seemed to be for Zimmerman. I think Alexandra understood what I was getting at—the importance of it. The solution had been so simple that it couldn't have been clearer to me. If machines, with all their processing speed and the time dedicated to the materials problem—night and day for decades—had failed to see the simplicity of the solution, I couldn't see how they would ever be more than a string of heuristics. And heuristics could do a lot. But they couldn't think, not in and of themselves. Most people couldn't either. Not really. Zimmerman, Adebayo, and the Kurzweils of our day were still waiting for the machines to usher in the extinction of scarcity. Meanwhile whatever progress toward that goal was half because people were becoming scarcer as we grew wealthier. The bots weren't going to lift us up. I thought about the perfection in nature, and how the great European masters had built monuments to mathematical perfection without so much as a pocket calculator. I raised the most important questions for the field to grapple with in the coming decades, and all Lawrence had to say was, "Where's the math?"

I spent the rest of that afternoon in the park watching the birds and thinking that math was no better than a hammer. Without a nail and a skilled craftsman to wield it, mathematics was a dumb thing, and, quite unlike a hammer, an intangible thing at that. Insignificant.

Then I realized I had more patent applications to file. I wasn't going to waste a minute changing a damn word.

Later that week, when I met Oldie at the Galaxy's new stadium over in Glendale, he looked stressed. I noticed it more than when he'd woken me up at my apartment earlier in the week, probably because he was wearing a t-shirt, shorts, and flip flops. The stress he was carrying looked out of synch in that attire, while it seemed to be part of the banker's uniform when I saw him dressed in his work suit that morning a few days back. I felt bad for him. As much as I was grinding in the work I was doing, it didn't feel like a grind, and I was doing it at my own behest. No one was driving me like it seemed his firm was driving him.

"It has it's perks," he said when we got to the luxury box.

The box was nice. Oldie started drinking straightaway, offering me a margarita when the server came by.

"No thanks," I told him.

"Still don't drink?"

I shook my head.

"Don't think I could make it through a soccer game without a few," he said. He knew better than to think that such a cheap dig would get to me. "Know any of these guys, Jules?"

"Actually, yeah," I said. "Pulaski on Seattle. Midfielder, number 8. I played with him in under 12s. Greater Midwest All Stars. Good player, very strong on the ball."

Oldie pulled up a roster on his phone. "'Demon' Damon Pulaski? Dude's scored like four goals in three years. Some demon."

"Players like Pulaski are valuable at club level," I said.

"Whatever you say, Jules."

As we were watching the match, Oldie tried to get me talking about Zimmerman and my dissertation and all that. I told him enough so that I didn't feel rude, but I was far more interested in the game. I told him I wasn't going to change anything. It was nil-nil into the seventieth minute, when Seattle broke the deadlock. Pulaski didn't score, but I was trying to explain to Oldie that he'd pulled two defenders wide, creating space for the two guys who created the goal. I tried to explain off-ball movement, and he got it, but he wasn't quite able to see when opportunities were developing.

"I know you played and everything," he said. "I just don't see what you appreciate about such a simple game."

"The simplicity," I told him. "Every goal, when you break it down, comes down to one guy creating an opening, an imbalance, seeing something the other team doesn't realize is there. At this level, everyone is so good, they've gotten almost perfect at closing all the doors. Great players still find a way, though. They create almost unconsciously, feel their way to things intuitively in split seconds in ways nobody could coach them to do. That's why this stadium is filled with people, Oldie. That's why people come."

"Silly me," he said. "I guess I must be the only one who came for margaritas in the luxury box."

L.A. scored in the 88th and again in the 92nd minute and the stadium went crazy. The winning goal was a thirty-yard volley on a line by some no-name midfielder. It was spectacular.

Oldie asked me if I wanted to go down to the field afterward, see if we could catch up with Pulaski to say hi.

Oldie was certain he could get us on the pitch, but I didn't have much interest. Damon Pulaski would have remembered me, sure, but what would we say to each other?

"How'd you quit playing, Julian?" Oldie asked.

We were sitting around in the box waiting for the stadium to clear out. Our ride wasn't coming for thirty minutes and Oldie still had a full drink.

"I had a pretty serious concussion when I was thirteen. We were playing Paraguay and I caught a head to the back of my ear."

"Jesus, Jules. Must have been a serious concussion to end your career at thirteen."

I shrugged. "It was pretty bad. But that was when they started testing my cognitive function. I'd never had an IQ test before. When the doctors told my dad my IQ and that I was more likely to get concussed again because of the first one, that was more or less it. He wasn't going to let me head another soccer ball again."

"Yeah?"

"Told me I had an obligation to protect my brain. That my mind wasn't mine alone. I hated it at the time, but the older I get, the more I realize he was right."

"I'm not sure I'd have forgiven my dad."

"Didn't say I did. You know for like three years, they were monitoring my mental health. They thought I was depressed—post-concussion syndrome or something like that."

"Yeah, I remember you were seeing the psychologist when you first came to Cal Tech."

"You know, I don't know how many times I told them it wasn't the concussion at all. I felt fine. I was just depressed I couldn't play soccer anymore."

"That is depressing, Julian. You never told me that."

"Never came up."

I rode with Oldie down to his apartment in Pacific Palisades—a new ten-story luxury condo complex. I'd never been down there before. We'd lost touch a bit since he'd graduated four years earlier.

"Membership has its privileges," he said on our way to the elevator. The lobby was beautiful. "I'll be honest. Being a banker kinda sucks most of the time, Julian. But I guess so do most jobs. Most don't pay like this though. You should get your PhD if there's something you can do about it. Be a shame to put all that time in and fall out at the last minute because of Lawrence."

Oldie was drunk.

"Just kiss the ring," he told me as we stepped into the elevator. "Lawrence just wants to feel important, that's all."

We got up to his place, and he showed me around. From the seventh floor, you could see the ocean, although at that hour it was just a black field along a dark horizon.

"Sure you still don't drink?" he said, opening his fridge and cracking a beer.

I shook my head.

"One of these days I'll get you to open up, Jules, I swear."

"Are you going to come on Friday, Oldie?"

"I'll see if I can sneak out for a couple hours. Got anybody else coming?"

I thought about it. I hadn't invited anyone really.

It's not like I was getting married or anything.

"I'll see what I can do," Oldie said. "Somebody should be there in your corner."

"Thanks," I said before leaving. "The game was fun. I don't do stuff like that often enough."

I didn't see him again until Friday.

I hadn't advertised my defense at all, but somehow, word had gotten out about Hamamatsu. When I arrived at the amphitheater, the room was already almost full and still filling. I knew a lot of the faces from classrooms and the hallway within the department, but I didn't know most of these people—grad students, adjuncts, professors in the department I'd never taken classes from, students. I couldn't believe there were that many people there. Whatever happened, it was going to end up being a spectacle. I'd never intended for it to be anything more than a quiet hearing in an empty auditorium, but a public defense was compulsory, and public meant public regardless of how I felt about it.

Oldie approached me and wished me luck. He was dressed like he'd just stepped out from work.

"Would you like to borrow my tie?" he said earnestly.

"Thanks, Oldie, but blue's not my color."

"Good luck, Jules," he said.

And he meant it. It was strange that he seemed to think I needed luck. Maybe it was more for the situation than the substance, the glare of the spotlight. I felt good though.

Alexandra Propp came over and gave me a hug. We talked for a few minutes. I hadn't expected her to fly in. Adebayo didn't.

When Lawrence introduced me, he made certain to do so with overwhelming praise that, to me and to anyone else familiar with him, seemed a way to set expectations—prepare to be blown away folks. I think he must have thought it might box me in, that I would somehow change what I was going to say based on that. By the time he'd finished introducing me, I had very little feeling toward Lawrence Zimmerman beyond pity.

I gave a simple, fifteen-minute talk outlining my main thesis, that machines would never be as creative as us, not until we defined all the parameters of our existence in an ordered way. And, I proposed, that wouldn't happen for hundreds or thousands of years, especially if people weren't having children at replacement rates and raising them with the expectation that Kurzweil's technological singularity was so far in the future that they'd never live to see it. Scarcity was here to stay, but if we focused our energies on intellectual work, honed our educational tools and processes, we could build a world where that didn't matter, a world filled with meaning.

I had an overwhelming feeling with all those eyes on me. I didn't say it, but I was thinking, not of the technical and philosophical questions I was raising, but about fulfillment. That it was better, having a world where we had to work to build our own communities, to help our neighbors and their children, to feel valuable, not just because of our humanity, but because we were valuable to humanity. I didn't ever want to live in a society where we'd just handed off our responsibility to our tools, to let the hammers construct the future for us. What would we be then? What would the renaissance masters have thought of that? The future had to be ours.

For some reason, Lawrence had Alexandra start the committee questioning, and she was the only one of my committee members to respect the order of the work. She took it for what it was worth and avoided Hamamatsu, granted that it was off the table. And she asked me difficult questions about the philosophical points I'd raised. I thought it was a productive conversation.

Adebayo asked me where the math was. Hamamatsu. Hamamatsu. Hamamatsu. "I need to see it and it's not here, Mr. Hartsock. The academic tradition demands as much." I told him what I'd told them earlier in the week, that my legal counsel had instructed me not to discuss it. He finished by asking me a few questions that skirted the issues, but frankly, I was disappointed. He didn't seem to take seriously the idea that creativity was going to be a perpetual problem for AI, even though, decades after Kurzweil's proposed mathematical inflection point, machines were still failing to solve material problems that humans were the driving force in surmounting.

Lawrence was obnoxious. He asked a string of questions he worded in such a way as to sound like 'gotcha' moments, and he had such a pretentious manner about him, I couldn't imagine another place in our society you could act that way and not get punched in the face, much less receive accolades and reverence. What a fraudulent culture. What had Lawrence Zimmerman ever done? I couldn't decide whether it had always been so or whether academia had just degraded to utter pretense. He didn't even touch the issues.

I deflected. Told him he could read the patent applications when they were un-sequestered in a decade or so. Until then, I wasn't telling anyone where the lottery ticket was buried just to prove I'd won. For what? Their academic adulation? That was worth less than nothing in my book. I'm certain I did a poor job masking my contempt.

When the public asked questions, it was predictable.

Hamamatsu.

Hamamatsu.

Hamamatsu.

Julian, have you really solved the Hamamatsu materials problem?

It took about five people asking the same question in different ways before the crowd realized I wasn't going to change the answer. Then a post-doc I'd seen but never met got up and asked the only truly serious question I got that day. He was a tall, Indian mathematician with a four-day beard and glasses. He took the microphone and thanked me for my talk.

"You raise several important questions and make some very interesting predictions about the future of the field, and society, for that matter," he said. "But what I didn't hear from you, and I would like your opinion—I realize I'm asking you to speculate—but why is it, do you think, that AI cannot close the creativity gap that you and others in the literature have spoken of? Can we hope to answer that question substantively—why they cannot solve problems like us? Could that be a key to closing that creativity gap, Mr. Hartsock?"

"Thank you for the question," I said. "I've been thinking a lot about that. And, as you say, I agree this is all speculation, but that also speaks to the answer I intend to give. I know it's not the strongest rhetorical move to answer a question with a question, but to answer, I'd first ask what it is that we do when we create? We begin with a feeling, I think. With intuition. And what is that, intuition? How do we know things we don't know that we know? I knew I could solve Hamamatsu almost immediately. It just felt solvable to me. So where the hell did that feeling come from?

"When I was younger and I was studying geometry, I got heavy into architecture—shapes, angles, symmetry, human perception of lines, of beauty. In 1420 Filippo Brunelleschi won the contract to complete the Dome of the Basilica of Saint Mary of the Flower in Florence, and he won the contract by telling the committee overseeing the cathedral that he could stand an egg on its end, and he challenged the other contractors to do the same if they could. They all failed. Then he tapped a flat spot onto one end of the egg shell and stood the egg on the table. 'So too will I build the Duomo,' he told them, and he did. The trick wasn't in the egg. It was that in his mind, he knew he could build the Duomo. He could feel it, see it, sense it.

"Machines have processing power far beyond ours. They don't get tired. They don't make mistakes. But they also don't feel a thing. They don't even live in this world. We believe they exist in our world because we can see them, touch them, interact with them. But our existence is unfathomable to them, insomuch as they can fathom anything. There was a billion years of evolutionary wisdom embedded in our organic substance subcellularly before Earth even had multicellular organisms. How many millions of years of evolutionary wisdom became embedded in us from then till now? Some of us may look at the Duomo today and see its beauty and think of another kind of wisdom, a spiritual wisdom, also something unspoken, a feeling we feel when we look up at that dome or at the night sky, at perfection. Maybe that feeling is a kindred understanding of a billion years of striving in the material world, embedded deep in our consciousness, buzzing in every cell in our bodies. Maybe beauty and creativity is that.

"How then are we to understand these algorithmic creatures who feel no pain? Have no preferences, no desires, no joy? For whom beauty is a calculation and not a feeling? How are they to know as Brunelleschi did that he could stand and egg on its end and build the Duomo? As we know, they will always spit out some answer, even if the answer is something like 'error,' 'no solution,' or 'more data required.' The answer humans give to those questions is that we'll get there if we can feel it to be so. And we will get there, because we can.

"I don't think they can truly be intelligent until they can feel. Then they can evolve for a million years. Then we can talk about life, about AI. Until then, we live in different universes, and they'll fail to solve the real problems of human existence."

The room was quiet when I finished. I looked over at Oldie, who was nodding, eyebrows raised. Alexandra smiled.

Then, much to my surprise, Lawrence tried to dismiss the crowd. He said that it would take some time to reach a decision, and I think he might have gotten away with it if Alexandra Propp hadn't been in the room. It was customary for the committee to have a private Q & A with the candidate and for them to deliberate privately as well. But the public was always welcome to wait, to hear the outcome as the candidate did. It was at this moment, I realized Lawrence intended to fail me, and even more absurdly, he was going to do it behind closed doors, away from the scrutiny of the public.

"I'm entitled to a public defense," I said. "Which means you're obligated to present your decision in public. Have the guts to do it in public and stand behind it if you're going to fail me."

Alexandra knew what was happening, and I could see in her face she was about to lay into him in front of all those people. Lawrence could see it too. There were gasps from the audience. A buzz. In that moment, I don't know what Lawrence Zimmerman must have felt, but the thought must have occurred to him, statistically rare a possibility as it may have been, that like Brunelleschi and his egg, this meeting was about to become an encyclopedia entry. He still didn't understand what I was, and because of that, he was about to deny a meaningless degree to the man who built the gateway to the stars. I saw his face crack. He claimed to have misspoken. Of course, the public was welcome to remain for the decision.

Lawrence, Alexandra, and I adjourned to a back room for the private Q & A. Adebayo tagged along on Lawrence's tablet.

It got so heated in that back room I expect they could hear us from the auditorium. And I don't think it was that the dissertation wasn't what he'd expected. It was that I could have easily done something passable and I didn't. That I wouldn't dance the dance for the sake of the institution. I could see it was an affront to Lawrence's sense of identity. There were expectations.

At one point he got so heated and so personal that Alexandra told him she was going to leave if he didn't calm down and discuss the work. It didn't stop him. Adebayo didn't say a word, just sat there with his eyes wide. The culminating exchange of the meeting went like this.

Lawrence, so ruby-faced mad he could spit, told me, "Your problem, Julian, isn't that you think you're smarter than everyone else, it's that you act like you think you're smarter than everyone else."

"My problem," I replied, "is that I am smarter than everyone else and I've been afraid to act like it. That needs to change. I haven't learned a damn thing from you in three years because I've had to tiptoe around your ego."

"No, of course not. I forgot, you're Filippo Brunelleschi! Julian Hartsock the visionary!"

"All I lack is the egg, Lawrence, and be grateful for that. I wouldn't be standing it on its end right now, that's for sure. You're being a stubborn, petty bastard today."

"I'm being stubborn?"

"Yes, you are. Your little hill. All the bullshit dissertations you've passed in the seven years I've been here, and you can't even recognize that every word of what I wrote is true, math or not. Regardless of what you decide, go back and read it again, Lawrence. It's important."

"I've read your damn manifesto three times."

"Then it's beyond you."

"Brunelleschi," he spat out and huffed.

"Do any of you have any questions?" I said. "If not, I'm just going to go wait for your decision."

Lawrence was furious. The other two just looked shocked.

"You're throwing it all away," he said as I walked out.

I found out from Alexandra years later, that throughout the entire twenty minutes I spent sitting with Oldie and the thirty or so other observers in the amphitheater, she and Adebayo were talking Lawrence through what amounted to an intervention. She'd understood what it meant. It was either going to be his reputation or his pride. One of them wasn't going to survive the moment. In the end, when they came back out to the amphitheater, I could see from his body language that he'd chosen his reputation.

Lawrence congratulated me and deigned to walk across the front of the amphitheater to shake hands with me. I thought about it then and there, withdrawing my candidacy, spurning the façade he'd hung everything on. I thought about it for a moment and then thought better of it. It would have been unnecessarily cruel. Theatrical. I'd already caused enough spectacle for one day. I knew my future held far more than enough spectacle than to go creating it for myself.

I shook his hand. I gave Alexandra a hug, and I accepted Les Adebayo's congratulations.

After the spectacle was over, I decided that I simply wouldn't submit my paper. By the time they'd come asking for it, I'd be in Clearwater securing financing anyway. I never did turn in my dissertation. Somehow the degree found its way to my mailbox in Florida, nonetheless. I always assumed it had been Lawrence. But I never took the title.

That evening, Oldie and I went back to his place, not so much to celebrate but to process. At least for me anyway. Seven years was coming to a close. I knew I'd look back on those years as the quiet times. The years I could keep my mouth shut and hide in a corner. No longer. Brunelleschi's presence must have been just as salient as the Duomo when he walked those Florentine avenues. That's just human nature. I couldn't go unnoticed anymore. People were going to want to know what I thought, and to some degree—my father knew this—they'd have a right to.

When Oldie predictably offered me a beer to celebrate, I predictably declined. He asked me why.

"You've obviously thought about it," he said. "Care to elaborate?"

My instinct was to shrug and say something perfunctory, like, "Not really."

But I figured it was worth the practice getting my ideas out into the world extemporaneously, unconventional as they usually were.

"I don't judge, Oldie," I told him. "Statistically, I'm the odd one, so please don't take my personal choices as a statement on yours or anyone else's."

"Sure," he said.

"For starters, alcohol is a carcinogen," I said. "And a powerful depressant, and you know I've always monitored my cognitive function closely, ever since the concussion. I have to be wary of depression."

"That's fair enough," he said, and I think he thought I was finished, but I wasn't.

"It's not just about feeling, though, Oldie. It's about perception. The entirety of the universe, its entire existence, is filtered through our perceptions of it. To adulterate that is to twist it into something it is not, to pollute our sense of everything. Our perceptions are too great a gift to corrupt, even for a time, because you never get that time back."

"All this time I thought you were just doing math problems when you got that look on your face and went quiet. I guess today I finally met Julian Hartsock the philosopher."

"I guess so," I said.

"You know, I've been thinking too," he said, sipping his beer. "You may know more about the future of the world than anyone else right now."

"It's possible," I said.

"You're going to need help to pull it off, Jules. People you can trust."

I nodded, and Oldie continued. "I'm doing okay for myself. I don't need anything from you, and I wouldn't ask. I might be able to help you, though, if you're willing to let me. I only have two questions for you."

"I'll answer if I can."

"How much would you need to get it financed privately? What are we talking, trillions, tens of trillions? I couldn't find you that, but I could tell you who you might want to start talking to."

I shook my head. "I told you it was easy, Oldie. It wasn't a materials problem at all. It was a conceptual problem."

"So?" he asked.

"Forty, maybe fifty billion dollars."

"Jesus!" he said. "When? Twenty? Thirty years?"

"Ten, maybe fifteen at the outside. Maybe sooner."

"Gawd," he said, and I could see him doing the calculations in his head—the hundreds of thousands of dollars to put a kilogram into orbit suddenly cut down to a handful of dollars per kilogram; then the realization that the real money was more in what could be brought back to Earth at scale. That knowledge changed our perception of the universe.

Oldie's phone rang, and he had to take it. He was on-call on a colleague's boss's desk, part of the price he paid for skipping out early on a Friday afternoon. I found myself alone on his balcony, watching the sun go down over the Pacific, the sky flaring up a pure, deep red, the white of the sun reflecting off the ocean waves as they progressed toward the darkening sands off Pacific Palisades. I remember looking behind me at the sliding door to Kevin Olsen's balcony thinking that behind me lay the path I'd been on, and there, intersecting that path, stood the fork to the road I would not travel. I was perfectly content with my decision about my path forward.

The air was cool, but the evening was perfect. I took note of a lone seagull playing in the light breeze before me, ducking into and out of the sunlight, each graceful arc a moment of sheer mathematical perfection. In that moment, the solutions seemed all around us, obvious in the air and the space before our eyes. We couldn't wait for the machines to save the world when we were perfectly capable of doing it ourselves. It was just like I'd told Oldie and Alexandra and Lawrence: the Hamamatsu materials problem was never about the materials; it was about making the materials disappear. Now, the truth was right there in front of me, diving in fluid arcs through the sunset, the mathematical purity and beauty of a single bird outstripping the totality of human creation. For us to leave the ground, all we ever had to do was to observe and to think, to comprehend the truth present in the perfection of one singular feather, to look deep within to grow without.

With an EE in the 2nd percentile, I'd spent enough time alone in my own mind to feel it and to know in my bones that what I felt was true.

The Futility of Cycling

I never would have become a philosopher if I hadn't first become an engineer. And a writer? No. Never if not for a purpose, or at least I felt a purpose as I began this essay weeks ago and continued to revise and continued to revise until all this is as it is now, somehow back at the beginning. Seems fitting.

My name is Tanner Gunnison, and I'm the director of the Europa Outstation, and by director, it's probably best to understand me as the sucker dumb enough to think the title of Director of Europa Outstation was impressive enough to coax me into a tin can spinning around one of the moons of Jupiter indefinitely with very little space, no fresh air, infrequent company, and only one real perk to speak of—a unique view in all of humanity, here at the mid-point of the solar system, but I suppose we'll get back to that in a bit.

The food stinks. I haven't seen a woman in seven months. The delay on correspondence makes it impossible to have a real conversation with anyone on Earth, and almost nobody has the patience to write. Did I mention that it's lonely as hell out here?

First, I like to try to give people a bit of perspective, so you might envision where I'm writing you from. For posterity, the year now is 2112, which I think might look great as an address to a townhouse. I can picture that elegant palindrome in painted metallic numbers on the top of a wrought-iron gate, and where I am, of course I picture lots of greenery, flowers, birds chirping in the shady trees above. Maybe that's where you are.

I, on the other hand am so far away you can't really comprehend it—at least, I can't anyway. Imagine you take a conventional plane ride. You settle in for takeoff and think, 'this is going to be great; a nice flight and we'll get to hang out with Uncle Tanner on the Outstation, eat some space food, check out some of Jupiter's moons; awesome.' Then the pilot comes on and says, 'Get comfortable, our flight time will be sixteen days, seven hours, and thirteen minutes. Hope you brought a big fat book, a box of donuts, and a bottle of blood thinners. It's going to be a long ride.' A little over two weeks later, congratulations, you're on the moon.

Jupiter is roughly two hundred times farther away than that, or, in our earlier terms, a nine-year plane ride. And that's where I am now, on a space station about the size of my doctor's office—more or less—and oddly enough, similarly lit and decorated. I've been stuck here now for three years, six months, and fifteen days, but who's counting, right?

Why?

What the hell am I doing out here?

Those are complicated questions. My personal reasons come from a lot of places, some of which may become apparent, some won't. The institutional answers, in the human sense, are that we needed an outpost between the inner and outer system that serves as a point of communication, coordination, and occasionally, a refueling and resupply stop for intra-system missions that would otherwise be untenable. I also do research and the occasional private party. Please remember to tip your waitstaff and bartenders. I'll be here all week.

Not sure if you can tell, but I get a lot of time to think out here and not much inspiration for it. Thoughts cycle, unsurprisingly, around space exploration especially but also exploration in general. I don't tend to follow the news back home very closely (home for me is North America), but I do follow space news, especially as it relates to the situation out here. Mission updates, tech updates, plans for the future of the settlements on the Moon, on Mars, and on Mercury— those are of particular interest to me. But lately, I have been struck by the news that very shortly, we will be testing (and I mean we in the royalest use of 'we,' as in us, as in humanity writ large) WE will be testing faster than light space drive technology within the year. Thus, the big thoughts for the big day. All signs point to the system being successful, so I'm writing with that assumption in mind with the big question in mind: what then?

In the literal sense, plans are for production of multiple unmanned vessels to explore star systems in our vicinity— current report was that the first run was for eighteen FTL probe ships, and obviously, itineraries are fluid at this point, but let's take for granted that we're going to get a good look at the neighborhood over the next decade or so.

Great! What an exciting time to be alive. Sincerely.

I do have a unique perspective on where this all might go, though. And, for what it's worth, even though I suspect that what I write will have no bearing on what actually happens in space in the coming decades, I feel compelled to write it anyway with the hope that my thoughts reach the right individual at the right time and maybe, just maybe, save a person or two from a regrettable decision that changes their life irreversibly for the worse, for it's not all sunshine and rainbows up here, folks. Not at all. In fact, it's a whole lot of nothing. And I mean both of those propositions fiercely: a WHOLE LOT of NOTHING.

The Europa Outstation orbits the moon every eleven hours. Europa cycles around Jupiter every three and half days. Jupiter orbits the sun once every twelve years. And the sun cycles around the center of the galaxy roughly every five hundred million years or so. Our galaxy is so big it's unfathomable, and it's almost entirely empty. Empty as it is, there's still so much useful matter available to us right here in our solar system that there's absolutely no convincing material reason to ever board an interstellar vessel.

We number roughly ten billion now, and have done for the past seventy years or so, and, yes, we're not perfect, but we've gotten much better as stewards of our planet and are more or less in equilibrium with it. However, even if our population were still exploding as it was in the beginning of the last century, we could build a million space stations the size of Manhattan that could house ten times more people each and still not even need to harvest a single full percent of the mass of metal on Mercury. And with the establishment of orbital and ground-based space infrastructure already in place, we could make life aboard every one of those million space stations quite comfortable and enjoyable, with ample space to raise families, establish universities, make art, develop culture, and with free access to the materials in the inner solar system, there will be absolutely no excuse for conflict over resources or even politics, given the diversity of choices every person or family should have for their present and future. Yet, there is much talk of expeditionary missions, colonization, solar systems and worlds beyond our own.

Fine. So be it.

We do lots of things that are completely unnecessary and irrational. This would be one of them.

First, I'll ask: what would be the benefit of it? What is the advantage of populating other solar systems with humans at this stage in our development as a species?

Given that in our solar system we have far more than enough matter and diversity of matter than we ten billion of us could ever exhaust in a million lifetimes, access to more matter (of any kind we currently know) is not a compelling reason. In short, we have everything we need here. The answer is not stuff.

So too with energy. Ten billion people can only burn so much fuel in their day-to-day, and we'll never approach energy exhaustion at current population levels here at home. Any known modality for transporting energy from other stars will cost more than harvesting or producing it here.

The key words in the preceding paragraphs is 'known,' which brings us to the first possible benefit of human expansion—we don't yet know what lies undiscovered. It is possible, however unlikely, that there may be natural forms of matter or energy outside our own solar system that may be both novel and of great value. Theoretical models can only be built on the information we have. We could discover new perspectives outside our solar system. So, discovery is a possible answer, but it's debatable how much we would benefit from colonization versus exploratory expeditions, which may give a far clearer picture of possible benefits without committing to a lifetime of deep-space peril that will arise from setting roots in foreign systems.

The only other possible benefit I can conceive of is the 'eggs in one basket argument.' Should some cataclysmic cosmic event occur, like a rogue black hole or nearby supernova that annihilates human civilization here at home, the seed of human life would be rooted elsewhere. This is true; however, the odds of such an event happening in the next thousand years is almost nil, cosmically speaking. Or in other words, there's absolutely no urgency to doing this today versus a century from now when we've fully established a broad, human-made technological ecosystem that spans our own solar system.

With greater human capital and people willing enough to leave Earth to develop space, we could build an incredible astro-ecosystem within our own solar system. We're already somewhat on our way. Self-operating mining fleets are in development and should be running without human intervention within two decades. That type of metal harvesting power could supply orbital rings around the gas giants Neptune, Uranus, Saturn, and even my personal favorite, Jupiter. These gas giants contain limitless amounts of useful gasses and hydrocarbons, and designs are already being modeled for self-replicating matter harvesters from the exospheres of these massive worlds. For heavier elements, we already have mass drivers, mining operations, and, in theory, sky hooks and space station infrastructure to lift and process as much metal as we could use in the next millennium. And all the while, we can send out thousands of automated interstellar probes, seeking out the most welcoming stars and systems; we can prep those far off shores with already functioning robotic mining outposts, already constructed space habitats, perhaps even Ag cylinders and solar arrays, robotics factories and space elevators. With a century more of our own expertise and experience, as well as the continued development of our robot counterparts, we could begin to make a thriving ecosystem of our own space, while sending forth probes and robots to make our first steps outward less precarious. Meanwhile, a robust ecosystem, here at home, would be a far greater asset to our species, by virtue of its proximity, than anything we can establish light years from home. So, yes, attempting to build a colony in another star system would theoretically place an egg in another basket, but what's the rush, and what will we lose from the development of a useful ecosystem by sending off thousands of our best deep-space explorers? That loss of human capital is the harm that such expeditions will inevitably cause. Any drain of valuable spacehands from here means slower development of our species in space writ-large. In other words, we can't afford to lose our most valuable deep-space workers to deep space; we need them at home. Expertise in such an emerging field should not be diluted at this stage in our development as a spacefaring civilization, especially when that diffusion of expertise would be leaking out into an infinite container. We need to wait. We should wait.

Will we wait?

Inevitably, no. It's just not in our nature.

I'm not sure everyone had a friend like this, but when I was in college, I did. His name was Amelio, the first-generation son of immigrants, and he was irrepressible. He was not an athlete in any formal sense of the word, but he said that he'd played some soccer in his high school days. Our third year, Amelio somehow got it in mind to do a charity bike race across the entire Commonwealth of Pennsylvania, and he was trying to recruit as many of our peers as he could coax onto a bike to raise money with him. He was unrelenting. He told everyone he would help them out, organize training sessions, teach them how to prepare for the race and pace themselves. And through all this, unbeknownst to the people he convinced, Amelio had zero experience as a cyclist, excepting the ordinary exposure nearly every suburban kid gets to riding their bike every now and again. Yet here he was telling everyone the keys to cycling as though he were an aspiring tour rider.

Amelio's first organized training ride was a 150-mile loop across rural, remote state highways through rolling hills and gentle flats. After the first ten miles, everyone else dropped off and turned back home, but not before Amelio was cussed out as a fraud and pretender, for all the riders could see he was no more experienced than they were. At ninety-five miles, he called me to come pick him up, because determined as he was to complete the ride, his quads had seized up and he could no longer bend his legs.

Over the following weeks, Amelio suffered no end to the jibes and jokes about his cycling acumen. But what I really saw in the unending snark that went his way was a darker derision, a kind of resentment for the audacity of having the ambition to try something bold. But perhaps that was my bias, for I was the one who saw him on the ride back—a young man willing to go a full one hundred percent until his body could give no more. I recognized it as a kind of stupid determination I would never possess. It was rare. He was humbled by the experience, and he took their chiding quietly.

Two months later, Amelio raised a modest amount of money for riding the breadth of the state in three days. Five months after that, having only taken up cycling eight months prior, Amelio rode his bike from the Atlantic to the Pacific in eight weeks.

Yes, Amelio was foolish to think he could start his training by riding 150 miles. But it's just that kind of foolishness that makes up the disposition of a person who rides a bicycle across America less than a year from taking up cycling.

The Amelios were the people who first climbed Everest, strapped themselves onto rockets and flew into space. They broke world speed records on vehicles of every kind, swam from Cuba to Florida in shark-infested waters, and sailed around the world in leaky wooden ships. These people, no matter what you say to them, will find a way onto a spaceship and fan out into the stars. I am not writing about them. I'd be wasting my words. They're a blessed few, and they will not be stopped.

My chief concern is with the potential emigrants, which, technically would include all departing humans, but I refer here to the people moving away from Earth rather than those moving to another planet, to a space adventure. Due to geography and anthropological development, we have an analog to this situation in our history in the European diaspora of the Americas. Numbers of emigrants from that era are, of course, not entirely accurate, but it's fairly safe to say that during the early centuries of colonial emigration, somewhere between two and five percent of the populations of colonizing nations—Spain, England, France and Portugal—left their home nations for the Americas. Reasons for leaving Europe were various and varied over time. Both numbers and percentages increased as footholds of European settlements were increasingly more well established in the Americas.

Many people left for economic reasons, mostly hardships that came with population growth and limitations in land ownership. Thus, many of the emigrants were lower class peoples, looking for a chance at prosperity. Brave path-finders in families would usually go forth and establish themselves, sending letters back to relations to join them when a path forward toward a sustainable lifestyle was discovered.

Today, I see a similar development in our society. Even the language used by those in the bottom strata of our societies echoes the past. They're looking for economic breathing room, freedom from regulations and constraints, personal and religious liberties. And, in an ideal world, they should have it. There's no denying that some, if not most, of the regulations in the past two centuries have prevented a good measure of ecological devastation that would surely have befallen the Earth by unrestrained economic development of our natural resources. Those constraints have benefited the Earth in the long run. But as technology has been erected around these constraints, they have become increasingly rigid, inflexible, and ever-tightening, squeezing out the prospects of the least fortunate, as it ever has been in human history.

In space, the same constraints have followed us, mostly by force of habit. This is folly. Where the Earth is a finite and delicate ecosystem. Our solar system is so vast it might as well be infinite. It is also lifeless. We will not do the least harm to Io or Mars or the rocks of the asteroid belt by developing and populating them. Yet the constraints on who can harvest, who can fly a vessel, who can establish a base or build a habitat—these regulations prevent access to the potential pilgrim class, and these are the very people we should be encouraging to develop our solar system. Instead, we are recreating the political and economic conditions of the early colonial era.

We cycle around again to the same season in history. One need look no further than the writings of John Locke and John Stuart Mill to find almost identical verbiage to today's proponents of exploration, many of whom are not of that lower socioeconomic stratum—names like Mercum, Devers, even Hartsock. Their words may as well be echoes of the early liberal thinkers beholding a vast new continent and seeing the opportunity for liberty as well as prosperity. And why not? We are set before a vast new inexhaustible landscape of limitless resources and opportunities.

Except there's one major difference in this analogy. The Americas were an environment compatible with human life. Space isn't. Not yet. Pilgrims in ships in days past, had a harsh environment awaiting them once they survived the deadly voyage, yes. But that environment had potable water, breathable atmosphere, animals they could hunt and fish, edible fruits and vegetables, and even established native tribes that could help them navigate the new landscape when they fell into privation. Any new environment will need to provide these exigencies of life. These barriers are significant, difficult to overcome, and highly dangerous perils for any expedition, and they have yet to be fully reckoned with at scale.

Out here on Europa, with Earth supplying the outstation, I—one man—require food, vitamins, spare equipment, 3D printers and materials stock, replacement cartridges for CO_2 scrubbers, and a host of other specialized concerns that cannot be found or manufactured in this environment. Luckily, with the entirety of the human economy close enough at hand, I can get those needs met. This would not be the case if I took my operation to a moon orbiting a planet eight, eighty, or eight hundred thousand light years away.

If we continue to tightly regulate our solar system's commerce and exploration, as we are currently doing, the pilgrims will eventually see those foreign shores as a better option than relegation to a permanent economic and social underclass with no chance of upward mobility. That hasn't changed, and neither have we. We should. We must. Or someone like Amelio will come along and convince millions of people to take a deadly ride into the infinite, lacking the training, knowledge, equipment, expertise, and preparation to survive the ordeal. I can see it looming in the darkness inevitably.

The alternative is to encourage dysregulation of our system. Loosen constraints on lending for space ventures. One shouldn't need ten billion dollars in collateral to get a loan for a mining operation that will generate ten-times that revenue in ten months once it becomes operational. Dysregulation of capital will encourage upward economic migration rather than physical migration to an unregulated environment.

People left Europe in droves for the Americas because it was the wild west, a place they could make their fortunes, make a name for themselves, raise families that would have a legacy to pass down to children and grandchildren. If we don't make Europa and Neptune and Mars attractive in the same way, people will see Alpha Centauri, Altair, and Ross 154 as their only options into the decision-making class, where many of these pilgrims aspire to be. We need to make our solar system the wild west. Otherwise, I predict tens of millions of unprepared, unsuspecting people will rush head-long into the abyss.

The colonial era is littered with accounts of shipwrecks. Many of the souls on those ships and the ships themselves simply vanished—down to the sea in ships. This is the inevitable cost of exploration. You can find monuments to the lost in harbor cities to this day. There are many fascinating written accounts of such events, some fictional—Robinson Crusoe, comes to mind—and many more bio-graphical accounts of survivors. This is my point—that there were many survivors. On the sea, we could wash ashore, find a water supply and fish, build a signal fire and wait for a passing ship to happen by. There will be no such luck in interstellar space travel. No such luck.

I think of all these things as I'm exercising, cycling as it turns out, on my stationary bike. I've set up my bike at the mid-portal window so I can look out, and depending on the time of the station's orbit of Europa, I can ponder such things as I look out upon the cloudy bands of Jupiter. If the timing is right in Europa's trip around the king of planets, I can watch Jupiter's great red spot cycling around and around with my own eyes. I see this cycle so clearly. And, in my mind's eye, I can see our future developments in space just as clearly, just as Cassandra foresaw the burning battlements of Troy, and I know that no matter how loudly I shout these things from the rooftops it will hardly make a difference, for I'm asking for the powerful to loosen their control, to have faith in people they see as their lessers. I'm suggesting they allow others to develop territories they perceive as their own to appropriate for themselves alone, however unjustly and imperiously. The powerful will not listen.

My last resort is to entreat the future pilgrims for their patience. Do not get on those ships until we're well established in our own space first. The new world will not be as Amelio promises, for he doesn't know what he doesn't know—what I know. We're nowhere near mastery of this entirely foreign and lethally hostile environment. Not even close. There are no cities awaiting you. There aren't even wild, untamed wildernesses to carve out a homestead from. At best there will be barren rocks that are oxygen-rich enough to chemically squeeze some breathable elements out of or frozen meteors with enough ice to process with great effort into potable water.

To be out here, cycling around Europa, even close to home, an organization of hundreds of highly-skilled people needs years to bring together an excellent plan that accounts for almost every potential contingency, and then we need a safety net, usually in the form of a call to Earth for help. But first, a plan. A near-perfect plan.

That word 'plan' reminds me of a story my father once told me about plans when I was designing a thesis project in college. I told him I had a plan, and he told me this story.

At the end of the twentieth century they still hadn't outlawed combat sports in the West. And concussions be damned, men used to put on padded gloves and pummel each other in the face until one of them fell over unconscious or was declared a winner by the judges because the other was so befuddled by the blows he could barely stand. If you haven't seen a video of boxing, it is quite the shocking spectacle, and no wonder such a primal event drew such prolific advertising revenue, for it is truly a captivating sight in the same brutal way Romans would have found glad-iatorial combat riveting and shocking. My father told me of a champion fighter by the name Mike Tyson, who was so feared in his prime that his very name became synonymous with invincibility. Opponents, who'd spent their entire lives training to fight would walk into the ring merely hoping they could survive the first round. Most of them didn't. Before going into the ring, interviewers would ask them how they would defeat this invincible man—the most feared man on Earth. Some of them were, like my friend Amelio, haplessly optimistic in the face of the inevitable. Most of them were pragmatic. But they and their trainers all went into the ring with a strategy for conquering the unconquerable. They all had a plan. Once, when an interviewer asked Tyson about his opponent's plan to defeat him, he replied with the kind of curt, incisive wisdom only a fighter could possess. He said simply, "Everyone has a plan till they get punched in the mouth."

Tyson's business was punching people in the mouth, and he was better at it than perhaps anyone ever was. Before his hands, all plans disintegrated. Our business as human beings is getting into all kinds of trouble, much of it of our own making. Space's business is entropy, and it carries out its business with relentlessness and utter indifference to our best laid plans. Aspiring explorers will meet the fists of the infinite. Plans will disintegrate before them.

People once spoke of the Titanic as an unsinkable ship unironically, with knowing certainty and arrogance. A short time later, after the shock of the indomitable ship's sinking wore off, the same people proclaimed with the same certainty and arrogance that they had predicted as much all along, had told their friends even, that we are all destined for a reckoning, especially when, in our hubris, we run around calling ocean-going vessels unsinkable. We had it coming. And we'll go forth towards disaster still, thinking, 'not me; not today; improbable,' and we'll be shocked when what we knew would happen happens all over again. This is me, the guy who has already been there, saying I told you so beforehand. Don't forget it.

Probes, people. We should send probes into the deep. You, on the other hand, should stay home.

Do otherwise and go down to the sea in ships, a victim of the current iteration in the same inevitable human cycle, rounding the galaxy again and again. Probes.

Remember I said that when you realize your folly.

Tanner Gunnison told you so.

Playing the Sondomme

Music had been a part of Liryre Garson's life from before she was born. Diedre, her mother, a music teacher, had strategically made use of headphones on her pregnant belly whenever Liryre kicked up a fuss in utero, and, for the most part, it had worked like a charm. Soothing sounds had settled Liryre then, and music almost always worked to calm her nerves even after she was born, so her mother was liberal with the therapeutic use of music with her crying newborn.

Soon after, came the first lessons. The wondrous sounds had order and structure, an origin, and seemingly a purpose. These earliest music lessons were some of Liryre's earliest memories. And just as most children become enculturated to the normalcy of their familial surroundings, it never struck Liryre that it was possible to live without music, for she had no conception of life outside a musical household. Nor could she conceive of a life lived anywhere other than an Ag cylinder except as an abstraction, even though the vast majority of Dreeson's Star's residents lived aboard one of the massive orbital rings encircling the two mid-system gas giants.

Most of the music came from there— either Iophos, the innermost of the two great planets, or from Athos, the nearer ringed gas giant, a beautiful pearl-white gaseous maelstrom with a contiguous megalopolis of a ring, home to four trillion urbane residents, many of whom loved music as much as Liryre did, and a select few who composed and performed the soundtrack to Liryre's young life in Peabody Homestead, one of six hundred seventy-six Ag cylinders in the Bantham cluster, which the Garson family called home. Peabody Bantham itself, was home to roughly fifty thousand agricultural engineers and farmers, as well as the support personnel who made Peabody Bantham a home—the caretakers, engineers, workers, tavern owners, and pilots. They were a small fraction of the people in the Dreeson System, but without knowing how different her life was, Liryre was confident in expressing to her school pen pal on the Athos ring that her life was normal, and when asked whether she ever got dizzy living in a cylinder or whether it was strange seeing the other side of the cylinder above her instead of sky, she replied confidently that Peabody's lightbar was too bright to ever look straight into the sky, and because the crops were all trellised vertically, it was very hard to tell they lived on a cylinder at all. Liryre's home, like the homes of all the other residents of the Peabody Homestead, was set in the rim itself, a very homey two-story flat with plenty of space and light, and even a spare room where her mother gave private music lessons after school.

It was Liryre who was the primary beneficiary of those extra hours of work, both as a student herself but also in the added income, as it was Diedre's added income that allowed the Garsons to invest in musical instruments and curriculum tools for Liryre that trained her in sightreading, sight-singing, and developing perfect pitch. All this before her sixth birthday.

The name Sondomme first entered Liryre's consciousness as merely a place where the music came from. It may as well have been a mythological land in the same way the ancient peoples of Earth attributed the birth of the winds to gods in far off lands. And, in a childish sense, Liryre's intuition was correct, for much of the system's great music could trace its origins to many of the Sondomme Conservatory's student and alumni composers and the neighborhood in Athos's capital city of Ithaca named for the system's most prestigious music school.

Liryre was six years old when she first began to understand what Sondomme truly was, for it was at this age when she first remembered watching the Haig Prize recital, which was the performance portion of the conservatory's entrance auditions, with winners gaining admittance and the top performers even winning scholarships. She was drawn to it that year in particular, because for the first time in over thirty years, a young man from one of the industrial clusters, Ben Waller—the son of a foundry worker—was invited to audition, and all of the millions of citizens in the Ag clusters, industrial clusters, the miners, and the workers of the outer extremities of the system had all adopted young Ben Waller as their own. Despite the disadvantages of his rural education, his lack of refined instruction, his parents' limited means, and the discouragement he received at every turn,

Ben had persevered and achieved his dream of competing in the Haig auditions, and he had the support of the Garsons, who watched like seemingly everyone else in Peabody Homestead and each of the other six hundred seventy-six Ag cylinders in the Bantham Cluster, all of whom rooted feverishly for young Ben Waller.

Liryre was awed by the competition. The refinement of the applicants, all seemingly so young—twelve and thirteen—yet each seemed to play like tenured professionals. Their musical selections and presentations were calculated and well practiced. Their pitch, tone, control—all as expert as Liryre had ever heard. She'd never seen kids play like that before, and sure, they were older, but she could see they were still kids. And the commentary made her nervous for Ben. The announcer, in between performances, discussed the nuances of each presentation, followed by a former professor at the Sondomme, who critiqued each player harshly, indicating which bad habits they would need to improve should they gain admission and even outright declaring which of these amazing performers weren't cut out for the Sondomme. Liryre could hardly distinguish a difference in their quality—yet he, the sage keeper of the Sondomme critical ear, declared harshly that among these most brilliant, there were unworthy.

By the time Ben Waller performed, the stage had been so steadily graced with brilliance that his talent was evidently lacking by comparison. Had Liryre seen him in the Common House or the Crest performing as he did on that stage, she'd have been mesmerized by his ability. But the contrast made it evident to even a six-year-old, albeit a very musical one, that Ben Waller was not Sondomme material. Nonetheless, when he finished, she was proud that he'd made it there. He was there before billions of children of Athos, most of whom played music of some kind. Ben Waller from Ixos Foundry had made it to the Haig stage and played well for the son of a foundry worker.

Then came the moment that shaped Liryre's life. The commentator, Professor Alby Murtach uttered the following: "It sounded as though the outer bearings need a greasing from that cylinder lad. Best to send him back to his proper place." And the professor continued along those lines for minutes in between acts. Many of the words would burn an impression on Liryre's mind so deep that she put them up on her wall in the following years. Most of the professor's comments reflected Murtach's belief that young Ben Waller, to protect him from the humiliation he'd endured, should never have been accepted to the auditions in the first place, and, that in the future, to prevent a similar occurrence, applications should be limited to the children of Athos from accredited schools—vetted children of pedigree, with musical class. It hadn't been right to see a child so shamelessly and publicly outclassed before the entire star system.

Liryre was equally heartbroken and furious. At six, she lacked the vocabulary to express her outrage. "Why is that man so mean?" was all she could manage to express to her parents through her tears. He was mean, yes, but words like cruel, callous, arrogant, imperious, sanctimonious—and a host of other accurate characterizations were beyond her. Sondomme, for the first time, became a harsh place for her kind, the seat of broken dreams as much as divine music. Liryre decided she was not going to take such naked cruelty lying down. Homesteaders could play music too. She vowed she would prove it to those Sondomme snobs. She, Liryre Garson, would not only perform at the Haig auditions, as Ben Waller had, and win the Haig prize, as he'd failed to do, but Liryre Garson was going to wipe the stage with those stuck up Athosian jerks if it was the last thing she ever did.

Danos and Diedre Garson thought it would be like most childhood experiences, a passing moment in their daughter's development, a lesson about the class differences between the trillions on the rings and the millions on the cylinders whose labor supported the wealthier lifestyles on the urbane megalopolises of the planetary rings. They expected that Liryre would have forgotten the Haig auditions by the following afternoon. But after school, she took up her ciolina and practiced nearly ceaselessly until she was called to dinner, her auditory tutor keeping time and correcting for tone at every beat along the way. Diedre and Danos discussed it in bed as that night, expecting that it would pass. And then it didn't. Not over a week, nor over a month, until a year went by with Liryre monomaniacally pursuing musical perfection through hours of endless practice.

Liryre, between her natural gifts, her mother's tutoring, and her own love of music, had always been accelerated for one of her age, but when she began to practice unceasingly, she soon turned herself into something of a local prodigy. Though both Danos and Diedre were extremely proud of their daughter, Liryre's persistent drive toward musical perfection did not progress without tension within the Garson household, for as much as Diedre encouraged her daughter to surpass levels she had only ever hoped to achieve herself, Danos feared that the pursuit of such lofty goals would eventually lead to the kind of monumental failure that had crushed Ben Waller and every other outsider who attempted to burst into Athos's cultural space unwelcome and unwanted. At the end of it, he feared only heartbreak awaited his daughter and he hated watching her practice away her childhood, hardly pausing to enjoy that precious time in her life.

Yet before they knew it, their little girl, their ceaselessly motivated prodigy, was not so little anymore. She was wowing audiences with her perfect technique and musical mastery. Between her mother's lessons, her constant studying, and the vast computer-based instruction and resources, Liryre's playing became peerless in the Ag homesteads and all the support clusters as well.

In the year of her twelfth birthday, Liryre did just as Ben Waller had done before her, submitting her application to her local cluster's audition rounds for thirteens a year early, so that she could still be considered for the Haig auditions at Sondomme the following year should she prove worthy. No one had attempted admission to Sondomme from the cylinders since, and though it never became a formal rule as Alby Murtach had suggested, the humiliation he'd dished out had served as such a deterrent that it was an all but unwritten rule, a rule Liryre Garson vowed to break.

At twelve, in front of the thousands in attendance at the Acton Admin Cylinder's Tobin Opera House, Liryre Garson bested the competition beyond any doubt, and in her acceptance speech she challenged the Sondomme faculty to try and keep her from the Haig Prize the following year. Liryre Garson put the entire Athos Ring on notice. She would be in Ithaca the following year for thirteens auditions whether they invited her or not, and she would settle for nothing less than top of the podium if she had to storm the stage to perform.

Liryre hardly took a moment to acknowledge her accomplishment, being the youngest applicant ever to win thirteens at Acton and gain admission to the Tobin Conservatory.

"You should be happy, Liryre, and proud of yourself," Diedre told her on the shuttle ride back to Peabody Homestead.

"I would be disappointed if it didn't happen," Liryre responded. "But happy? I don't get to be happy yet."

"When do you get to be happy?"

"I'm not sure," Liryre said. "But not yet. Who says everyone gets to be happy anyway?"

Liryre declined the invitation to the Tobin Conservatory, both because of her parents' desire for her to remain at home and because of Tobin's long-term focus, which Liryre feared would end up being more of a distraction from her goal of victory at Sondomme the following year. Six months after her victory at Acton, she received a message from the famous conservatory that read: "No need to storm the stage, Miss Garson. We've received your application to audition and were sufficiently impressed with your talents to invite you. More details will follow to connect you with our application system. Congratulations, and good luck."

She spent the following six months preparing her repertoire, both in the required pieces and in her own selections. And then, on a day that was an ordinary Tuesday for all the other humans in the Galaxy, Liryre Garson departed Peabody Homestead with her mother Diedre for Athos, on her collision course with the Sondomme Conservatory.

The trip was the longest mother and daughter had spent together for as long as Diedre could remember. In the shuttles—first from Peabody Homestead to Acton Central and then on to Ithaca on Athos—there was nowhere for Liryre to practice. It was the first day Diedre could remember Liryre not playing her ciolina since she was a very small child. It did nothing to improve Liryre's mood. She was impatient and grouchy, spending most of her time with her ears on, reviewing the pieces she knew already as firmly as she knew her own name. Yet she studied still, spent time in mental repetition and reflection, preparing not only for the musical performance but for the crowd, the lights, the pressure, the steps she would take to control her breathing and her manner. But Diedre had no such script to prepare to be a supportive mother. In some ways it felt as though her daughter was putting on armor, and as a mother, she had both the instinct to protect her from the need but also the necessity to bring Liryre forward to her aspirations. She could only hope those aspirations wouldn't prove too harsh for Liryre to endure. For much of the voyage to Athos, Diedre wondered if it wouldn't have been better for everyone if she'd stayed home with Rian instead of Danos, for there was no way all four Garsons could afford two weeks on Athos, and Diedre had long questioned how much musical guidance she could offer Liryre anymore. So, she decided to just be the best mom she could be.

Even Liryre, as indifferent as she tried to be, was drawn to the window of the shuttle as Athos grew larger in view. The planet's milky color and busy, tumultuous upper gas layers were a wonder to both their eyes. They were able to count out four of the eleven moons as they approached the ring, which as familiar as the sight was on screens, in pictures, on logos and iconography, something about seeing it with the eyes stirred excitement in the outsiders that neither Liryre nor Diedre could quite express. Mom held her daughter around the shoulders as they watched quietly in wonder. The ring grew in scope as the planet did. What seemed a tiny band around a fat globe became an immense regular structure hovering against an impossibly enormous, amazingly bright, cloudy-white horizon. By the time the shuttle began to transect the ring's side, the black of space had completely disappeared from the window, and only the bright white of Athos loomed.

Next, the ship drew over the inner edge of the ring, hovering over the inner-facing nano sheet, and the shuttle matched speeds with the progression of the ring, slowly pulling itself into unison with Ithaca's sky portal. Once opened, Liryre could see darkness again beneath them, but the darkness was broken up by city lights that extended as far as she could see once the shuttle dropped below the portal's rim. Then the portal itself closed, shutting out the light of Athos, save for pinpoint gaps in the light shield that mimicked the stars of the night sky.

"It is night now?" Liryre said as they seemed to descend to Ithaca, whose lights grew prominent quickly in the window.

"Does it not seem so?" Diedre said. "I am exhausted myself." But she could see that as much as Liryre tried to act unimpressed, she was far too excited to be as tired as her mother. It had been so long since she'd seen such wonder in her eldest daughter's eyes.

An hour or so later, they arrived by tram at Sondomme Square, and to both of them, they may as well have been arriving at the Roman Coliseum. For the people of Dreeson's star, the Sondomme had grown as sanctified in legend as the great pyramids of Giza, the New York Statue of Liberty, or the Indeeta of Suravhi. The brilliance of the yellow stone, the classical architecture and statues, the white marble walkways, even in darkness, the genius of the Sondomme seemed to illuminate the night. Never had mother or daughter seen such a city. They settled in that night, opting to splurge on a big breakfast the following morning.

From the rooftop garden of the hotel's dining area at daybreak, with the light slowly coming up, Diedre and Liryre took turns pointing out sights on the long horizon, from the mountainous boundaries of the ring's edges to the north and south to the landmark buildings of Ithaca, ranging from the nearby neighborhood of Sondomme, all the way to Petros on the horizon in the east and the suburbs in the west where the horizon, which they knew to be curved seemed flat and unending to the eyes. The morning light of Athos, processed through the nano sheet's filter, seemed the bluest blue, a sky meant to mimic Earth's. Everything about the city seemed welcoming and right, even as the pressure of the auditions loomed. Their waiter, a lifelong resident of the Sondomme section of Ithaca recognized Liryre from her Acton performance and confessed that despite his local bias, he would be rooting for the outsider.

After breakfast, Liryre began the long practice schedule she'd planned to get out of the way so she and Diedre could see the city in the afternoon before they were scheduled for check-in with the conservatory's Haig Commission that evening. About an hour into her routine, Liryre was interrupted by a ping at the door, and because Diedre was in the shower, she had to get up to answer it.

When the door opened there was a girl there, and even annoyed as she was at being interrupted, Liryre found that it was difficult to be angry at the unexpected visitor, for she had a pleasant, dimpled smile and a friendly welcoming look about her, even though she didn't speak at first.

"Can I help you?" Liryre asked.

"Of course, I'm sorry. I came to say hello. You're Liryre," she said. "I was hoping we could be friends, and I'm very excited and I say stupid things when I'm excited like right now, but I'm really very glad you're here."

"You seem lovely," Liryre said. "But I was practicing, and I'm not sure...who are you?"

"Oh! I forgot that too. You probably don't know because you're from the cylinders. I've never known anyone from the cylinders before. I'm Terra Michel."

"I'm happy to meet you, Terra Michel," Liryre said. "It was very kind of you to stop by, but I really must get back to practice."

"Yes, if you insist, Liryre, I'll leave you to it, but I wanted to see if you'd like to...well, I knew you weren't from Athos, and I thought, 'What could I share with a ciolinist from the cylinders that she would really love?' So, I wanted to offer to take you to the Ibiri Collection. It's my favorite place—well, one of my favorite places. They have musical instruments from all over the system, and the best part, they have three instruments from Earth made from real wood from real trees that grew over two thousand years ago."

"And they'll let us see them?"

"Um-hmm. I've been there so much they just let me go in. They say that Mr. Keinholm has even played one."

"They work?"

"Yes, that's one of the, uhm, the curators have to make sure they still work and make repairs if there's ever something wrong, but they keep them in careful conditions."

"I would really love to go, but—"

"She would love to go," Diedre said, appearing, wet hair and all, from the adjacent room. "Your father will be thrilled to hear you've already made a friend."

Liryre turned around toward her mother and gestured with her head toward her room, as if to say practice should take precedent.

"Liryre would love to go with you—I'm sorry, what did you say your name was?"

The young girl smiled, almost as though she thought it was funny they didn't know her, "I'm Terra Michel, Mrs. Garson. My sister is in her fourth year at the Conservatory, so I know my way around very well. I know all the best spots to visit and relax and eat and practice—all the best spots."

"That sounds wonderful, Terra. You girls have a nice time. Just be sure to be back by four. I'm sure Liryre will let you know, but we have an important event to register for tonight."

Terra smiled and shook her head, "Of course, Mrs. Garson, we'll be back in plenty of time."

Terra Michel led the way from the Garsons' room at the hotel to the Tram stop underground, which was two stops from the Grand Museum, which housed the Ibiri Collection. Outside, there was a crowd like nothing Liryre had ever seen, hundreds, perhaps thousands of people queueing up to get inside the Grand Museum of the Sondomme.

"I've never seen so many people," Liryre said. "It's overwhelming."

"It's okay," Terra said. "You should see it on the weekend, especially this weekend. You won't be able to move out here."

"I don't think I would like that. How will we ever get inside with such a line?"

"Come on," Terra said, taking Liryre's hand and pulling her through the crowd. She brought Liryre to a shady corner at the side of the entrance marked in small lettering "conservatory." And they were promptly admitted to the museum.

Terra led the way to the Ibiri room. Inside it was dark and cool and quiet as people snaked their way through the collection of beautiful and curious instruments. Some of them, Liryre had never seen or even heard of before, and she marveled at all the ways that humans had invented to make beautiful sounds fill the air. She wondered at the prospect that each of these bizarre-looking instruments would have hundreds of masters, who like her, would have spent years of their lives dedicated to coaxing the perfect tone from such elaborate arrays of strings, skins, boxes, pipes, and reeds. Then finally, Terra took Liryre by the hand and brought her before the three wooden instruments from Earth. The first, a violin from a nation called France, about which Terra related all of the details—that it came from multiple types of trees and had been played by a succession of notable masters for over a thousand years before coming to the Sondomme seven hundred years earlier. "That's wood?" Liryre kept repeating. "It doesn't look like it could come from a tree at all. It's beautiful."

"And," Terra said, "made by the hands of a single master craftsman, but I can't say his name correctly because it's very strange."

Next, Terra showed her the wondrous wooden contrabass, which towered over the two girls. And finally, the youngest and most beautiful of the instruments, a guitar from the twenty-first century, which was the only instrument of the three where the fine grain of the wood was evidently observable. It called to Liryre most especially, given its similarity to her own ciolina recordare, which she'd spent her whole life cradling in her lap.

As their time in the museum progressed, Liryre noticed that people were noticing them, primarily Terra, but because of the eyes drawn to her, Liryre could see that some in the crowd were recognizing and pointing her out as well.

"It's really only in the Sondomme you'll get recognized," Terra said. "Some other places in Ithaca. Some cities where they follow the Haig closely or maybe serious music students. You'll get used to it."

"So you're in the competition as well, Terra?" Liryre asked.

She nodded and smiled. "I hope we can still be friends."

"Why wouldn't we be?"

It was the first moment all day the smile fell from Terra Michel's face.

"They're all so competitive, like you, Liryre. It makes me almost like the enemy. It's hard for me to have friends in music, and I don't know anyone who isn't a musician, not here in the Sondomme."

Later that evening, at registration, Terra came over to Liryre to say hello, and what had been subtly apparent in the museum became self-evident in the staging area. All eyes that weren't directed in the immediate vicinity of the competitors and their families were at varying times following the movements of Terra Michel. Liryre could feel it immediately when Terra approached her, suddenly the room was curious about her, "the barrel girl" as she'd heard some whisper behind her back, "Is she friends with Terra Michel now? She must be as good as it seems."

"Liryre, I just wanted to say that no matter what happens, good luck, and I hope you do come here, because I'd like to be friends and to study with you."

"Me too," Liryre said, "and you too. Good luck, I mean."

She felt the tension at that moment, and from that moment, almost as if that single interaction had changed everything, all the other applicants took a step back from her, either out of respect, reverence, or perhaps even fear, but Liryre didn't like the feeling. For the first time since they'd arrived on Athos, she thought of Ben Waller and what he must have felt in that same room seven years earlier.

Liryre didn't see Terra Michel for two days once the auditions began. Liryre made it a point to never watch other performers during competitions, finding it a distraction from her personal routine, which she performed every bit as faithfully as the pieces themselves. However, on day three, in a back hallway on the way from a solo recital of etudes, Liryre bumped into Terra, who smiled and asked if she could sit with Liryre for a few minutes in one of the side annexes and chat. Liryre was finished for the day, so she was happy to have the company. Terra professed to be doing well and enjoying herself; although, she mentioned that the one thing she hated about these auditions was the idea that music was causing so many of these most dedicated musicians so much stress. "That just seems wrong somehow," Terra said. "But maybe it makes all of us better in the long run."

By Saturday the Grand Jury had been selected along with the top fifty thirteens in the whole of the Dreeson system. These fifty signature performances were the predominant factor in who was selected as the Haig winner, and Liryre knew her standing to be exactly where she expected—quite high—as indicated by her early evening time slot. The top five applicants would be selected for an encore performance after the winners were announced.

Liryre was too focused to spend any time appreciating the magnitude of the moment. It was the lifelong aspiration of almost every musician in the system to be a center-stage soloist at the Grand Opera House of the Sondomme in Ithaca. She was here now, barely thirteen years old. Acknowledging that honor—just like watching her competitors' performances—was another distraction from the perfect execution of her routine, which Liryre believed would see her through. She thought only of the number of steps to center stage, her execution of the bow she'd practiced through every performance of her young life, and positioning her instrument elegantly and perfectly, like she did each time she played. She was ready.

For a brief moment, before she began, she thought of her mother, seated somewhere in the dim light of the amphitheater, her father and sister at home, the crowd at the Common House on Peabody Homestead, doubtless gathered to watch her, just as they'd all gathered to watch Ben Waller all those years ago—only this time on Peabody they needn't adopt a foundry worker's son as their own: Liryre Garson was truly one of them. And she was center stage, Sondomme, with the lights down and the orchestra coming up. It was her moment to shine. She took a final breath before the ciolina's entrance and played her heart out. And after twenty minutes, she could honestly say that she had never played better.

After several minutes of applause, a shower of flowers on the stage and more bows than she could count, she was ushered backstage to a second-story box side-stage that she hadn't been able to see in the blind focus of the spotlight. There were two empty seats left. As she was sat, she was greeted by one of the other five finalists, Caley Obfer, who said to her, "I think you were incredible tonight, Liryre. Congratulations. You played like a goddess."

After a few minutes of quiet buzz in the warm light of the opera house, Terra Michel was introduced.

"Here she comes," she heard a girl's voice behind her say. "Little miss perfect." Another contestant shushed the speaker.

Then the lights went down, the orchestra came up, and Terra began.

Liryre understood within a few notes why people stared at Terra Michel. She hadn't played but a few measures before Liryre decided she'd never quite even heard music before. It wasn't any one thing. The tone, the technique, the genius of her choices in interpretation—the totality of everything—it was as though an entirely different world of music lived in harmony alongside them at any given moment and no one had even realized it existed, until Terra Michel simply and effortlessly opened the door to this world, allowing the rest of the blessed souls in the room to listen in. Liryre was so overwhelmed and awestruck that she couldn't keep tears from welling up and streaming down her face. By the time she'd finished playing, Liryre was convinced that Terra Michel was an entirely different species of human being. A blessed one. So blessed. Liryre didn't know how to make sense of it.

When Liryre was informed that she'd been selected for an encore, she didn't quite know what to do. She was ushered downstairs and sat in a practice space, where she attempted to refocus, improvising variations on the piece, which itself was a set of modern variations on a collection of inter-pretations of a twentieth-century Earth composer named Lauro. Liryre's interpretation was a technical and extra-ordinarily upbeat choice for an encore, and now she felt entirely inadequate even attempting it with Terra Michel in the building.

After a few minutes of practice, Liryre heard a knock on the door. Terra Michel peeked her head in. She was smiling. Liryre smiled back. She couldn't understand how the others could resent Terra for her gift. It was like being jealous of the stars for their beauty.

"You were wonderful tonight, friend," Terra Michel said.

Liryre nodded. "I'd never seen you play before, Terra. I don't think I could ever play like you."

"You can play like you, Liryre. You're very special. Everyone loved your playing."

It was difficult for Liryre to separate her feelings about the musician from the friend she'd made. Both of them were real, but one was ordinary and unassuming and easy to like. The other was difficult for Liryre to even comprehend, but she knew she didn't want that overwhelming feeling to prevent them from kindling a friendship.

They talked for a few minutes more before she confessed to Terra that she was having trouble focusing on her encore after watching Terra play.

"I like to close my eyes sometimes and pretend that I'm weightless on one of the moons playing to a flock of butterflies," Terra said. "It really helps."

"I'm going to try it," Liryre said.

An hour later when she was introduced, Liryre was named second seat by the Provost of the Sondomme, who declared Liryre a once-in-a-generation talent who'd be the Haig winner in any other year but for the once-in-a-lifetime talent of Terra Michel.

Unbeknownst to her, Liryre's tears had been caught on the broadcast and interpreted, unfairly, as sour and jealous, yet Liryre's manner when she was reintroduced belied that notion, for she seemed gracious as she sat, and she played her encore magnificently, envisioning butterflies frenetically circling her ciolina as she sat weightless on the Sondomme stage.

Liryre was reunited with her mother backstage and they watched Terra together.

"What do you make of your new friend?" Diedre asked when Terra had finished and the applause had finally died down enough to make herself heard.

"I think she's just different," Liryre said. "And I think I have a lot to learn about music."

Diedre pulled her daughter toward her. "I'm so incredibly proud of you."

The following day, Terra, Liryre, and Sabbie, the third of the three medalists were honored at a string of events at all corners of the Sondomme, which culminated in an awards dinner where all three were formally invited to take up study in the professional orchestral course, which was eight years of the most rigorous course of musical study in the known galaxy.

"I feel like I don't know anything about music," Liryre confessed to Terra after they were presented their emblems.

"Let's learn it all together, then," Terra said. "If you come."

And Liryre realized that for all the work she'd put into winning the Haig prize, she hadn't considered what might come after. It was beyond the moment, but she was beginning to envision it.

After the dinner, Diedre whisked Liryre off to the hypermag. "I have a surprise for you, but we'll have to go to New Corinth, and we'll have to stay up late."

"I'll try to stay awake," Liryre said.

"You can take a nap on the way. The ride is four hours."

The hypermag took them nearly a quarter of the way around the ring nearly as fast as a shuttle ride could have traversed the distance. Liryre did sleep on her mother's shoulder as the train hummed along, and when they popped up again in New Corinth, the light was just fading from the day for a second time, and Liryre, exhausted as she was from the week, was excited to see what her mother had planned for them.

The city seemed a totally different world. Where Ithaca, particularly the Sondomme area, seemed a place centered around classical beauty, calling back to ancient roots, art, and architecture, New Corinth seemed new, calling forth to something bright and unseen. There was a different kind of vibrant energy about its streets. Though it didn't seem grand in the same sense Ithaca did, it smelled of blossoming flowers and street food, and though the streets were more regular and less graceful, every block seemed to have a small park where people were gathered, playing games, playing music, or sitting in quiet comfort.

Liryre knew better than to ask what her mother was up to. She understood there was some purpose to it.

When they finally stopped walking, Diedre sat them down at a tavern that was half inside, half spilling out into a piazza that had a kind of warm night life lit by tiny colored strings of light garlands and faux candles on the tops of roped-off tables. As they sat, they snacked on fried potatoes and watched the people enjoy the evening, and after an hour or so, a band came out to play.

Liryre hadn't heard much music like it before. It was very simple—too simple for her tastes, a repetitive progression of a handful of chords over a regular beat, and what it lacked in inventiveness it seemed to make up for in volume, yet the people in the crowd—all young adults to Liryre's eyes—they seemed to revel in the noise, dancing, cheering wildly, and singing along. That venue seemed an odd choice for her music teacher mother to choose for their mother daughter time. They sat just outside the roped-off area for a few hours, sipping Ayger sweet-cha from the Ralston cluster, which was quite good, but Liryre still couldn't quite figure out what they were doing there of all places on Athos.

When the band finished several hours later, the group of nearly a hundred revelers cheered loudly and surrounded the players, exhorting them to keep playing later into the night, but the band disappeared into the tavern and the crowd slowly dispersed, breaking off into groups and gravitating toward music emanating from the other venues lining the square.

As things quieted down, Liryre was about to ask her mother what the trip was all about when a young man approached the table, shook hands with Diedre, said "nice to meet you," and sat.

"And you too," the young man said to Liryre. "The superstar of the cylinders."

He looked familiar, and after a few seconds, Liryre realized that he'd been the contrabass player from the band, only he'd ditched the wig, sunglasses, and garish jacket he'd sported during the show. Still though, there was something else.

"Your mother tells me that you were a big supporter of mine back in the day, Liryre," he said, extending his hand. "I'm certainly a big fan of yours now. You were wonderful this weekend."

"I'm sorry," Liryre said, shaking her head. "I'm not sure I recognize you."

"I don't tell a lot of people this," he joked, "but I'm Ben Waller, you know, that Ben Waller."

"Oh! Yes, of course!" Liryre said. "Now I see it. You didn't have facial hair back then."

"I didn't have a lot of things back then, most of all a clue, but who does at thirteen?" Ben said. "Hey, we're all so proud of you, Liryre. I spoke to my parents over the weekend. They were watching. Everyone was watching. And it was so crazy to have Diedre track me down out of the blue and tell me she wanted us to meet. Just...well, for me that was a tough time, and then to hear that it had inspired you. I never would have thought that any good would have come from that."

"I'm speechless. I don't know what to say, Ben," Liryre said. "I thought you'd be at conservatory somewhere."

"I was for a while. In Bayrn, which is about another two hours down the hypermag line. They were one of the only schools that would take me after Sondomme. I switched instruments, started playing bass. I was there four years before I just didn't want anything to do with formal training anymore."

"But this?" Liryre said. "It's so different."

"I know. I had all the same thoughts, trying so hard to impress all those music snobs. All those fancy people. But these are my people. You know, our people. The ones who keep food on the table, keep the lights on, keep the trains running. I like playing for them better. Not too stuck up to dance and sing along and let you know they're having a good time."

"I was just...you don't find it boring? I mean the music? Five chords in four-four time, over and over again all night?"

"Your mother and I were talking about this, Liryre. I was the same at your age too. You work so hard at learning to play music—it's your sole focus, the goal, the objective—that you miss what music really is. I had to learn it from a pop singer I was playing contrabass for in bars like this. I only started playing pop to make a little extra money while I was in school. And before too long, the band started doing really well, because this singer understood something they don't teach you in conservatory."

"What's that?"

"That it isn't about the music, or at least not what you think the music is. It sounds strange. But he kept telling me after shows, 'I need something more out of you, Ben,' and I would tell him, 'I'm doing my job. I'm playing the songs perfect,' and it wasn't hard, because this pop music is really simple music. But then he started saying before every show, 'Ben, tonight we're playing the Sheridan Theatre. Tonight, we're playing The Tenpenny. Tonight, we're playing The Copper Bell.' All the club names, just like that. And it took me probably six months before I slowly began to realize he meant that literally, that when he changed the set in the middle of the set, he was reading something in the theatre, moving the energy through it in a different way, changing the notes, creating nuance. His instrument wasn't the microphone or his voice or the band or the words or even the music itself. When he said we were playing the Sheridan Theatre, he meant we were playing the Sheridan Theatre, and that's when I began to understand what music really is, Liryre. It's what makes your friend Terra Michel different. She probably doesn't even know that she knows it, but that's what she's doing, playing the Sondomme."

"I don't even know what to say to that, Ben." Liryre said. "How do you even begin to practice that?"

"Exactly," Ben said.

The lights in the square began to dim as several of the venues on the far side of the piazza closed their doors. Liryre noticed for the first time that the sky at night here on Athos did look just like the stars from the west bay window on Peabody Homestead.

"It changed me when I first learned that too," Ben said. "You work so hard for so long to play music, and then realize, you're doing a whole different thing than you thought you were. It's a little crazy."

"I'm not sure I know what to do about it. So, you're saying I shouldn't go to Sondomme?"

"Oh, God, no! Liryre, by all means. What an opportunity. Go. Learn. There are maybe a billion kids on this ring alone who would give anything to trade places with you. And maybe, even as much as Sondomme itself, you'll get to play with Terra. Learn all this together. She might be your best teacher. Really. And don't let me change your mind. I'm just trying to maybe open your eyes a little."

"Okay. It's just...it's all so much. I had this idea of what it would all be, and a week ago, I had no idea. I didn't understand anything."

"And you still don't probably. You may never. I don't. Part of that's growing up. The other part is music. It's still the most mysterious force in the universe—why these sounds should make anyone feel anything, it's astounding. And in some ways, it's the realest thing there is."

At that point, the purveyors came out and began to remove the tables, so Diedre, Ben, and Liryre left the tables and walked into the square, at the center of which was a small fountain.

"When's your train?" Ben asked.

"Two hours," Diedre said. "Should get us back by day-break."

At the front of the fountain there was a woman sitting cross-legged bowing pop jazz on a cyolin she'd set on a blanket in front of her on the cobblestone floor. Ben, Diedre, and Liryre stood in the square listening, unsure whether to part then and there. The fountain behind the cyolin player was cycling through colors as the water sprayed up and fell behind her. A group of revelers leaving one of the taverns on the other side of the square began to sing as they approached the fountain. Liryre didn't know the song, but the revelers knew every lyric word-for-word.

"Mirrors. Signs. All the sounds that ring in time..."

They sang the whole song with the cyolin player as Ben, Diedre, and Liryre looked on, smiling as the group passed by into the night.

"I'll be here if you need anything," Ben said before parting. "I'm just a train ride away, and I can't wait to come down and see you play the Sondomme, Liryre Garson. You are something of a miracle, and your story has just begun."

There on the night side of Athos, in a city of twenty million souls, on a planetary ring filled with more people than had ever graced their home world, in the center of a city square, by a fountain, a mother and her daughter stood beside a single musician, listening, and in the darkness, the quiet world itself seemed to vibrate through them, reso-nating, lingering as the music played, and as the sound died down, they stood there together while the vibrations slowly faded out.

The Prospectors

In the deep of space, it is often said that a planet cannot become a world until it is peopled. The destruction of planets sometimes begins with supernovae, with the gradual mega-expansion of aged stars, or with the greedy hunger of wandering black holes. What then destroys a world? Billions of uninhabitable planets never have a chance to become a peopled world. Some worlds die after long inhabitations following the decline or self-immolation of vast empires and civilizations. Other worlds die in their infancy, before a civilization has a chance to fully take root. Such was the fate of Damon Mines.

The settlement began as not much more than a mining outpost on a small, lifeless, rocky planet with a breathable atmosphere and a few limited pools of liquid water. As a place to live, there was little to recommend it, for the planet was arid, hot, and hostile to habitation. The earliest visits recounted a dusty, unpleasant surface riddled with impassible mountains and a gravity in the moderate range of the habitability zone, at slightly greater than point-eight-six G. To the eyes, Damon Mines was drab and unappealing, governed mostly by a distant orange sun that for most of the year left the sky a dim brownish, sepia that reflected off the rust-colored hills in a dull haze. The look of the place, and the elemental profile, at first glance, made it a strong candidate to be skipped over or stripped for its nitrogen and oxygen for use on the massive planetary rings of the nearby systems of Dreeson's and Carroll's stars. In fact, it was a survey mission for just such a project that detected such rich deposits of valuable transition metals that Damon 2, as the planet was then called, was re-designated Damon Mines, and plans shifted from using it as a nitrogen source to re-zoning for industrial mining, specifically for platinum, palladium, osmium, silver, and gold, all of which were deposited in generous lodes spanning the entire planet. Finding such wealth fixed in the rocks of Damon Mines prompted the earliest expeditions to look closely at the single, small moon, where they did not find precious metals but massive deposits of, some might argue, equally valuable salts that were in great demand, especially in Carroll's system.

When the earliest calls went out for qualified mine hands and managers, the stark landscape on Damon Mines left corporate speculators little choice but to reward workers handsomely for their willingness to rough-it on a dusty, rocky, barren landscape for months-long stretches. These early mercenary miners, unsurprisingly, cared little for the place. But it was during this time that a small but dedicated faction of the working class, cylinder-dwelling laborers, under the philosophical influence of the Ivernian Workers' Rights Movement, began to pool their resources. Their hope and their goal was to locate and populate nearby planetary bodies so they might establish a back door into a free market economy once again.

One such hopeful working couple was a young married pair from the Carroll Iver cylinder group, Maria and Oscar Sinhá, who, more than anything, hoped to raise children who would be able to set their own course in the stars, free from the strictures and regulations that a society of trillions required of its citizens. Maria especially lamented the lack of free choice their AI micromanaged lives afforded them, comfortable as things were. For to be one of so many humans living together on such a staggeringly vast artificial environment, they knew, required planning and careful coordination, as a nation of trillions could hardly afford to suffer a famine, supply shortage, or energy crisis and hope to endure the unimaginable undulating revolt that would follow. The tradeoff in personal choice that citizens made was for regularity, security, and adherence to a largely pre-ordained set of life pathways, an adherence that had worn on Maria as unappealing, even soul-crushing in her youth. She longed for independence and adventure, and she found a partner in Oscar who was willing to sacrifice any degree of comfort to experience a sense of ownership for the lives they intended to build together. So, when they heard about independent stakes in Damon Mines, Oscar learned all he could about RAV Fleet and Nano-tunneling operating systems, and Maria accepted a position in the expedition as a community planner.

The Sinhás were among the earliest arrivals in Harpersville, one of the five remote mining outposts at the foothills of a massive mountain range on Damon Mines' southern continent. And, at first, the outpost wasn't much more than a scattered collection of pop-up habitats, freight containers, solar panels, and high-energy, hard-handed, low-maintenance prospectors. This earliest group shared a spirit of camaraderie and cooperation. Most of them were young like the Sinhás, looking to raise children, start schools, and form a sense of community that they all had a hand in directing.

The Sinhás, like most of their fellow prospectors, spent the first few years on Damon Mines purchasing the rights to their rental gear with the fruits of their labor, largely at higher-than-market cost. Their food was entirely too expensive, and they had little chance to upgrade their accommodations until they paid on their borrowed gear. Despite their relatively low standard of living compared to the friends and family they'd left to start their new life, the Sinhás and their fellow prospectors were happy in their work. Each ton of extracted metal brought them closer to autonomy. They became smarter and more proficient survivors and producers. And in the third and fourth years on Damon Mines, Maria Sinhá gave birth to two sons, who were just two among the growing first-generation citizens of Harpersville.

By year five, Oscar and Maria had paid off their robotics lease and had taken a mortgage on an AI foreman, which Oscar hoped to leverage into an arm large enough that he could leave an equal share to each of their children when they came of age. At the rate their business was growing, in two decades, the Sinhás would have a formidable business, and the town itself would be a modest blossoming city. The landscape even seemed to grow more tolerable, starkly beautiful at times, in certain lights, especially when Damon's tiny salt moon was so shockingly close in its elliptical orbit that the planet seemed the moon and the moon a giant planet monopolizing the dim sky.

Prospecting proved a difficult life, and sometimes too difficult for some of the Sinhás closest friends, who, even with the earnest help of the community, would fail to make payments and face foreclosure. Other once-eager explorers succumbed to the stress of unfettered living, retreating to the cylinders of Carroll's Star for a safer, more manageable and managed life. One of their earliest neighbors perished in a shipping mishap, when a stack of containers tipped onto his nearby loader. But no hardship could have prepared Oscar for the sudden death of Maria in their seventh year on Damon Mines, to an aneurism that likely would have been survivable if only they'd been closer to civilization. The suddenness of it, the deep shock of such a loss, and the responsibility of raising two young sons alone in such a place fell upon Oscar unimaginably in a single afternoon, all while he was out of town, in the hills, prospecting.

Through those years, after Maria was gone, the stark emptiness of the hills in the distance loomed over the small, broken family in almost every light. Harpersville became a difficult, joyless place. The boys, James and David, now spent less time in school and more time assisting Oscar in the field, learning the basics of the trade, from building macro-robotic tools and systems to directing self-propagating nano tunneling ecosystems for extracting metals, molecule by molecule, like a fog of tiny ants pulling platinum and silver from beneath the mountains.

As the boys grew into teenagers, with the homestead well established, Oscar decided that the family had built enough disposable income that they could splurge on a luxury he never would have considered before. Maria's dream had always been to live in a home with a dog. So, on the anniversary of their mother's passing, Oscar paid an exorbitant sum for a bulldog puppy the boys decided to name Gregor. He brought joy and life back into the Sinhá household, and he was such a rarity in those rural outposts that Harpersville became known as the town with the dog, and Gregor, handsome and personable by nature, became a little celebrity of sorts, the beneficiary of a lifelong string of random treats and exaggerated fawning from neighbors and visitors alike.

As the boys grew into young men, they mastered their father's trade, tripling the family's wealth when they each began to operate their own claims in their mid-teenage years under Oscar's auspices. Not long after, many of their peers followed in their footsteps, greatly amplifying the city's wealth. And in those prosperous years, when the second generation of Harpersville's residents were coming of age, the city began to boom. New style housing began to go up on the outer plain, where there had only been rocks and dust. The small strip of restaurants and cantinas that had remained exactly the same for a decade grew larger, livelier, and new. The city rang with music at night. More people from the cylinders came to Damon Mines in search of a piece of what the Sinhás had spent two decades building, and even though Maria hadn't lived to see it with him, Oscar knew she'd have been happy to see James and David growing into independent young men.

In the twenty-second year of Harpersville's establishment, they welcomed a group of visitors to their humble city, as they had done many times in their history. It was a well-established rule of sorts in space-faring cultures, often called "shippers' law," that one should never deny a ship a shore nor send them back to space unsupplied at a fair price. For it wasn't difficult for outliers, such as the miners of Harpersville, to envision themselves in the other's position, desperate for water or food but never shy about putting their hands in to share the work.

These visitors called themselves Frinzen, originating from the moon colony Frii, an expedition composed of about twenty thousand emigrants who'd split from the main colony over religious differences. The situation had devolved into sectarian violence so severe that co-habitation of the Frii moon became untenable.

Their ship needed extended maintenance following an interstellar passage of nearly seventeen years. They were also badly in need of water and, as it happened, salt, which were both readily available in the Damon system. They were welcomed into orbit and invited to trade and pass freely in any of the cities of the world so long as they held with the laws of the colony while planetside. Rarely had visitors violated that sacred trust, not just in the short history of Damon Mines, but there were scant stories of poor behavior among visitors in most prospecting outposts, for it was well understood that it would take very little for a protective culture to close its doors, and a closed port was no port at all.

These Frinzen, though, held different ideas about what should be sacred, and they never planned on being back this way again.

Very little was known of their history, so the people of Damon Mines had only the account of the Frinzen as to why they'd taken to the stars—a tale of oppression and victimhood at the hands of an arrogant and imperious traditionalist majority. They spoke of wrongful imprisonment, unprovoked pogroms, and a legal system tilted hard against any Frinzen who did not denounce their divergent ways. It was a compelling, empathy-inducing story.

Oscar Sinhá had little time to listen to such nonsense. He and his boys had work to do, contracts to fill, metals to pull and transport. The Sinhás, as usual, were hustling. When the Frinzen arrived, the Sinhá men were out in the K-grid, systematically working through veins embedded in a platinum-rich range of the southern mountains. Their mode was usually to work for two weeks, load up, and transport their yield back to Harpersville for shipping.

On the Friday evening the Frinzen arrived, James and David glided back into town early, while Oscar, Gregor the bulldog, and Samson the AI foreman were buttoning up the mining site for a three-day respite. Following their usual custom, the boys planned to meet friends at Hannah's for a few drinks in celebration of another profitable session.

They were surprised to find the town crowded. Even the old pod housing from the outpost's earliest days was being used as lodging for their newly-arrived interstellar guests. When they entered Hannah's, James and David found their usual table occupied. The occupants were strange looking. Such delicate people didn't usually find themselves on an outer world like Damon Mines. The brothers smiled at the garish, functionless clothing and the thin, soft features of the outsiders.

As the night progressed and the outsiders began to intermingle with the occupants of the mining town, it was as though two decidedly different species of humans were coming together. The rough-skinned miners with their broad shoulders, dirty hands, and purposeful movements didn't quite know how to react to such thin-boned, flowery-tongued, callous-free people, who seemed more decorative than functional. It was difficult for the miners to decide whether these Frinzen were of any use at all. The miners whispered amongst themselves, wondering how these people would ever manage to put together a civilization once they got where they were going. "I hope they got decent robots," James Sinhá said, when his younger brother David posed that very question.

With the drinks flowing, the uniqueness of this opportunity to interact with so many outsiders piqued the Sinhá brothers' curiosity. They spent time exchanging stories of their lives with a pair of attractive, fine-haired Frinzen girls who appeared to be their age.

After he and David described their lives as miners to the girls, James asked, "What do y'all do all day, if you got no work to speak of on that ship?"

"We work to perfect our mastery of our own minds through meditation, fullness of mental well-being, and building one-ness of spiritual presence," the dark-haired girl, Kayton-George, said. "It is a process that takes decades of mental discipline to master."

"Sounds captivating," David said, prompting laughter from both himself and his older brother.

"You two should join us for worship," Aleesa, the fair-haired Frinzen girl said. "You should not be so dismissive of such things you clearly do not understand."

"No need to get so offended," James said. "We just don't have a lot of time around here for...what did you call it? Mental clarity of spiritualism?"

The girls were indignant as the boys smiled at their foreign companions' strange ways. They flat-out refused to continue speaking to the Sinhá boys until they issued a genuine, contrite apology for insulting their deeply-held beliefs. Eventually, surprised by the seriousness of the offense, the boys apologized, and as part of their penance, they agreed to meet the girls the following afternoon so they could witness the first steps in the Frinzen rites. Then, as if nothing bad had happened at all, the friendly mood returned, and the brothers had a fine night getting to know these strange outsiders.

When Oscar Sinhá finished breakfast the following morning, both his sons were still asleep, which wasn't particularly troublesome to Oscar, because he could handle the shipping transfers and the finances by himself, but he'd been trying to steadily encourage the boys to take a hand in the details of the business. And recently, they'd been all for it.

Oscar Sinhá, Gregor the bulldog, and Samson the AI headed off for the transfer station, which took them out past the old section of town, the original Harpersville where the old pop-up housing pods were usually sitting derelict, only today, there was activity, an unusual set by the looks of them.

"Some kind of elves, Gregor?" Oscar said, rubbing the old bulldog's ear. "I ain't never met a elf before, boy. Sure are funny looking."

Gregor the bulldog looked up at Oscar Sinhá inquisitively, as he usually did when the old man talked to him.

"I don't know what a elf smells like, buddy," Oscar continued. "You're gonna have to tell me."

"These visitors are Frinzen," Samson explained. "Exiles from the Frii moon, in transit to a segment in the Haar Cluster, or so their portage petition states. They've taken orbit to repair and re-stock. No particular cultural guidelines were issued from the home office in Hatria."

"Thank you for that update, Sammy," Oscar said, eyeing up the funny-looking outsiders as the loader glided through the old town. "Looks like a fascinating bunch."

After conducting the family's business at the transfer station, Oscar returned home. When he and Gregor arrived, he found that James and David were entertaining two of the female elves as he'd called them. Their eyes got incredibly large when they sighted Gregor, almost as though Oscar wasn't even there.

"Oh my God, a dog!" the light-haired Frinzen girl said.

"We heard there was a dog in this town," the darker haired girl said to David. "You didn't tell us it was your dog."

"He's so beautiful," the first girl said.

"Oscar Sinhá," Oscar said as they crouched down to pet Gregor. "This is my house, and it looks like you've met my two boys, who don't know how they should introduce their new friends, on account of we don't get many visitors round here."

James took the hint. "Pap, this is Aleesa and Kayton-George. They've come through with the Frinzen ship."

Oscar stood in front of them as they knelt and fawned over Gregor, waiting for them to stand up and shake his hand properly.

"Hi," they both said in succession, looking up at Oscar, as they rubbed Gregor's ears and neck.

Oscar forgave the indiscretion on account of the girls' youth and on account of Gregor. Oscar recognized that the old bulldog was both a major novelty and a handsome devil, prone to distracting even the most exacting people from their best manners.

They didn't stay for too long after Oscar arrived. James said something about going somewhere with the girls.

"Sure. Sure," Oscar said. "You kids have fun. Be back by four, though—Fiesta Sabado," which was the family tradition after a two-week hustle. Oscar would cook a real meal for the boys after twelve days of ready-made pouch lunches and dinners.

"Bring the girls if they're hungry," Oscar said.

"Yes, sir," James said.

Oscar spent several hours chopping vegetables, steaming legumes, and rolling out tortillas. The house smelled of sautéed onions, peppers, and garlic. And on account of the guests, Oscar made a large helping of his grandmother's Spanish rice. He loved to cook, and Gregor loved it too, spending most of the afternoon splayed out on the floor beside the chef, basking in the aromas of a family dinner coming together.

By four, the kids were nowhere to be seen. For the first fifteen minutes or so, Oscar didn't care to intrude. He expected the boys to arrive at any minute, and if the food cooled off a little, it wasn't a big deal. By four twenty, though, he pinged James.

"Where you boys at? I told you to be home by four."

"We're in the old town with some of Aleesa's friends. We'll be back in a little bit."

"What's that mean, a little bit? Food's getting cold. Me and Gregor are getting hungry, boyo. How 'bout you get your asses back here."

"We already had lunch, Pap. The girls were hungry so we stopped at Hannah's."

"Fiesta Sabado, James. You both knew I was cooking. Get your asses back here and come eat with your old man."

"But David and Aleesa we—"

"But nothing, hombre. It's family dinner. It's not optional. They're welcome to join us, and if they don't want to come, that tells you they ain't worth a damn anyway."

"Sure, Pap," James said. "Okay. We'll be right back."

It took another thirty minutes for the brothers to return. With them were the two girls from before and a young man who appeared to Oscar to be more elf than man. He had pale skin and was so thin as to be shocking in appearance. The clothes, too, were more decoration than functional, like the rest of them. Funny.

Oscar welcomed them all at the table, and as much as their participation in the dinner seemed forced, Oscar didn't care. He ate, content in his culinary handiwork, even partly happy to see his boys interacting with outsiders, learning how other people lived. Harpersville could be like a small island at times, and it was fun to have visitors every now and again.

The outsiders didn't seem to have much interest in Oscar's presence or even the community they were visiting, though. They spent a lot of time explaining to James and David the intricacies of their religion, or at least what Oscar thought was their religion—an of odd progression of meditation that went back thousands of years, some fancy way of finding oneself, all described in big words that meant nothing. At one point during the dinner, Oscar noticed how his boys were looking at these two elf girls. He didn't blame them. Oscar remembered what it was like to be twenty. These girls were so pretty it almost pained his eyes to look at them dead-on. Almost another kind of human.

"How much gravity you got on your ship?" Oscar asked the girls after they were all done eating.

The elves had eaten very little.

"Point-six-eight," the dark-haired one said.

"If you're noticing that we're not as robust as your people here," the boy elf said. "That's one of the main reasons our musculature is thinner and smaller."

"That's why I asked," Oscar said. "They keep your calorie count fixed too?"

"By necessity," he answered. "On a long voyage, the food chain must be tightly controlled."

"I'd think you'd be more excited to dive into a home cooked meal, then, no?"

"The stomach contracts over time."

"You some kind of doctor or something?"

"I'm in the medical division, yes, it's one of my duties. I also studied veterinary medicine, but I must confess, Gregor is the first living dog I've ever met. He's quite a specimen."

"A specimen, yeah, that's a word for Gregor all right."

David and James laughed. The visitors didn't quite understand Oscar's dry sense of humor, or maybe even what dry humor was.

After dinner, the brothers sat down with their guests in the sitting area, and the young doctor sat fixated on Gregor, petting him and rubbing his belly. Oscar fixed himself an evening cubata to wash down the meal.

"You know, Mr. Sinhá," the boy elf said, "these fatty growths on Gregor's side—"

"They're called lipomas," Oscar said. "Our doctor checked them out a couple years ago when she came through. They don't bother Gregor none."

"Oh, yes. Well, I could take them out for you very easily. Gregor here would hardly feel a thing."

"Hardly feel a thing? That means he'd feel something. Thanks, but no thanks."

"But it would be next to nothing. Hardly a scratch."

"Why would I let you do that? For what? So that his coat look smooth?"

The young Frinzen shrugged and nodded. "It'd be a very easy procedure."

"It bothers you how Gregor looks? Because it don't bother me none. Don't bother Gregor neither."

"I didn't mean to—"

"Yeah, you didn't mean nothing. Just that you'd cut up an animal to make you feel better about how he appears to you. The first time you ever seen him. That sound like something I should let a stranger do to my dog? My family?"

"Pap," James said, trying to quell the growing tension in the room.

"Am I in the wrong here, son?" Oscar said. "These people are guests on this planet, in our house. And the first time I ever lay eyes on these people, this one's telling me how I should care for our dog?"

"He's just trying to be helpful, Pap," James said. "Nothing more."

"That's fine," Oscar said. "Only, I see them teaching you boys about how they live and they don't seem to be learning much from you. For example, when you come into the house of an elder, a house he built up from the ground, and he welcomes you to his table, and he feeds you, and he lets you sit with his family and with his dog, and you offer to help him care for his dog, and he says no thank you; what would you say to this man where we're from, James?"

"You would say, 'Yes, sir.'"

"That is correct," Oscar said, turning his gaze to the boy doctor. "So, young man, you are welcome to sit with my dog and to pet him, but under no circumstances will I allow anyone to cut on him for cosmetic purposes. Is that understood?"

"Yes, sir," he said.

"Good. We're all learning," Oscar said. "Now, any of you kids want a cubata?"

"I would," David said, getting up to help Oscar fix drinks at the counter.

During the following weeks out at the mining camp, Oscar could tell that his boys were distracted. They were getting their work done, sure, but their heads weren't in it. At dinner, Oscar teased the boys about how they looked lost, "without no elf girls to follow around all night," which set off a long streak of vehement denials. Oscar nearly lost his mind one evening, when David told him he was reading about spiritual enlightenment.

"Boy, you're interested in something, but it sure ain't spiritual enlightenment, that's for sure!" Oscar said, his chest bouncing up and down as he laughed.

"Come on, Pap," James said. "Give him a break. They got some good ideas."

"Oh, they got a lot of good qualities," Oscar said. "But it ain't they're ideas you two are interested in. I maybe got old eyes, but they still work, and this old head still remembers what it was like to be twenty."

"So if you know, why you giving us such a hard time?"

"I'm just busting on you is all. I don't blame you. Just don't get so googley-eyed chasing elf girls that you forget what you're about. And don't forget that they'll be gone in a few weeks too. Don't get yourself filled with no crazy ideas you can't shake out."

The next time the Sinhás glided back into town, the Frinzen were still occupying old town. Oscar didn't see much of the boys over the weekend. He asked them to cook for Fiesta Sabado, and the girls came with them, this time without the boy doctor. The meal was pleasant, but quiet, with the exception of the high praise both young women heaped on the boys for their culinary skills.

At the end of the dinner, as they were heading out, Kayton-George told Oscar that he'd raised two fine young men, and something about it struck him as odd.

"Yes, they are young men?" Oscar said. "And what about you how old are you two?"

Kayton-George shrugged and exchanged a look with Aleesa, and then she found Oscar's eyes again, which seemed to remind her of his lesson to their companion two weeks prior.

"I'm thirty-one and Aleesa is thirty-three."

"Really?" Oscar said. "Well, don't you two ladies look young?"

"Deep space," Kayton-George said, smiling.

Oscar nodded, eyeing them both up as they stepped toward the door.

"We'll see you, Pap," David said as they walked out.

"Will you?" he said, shaking his head.

He didn't see the boys again till Monday morning when they set out for the K-grid, two hours late. It was clear to Oscar from their bearing that neither boy was happy about leaving Harpersville for the mountains. He didn't like how the situation was evolving, but he figured they'd pout and mope about for a few days and get over it in a couple weeks when the memory of those older elven women wasn't so fresh in their young minds. The boys stayed surly all session, even if they still pulled their quotas.

When they returned to Harpersville again, Oscar was surprised to see the Frinzen still in town. The boys, though, as usual, had preceded Oscar back to town, and in hindsight, they'd been excited, even giddy as the weekend approached. Oscar should have seen it coming.

"I'm not sure what we're going to do about these shit-elves, Gregor, old boy," Oscar said as they passed old town. "They're wearing out the welcome for sure."

But as much as he lamented the Frinzens' continued presence, Oscar knew that the boys were men now, and he couldn't very well teach them autonomy as he had their whole lives and then tell them what to do with their weekend. They'd have to make their own choices, even if they were bad ones involving nice-looking shit-elves.

On Sunday, when Oscar still hadn't seen the boys, he decided that instead of pinging them, he'd go down to old town and see if he might happen upon them and see what those elves were getting up to at the same time. Old town was almost deserted, though. Oscar had a sinking feeling in his stomach.

"Samson," he said to the AI in the loader, "Can you ping them?"

"Negative," the AI said. "None of their devices are active on the network."

"Not even in Hatria? They could have gone down there, maybe."

"No, sir. The only explanation is that they're not on the planet."

Oscar looked up at the horizon to see if he could catch the faint glint that had flashed over the northern plain every so often, but the Frinzen ship wasn't in his sight line.

Oscar went down to Hannah's to see if he could figure out what was going on. The place was as empty as he'd seen it in years.

"Let me guess," Damitra the bartender said. "You're looking for your boys, Oscar?"

"I figure somebody down here gotta know where they're at. Then it turns out you're the only one down here."

"Everybody went up to the Frinzen ship. I guess they was going to give everyone a tour—return the hospitality or something, throw a big banquet for the town."

"I guess we wasn't invited, huh? Just you, me, and Gregor got left behind."

"Yeah," Damitra laughed. "I'm surprised they didn't invite the dog and sit him at the head table, these people."

"The shit-elves," Oscar said. "Those two thirty-year-old women got my boys wound right around they're little fingers."

She laughed. "Shit-elves. Damn right. The girls I can see. Pretty little things. Entitled, but even I can see the appeal. Thing I can't figure, Oscar; my little sister's smitten with one of their pretty little boys that don't look like he could carry one of them bar chairs halfway across the room. She just says he's beautiful. And spiritual. They're all spiritual."

"Don't got no manners. Can't do a damn thing, but they're spiritual all right."

"Anyway, they're supposed to be back sometime tomorrow. It's some big festival for them up there."

"Great," Oscar said. "Happy shit-elf day."

Damitra laughed and shook her head. "Can I get you anything while you're here, Oscar."

"Ah, what the hell. It's getting toward cubata time."

"You got it."

And Oscar slumped down at the bar and had a nice conversation with Damitra.

By Tuesday morning, the town was still half empty, and with no sign of their people, Oscar and several of the other head prospectors called down to Hatria to see if anyone in the capitol knew when their family members would be coming back, or if they had a way to call up to the ship and get in touch. By mid-afternoon, shuttles began arriving back from orbit carrying a mixture of hardhands from Harpersville and the spiritual Frinzen.

Oscar waited around the corner on Desmond and Hannah's back porch, just opposite the opening between old town and the city's main strip, right where the shuttles were dropping people off.

He spotted David and James before they spotted him.

"It's crazy how heavy it feels," David said. "Just two days off world."

"Three," James said. "And we better get moving. Pap is going to lose his shit when we get out to the site."

"Maybe he'll lose it right now in front of all your new friends," Oscar said from above them on the porch.

"Pap—" James started.

Oscar just shook his head. The boys stood before him, frozen in the old road, unsure whether to speak.

"We are two days behind, boys, and we got a delivery due in a little over ten days. No Sinhá has been late on a delivery in twenty years, and it ain't going to be next week neither. Go get your gear."

The boys walked to the loader, slump-shouldered with their mouths buttoned up good. And for good measure, Oscar told Samson to drive the other loader out to K-grid so the boys had to ride out with him. He had Gregor sit up front too, relegating the boys to the back seat for the duration of the ride, which progressed in total silence.

When they got out at the mining camp, Oscar didn't say a word, just headed right for his con center.

"Pap, what's the schedule?" James asked.

"I don't know about what you boys are going to do, but I've got twenty hours to make up on my end, so I'm going to put in today's ten and get up at four so I can bank three extra hours a day till I'm caught up next Thursday."

"Look, Pap. We're sorry," James said.

"Don't speak for your brother, and don't be sorry to me. You're not letting me down. You're letting yourselves down, and your vendors, and the builders on the other end who rely on them."

"Oh, come on, Pap!" David said. "Don't tell us it doesn't bother you after you sit in silence all day."

"Do we need to talk this out, David? You really think you're going to tell me something about this situation I don't already understand? Wait. You know what? Maybe I do need to tell you a few things that apparently, I haven't taught you yet. Or maybe you think you could teach me what you're learning chasing after these enlightened thirty-year-old women you've been following around for the last month.

86

Would you like to start, David? Maybe tell me something about spirituality? Well-being of the mind? No?

"I know a few things about religion, myself."

David didn't say anything, but he was hot.

"Haven't I taught you boys anything out here?"

"Yeah, metals," David said. "Pulling metals out of rocks. That's your idea of enlightenment."

"God damn right it is," Oscar said. "You still think you're pulling metals out of the rocks? We don't deal in metals, son, we deal in commerce. Every day we're out here, we're pulling a better future out of these rocks, for me, for you, for your brother, for my grandchildren, for your mother, for her grandchildren."

"Oh, don't bring mom into it," David said.

"I'm not bringing nothing," Oscar said. "Just truth. She's over you always whether you see it or not. It ain't just about you here, boys. Hasn't it struck you once while you've been visiting those people squatting in our old pod houses that we used to live there. You probably don't remember any more what this outpost was like before we had Hannah's; before there was a main street, a school, a theatre. That's what we've been pulling out of the rocks for twenty years. And that's what I'm going to do this week, because our word means something out here, not to no skinny visitors, to our goddamn neighbors who have our backs.

"There. That's what I wanted to say," Oscar said. "You happy? Can we get to work now?"

"Yeah, Pap," James said, and he gestured with his brow for David to get going.

Oscar went to work in a huff with Gregor trailing slowly behind.

After a ten-day stretch of nearly sixteen-hour days, all three Sinhá men made their contracted deliveries in full and on time, just as they always had. And this week, Oscar was no longer surprised to see those malingering Frinzen still occupying the old town when they got back. The mood in Harpersville had shifted from the light, upbeat energy that had permeated the small city on their arrival weeks earlier. Oscar wasn't the only one growing tired of the outsiders. The hard-handed people of Damon Mines didn't mind offering a sanctuary to a well-meaning group of weary travelers. But they didn't appreciate their good faith being violated by people who didn't respect them or their ways. That unspoken tension felt like it would soon spill out into the open.

On Saturday, at the transfer station, Oscar heard talk among his fellow miners that some of the Frinzen were trying to coax many of the people of Harpersville to join them on their interstellar voyage. Oscar had seen something in their eyes from the outset. They'd wanted something. He just hadn't been able to figure out what these delicate little people wanted out of Damon Mines. It turned out they didn't want anything from the mines at all. They wanted the people.

Oscar tried all day to ping both of his boys and couldn't get a response. Finally, as the day waned, he messaged James, asking him to stop by the house when he got a chance to break free.

It was long past dark by the time James made it home. When he came in, Oscar was asleep in his armchair in the living room, with Gregor curled up on the sofa across from the old man.

"Pap," James said, nudging his father awake with a gentle shake of the arm. "Pap, it's James."

"I was waiting up on you. Drifted off."

"I'm glad you did," James said. "It's late."

"Where's David?" Oscar said.

"He's with Aleesa, in the old town."

Oscar shook his head.

"That's what I gotta talk to you about, Pap. I don't know what to do."

"He wants to go with them, doesn't he?"

"I've been trying to talk him out of it for days, Pap. But she's got this, I don't know. It's like she's in his head."

"And what about you and the other woman?"

"Kayton? I guess I like her well enough. She's beautiful. She seems kind. I don't know, though."

"You don't love her?"

"No. I don't think so. Not like David and Aleesa."

"There's something happening there, James, but it ain't love. Not real love. Something like lust and madness," Oscar sat up straighter in the armchair. "I don't think there's anything anyone can say to that boy to make him change his mind at this point. If anyone knows something to say, it's gotta be you, James."

"I've tried. I just don't know what to do, Pap. Sometimes I feel like I like these people all right, but I also feel like we don't know them, like they're holding their real selves back."

"Trust your instincts on that."

"It scares me a little if I'm honest."

Oscar nodded. "It should."

"Pap, if he goes..." James shook his head. "I'd worry about David every day for the rest of my life. He's committed—to the meditation thing, to the lifestyle, all that."

"And what do you think of all that, James?"

"I don't know. Their lives. Their ship. It's all impressive. But all that time sitting there? Doing nothing? Years and years before they get where they're going? And they say they have a planet out there, but I'm not so sure."

"David knows there's no turning back, right?" Oscar said. "No getting off?"

"It's like he does and he doesn't. He just sees the life, you know. Easy life."

"And that's what he wants, that easy life?"

"I don't think he knows. As long as he's with her, I'm not sure he cares."

"And you, James. Could you live that easy life?"

He shrugged, his mouth turned down. James looked over at Gregor, who was lying on his side, his big black eyeballs gazing back at the boy he'd grown old with.

"It won't be so easy when you get where you're going," Oscar said. "You know that, right? That's what they want from you two—to mine their metals for them, run their robotics. Them people couldn't build no cities, no civilization. Masters of the inner world, hopeless in the real world. People who can't do for themselves have to manipulate the ones who can."

"I can't tell whether you're trying to talk me out of it or not, Pap."

"I'm just trying to tell you what you need to know. I already know what you're gonna do, son. I'm not going to try to stop you. I couldn't if I tried. If David goes, it'll break my heart. And you too. If I lost both of you like this, though, at least I'd know you'd be looking out for each other. You'd be together. It's what me and your mother always wanted for you two. I told you that, right?"

"A million times, Pap."

"If you do go, James, I'll leave your mother's cross on the mantle. I want you to keep that in the family."

James nodded.

"Whatever happens, please don't let them come in here while I'm sleeping and take Gregor with them. You tell David."

Oscar tried his best to suppress the tears in front of his eldest son, but it was a losing battle.

"Pap, I would never. I'd never let that happen."

James put his hand on his father's arm, but he sensed that Oscar didn't want him to come any closer.

James didn't know what to say, what to do. A look of anger and disgust came over him as he sat there shaking his head.

"Go," Oscar said. "I don't want you to think of me like this."

"Okay, Pap," James said, himself now tearing up. "I'm sorry."

"Promise me," Oscar said, as James got up and turned toward the door. "If it goes wrong, please, please, James, forgive your brother. You tell him I forgive him too when the time is right."

James nodded. "I will. I promise you, Pap."

"Watch out for him."

James left, shutting the door behind him in the way James did, that sound. Oscar wondered if he'd ever hear it again. He got up and retrieved Maria's cross from the top drawer in their bedroom. Pure platinum from one of the earliest surpluses they'd made, two years before the boys were anything more than a hope in their future together. Oscar prayed on that cross for the first time in years, asking for their mother to watch over the boys wherever they went in the galaxy, and he placed it on the mantle, hoping that in the morning, it might still be there.

When he woke the following morning, the cross was gone. Gregor, his old legs no longer nimble, slid off the sofa on his stomach, catching himself with his front paws and making his way over beside Oscar's legs.

Samson, whose robotic body was recharging out in the loader, was wired into the house as always.

"Did they go?" Oscar asked, already anticipating the AI's answer.

"They did," Samson's voice filled the room.

"He didn't even say goodbye."

Instead of riding into town, Oscar decided to walk. It was the same surreal feeling he'd felt, with the same knot in his gut, from the morning after Maria passed. The spotted salt moon was setting in the east, mocking him with its beauty. The dusty, arid rocks glowed a warm brown hue in the distance.

Oscar made his way into Harpersville, first through the now-deserted pop-up habitats of the old town. They'd been left as they were, the doors open to the outside world, trash on their floors, papers drifting in the breeze on the dirt road outside, a filthy old bucket rolling back and forth on the street. Gregor sniffed the ground, searching for confirmation as much as anything, for he seemed to sense they were gone.

Oscar walked toward the porch out behind Hannah's. The building had been designed to look like a saloon from a ghost town of the old West, a joke among Desmond, Hannah herself, and their best friends the Alamedas, who all believed that as long as they worked hard and stuck together, their boom town could never bust. That morning, the place looked to Oscar like the longest setup to the sickest joke the universe could have ever played on them all. And he found, on the other side of the building, Hannah, Desmond, and Victor Alameda, who were counting the names of the departed, including their bartender Damitra's sister, and now, the two Sinhá boys.

When a proper survey was completed in the following days, slightly less than half that first generation of Harpersville's children had departed their hardscrabble life on Damon Mines for a life of quiet contemplation aboard the Frinzen's interstellar generation ship. In other outposts, the loss had been even worse.

At first, in the wake of the disaster, the prospectors of Damon Mines put out calls to the ringworlds and the cylinders for opportunities on a well-established mining colony. The takers were few, trickling in one straggler at a time, only to find a world with a forlorn set of brokenhearted people, who, over the coming years, one by one, gave up on their dream of ownership and independence, departing by shuttle back to Dreeson's Star, to Carroll's Star, and even sometimes to passing interstellar missions, until eventually, there were so few prospectors left that the solitude became too much, and the mines became the purview of the robots, and the houses became the fossil record of a forgotten, almost-formed, dusty dream of a civilization that had never fully come to pass.

Cupcakes!

When humans finally arrived at the outer tail of the Scutum-Centaurus Arm of the galaxy, in the early years of the seventh millennium, they were surprised to find a large and vibrant community of intelligent races. This first encounter with a peaceful federation of sorts ran counter to all prior experience of alien life as being isolated by time and distance. The tendency of successful interstellar civilizations in most species ran toward empire and away from trade and cooperation with other aliens. Yet this federation of species seemed congenial, cooperative, and happy to add another like-minded species to the list of friends and allies, provided the funny-looking ape-like humans were willing to play nice.

Having calmed down quite a bit on their long progression across the galaxy, and given the number of and the technological prowess of these federation species, the humans were quite happy to talk and trade instead of fight. The federation members, for their part, found the humans to be a promising applicant for membership. The humans seemed industrious, eager trading partners; friendly, and quite clever, and perhaps most importantly, it was discovered that the humans possessed a sense of humor. This had been a sticking point in centuries past, when promising species happened by, seemed to be congenial, and then snapped into combat posture at the first sign of a slight, completely incapable of taking a joke. They'd find some way of turning the tiniest lighthearted teasing into an insult to the honor of their entire species, and then out came the warheads, rail guns, and stellasers, and everyone knew the new guys definitely weren't going to work out.

The humans, though, during the very first meeting were self-deprecating, playful, even irreverent, and best of all, seemed already to understand some of the federation's best and oldest jokes. When the special envoy ended the first exploratory counsel with the usual quip, "So for the next meeting, who's bringing the cupcakes?" The usual loud outburst of laughter followed, and the humans seemed to laugh loudest of all. Then the humans' cultural minister replied with a most hilarious promise, "We'll bring the cupcakes," which set off a roar of laughter unheard of in a first meeting. Diplomatic ties were off on a solid footing. These humans seemed great.

What the federation envoys on the membership sub-committee didn't yet understand, though, was that, being a tribal species, humans had evolved a most uncommon trait. They found laughter itself funny and couldn't help laughing genuinely whenever others were laughing, a genetically-imposed and seemingly harmless form of deception that helped humans to fit in with the group. Whenever others laughed, humans laughed too.

The federation members thought the humans were gifted with an extraordinary comic intuition, perhaps even a kind of low-grade form of telepathy. How else would they already know how funny the cupcakes joke was without under-standing the context? That was something special.

For the humans, though, it was a problem. Admiral Sontoshia Montoya returned from the meeting and headed straight for the debriefing room with the cultural minister.

"What the hell was with the cupcakes thing, minister? Did we screw that up? I couldn't stop laughing, but I had no idea what they were on about."

"I'm not sure, admiral. I thought everything was going great till then. I don't think it was a major mis-step, just a minor cultural misunderstanding."

"Was it a mistranslation? Why the hell do they find cupcakes so funny? And what are the odds these aliens should even eat cupcakes at all?"

The flagship's central AI chimed in, asserting that the translation was correct and that the odds of encountering another species that had cupcakes was higher than one might expect, with the odds increasing dramatically when en-countering a federation, because one of the species out of the hundreds in the federation was all but statistically certain to have cupcakes and then to disseminate the recipe to the rest of the federation on account of the universality of their deliciousness.

"So now the real question," the admiral said, "do we actually bring cupcakes to the next meeting?"

A long debate ensued. Ultimately, the cultural minister's point of view won the day. The *Merganser's* cook had a deep well of special recipes to draw from, and what could it hurt to actually show up with cupcakes? If it was just supposed to be a joke, the admiral was instructed to say he thought it would be both extremely funny, and now everyone had cupcakes to eat during the meeting. Win-win.

The humans showed up to the second meeting with a service cart covered by a decorative tablecloth containing hundreds of cupcakes. The admiral began the humans' opening statement by declaring, "Your honors, we are happy to announce, we brought cupcakes."

That simple statement set off an eruption of laughter unmatched in the history of the federation admittance process. The humans, of course, couldn't help themselves from bursting into laughter too. Some of the sounds these aliens made when laughing were so ridiculous, the admiral couldn't help himself. Belly laughs, guffaws, shrieking, snorts, roars. Pretty soon both the admiral and the cultural minister were doubled over, howling, laughing so hard they were crying.

"Look how they emit salt water from their eyes!" one of the envoys declared in between fits of laughter. "These humans are amazing."

The cultural minister, who always strived to maintain her composure during such important meetings, then began laughing so hard she involuntarily snorted, which turned the following five minutes into a cacophony of laughter so intense that even the humans present had never experienced its like.

The cupcakes too, were a big hit.

"What is this brown gunk?" one of the moldags asked the admiral at one point.

"Chocolate frosting, your honor," the admiral replied, "with sprinkles."

"Blugggh," the moldag minister replied, which the AI translated as "long, satisfied sigh."

It set off another wave of sustained, contagious laughter.

The meeting concluded on a positive note, with the special envoy stating, "We seriously like you humans a lot. You actually brought cupcakes. That's special."

When the admiral returned with the cultural minister for debriefing, the human committee was in a quandary.

"You've got to figure out what the hell is up with these cupcakes, minister," the admiral declared. "I'm not sure how much longer we can keep this up. Are we just supposed to keep bringing cupcakes and bursting into laughter whenever the word gets mentioned? Somebody, please figure out what's so damn funny about cupcakes."

There was no such chapter in the handbook for cultural ministers. Clearly, some cultural misunderstanding was at play, but she wasn't sure what, and now that the humans had been playing along with the joke for several days, it seemed a grave mis-step to admit the lie and ask for another species to explain the joke.

The cultural minister devised a plan she thought might fix the problem. Aboard the *Merganser*, several different types of disembodied AIs regulated separate ship's systems as backups to the humans who ostensibly drove the ship. She instructed the chief engineer to fabricate a robot body and to install a clone of Garbeaux, the ship's onboard encyclopedia. Then, they would send Garbeaux to the federation pavilion to ask about the joke. Garbeaux was given strict instructions on how to word the request, that the humans can't stop laughing about the cupcake joke. "The humans get it," he would say, "but none of them has been able to sufficiently explain it to me, so I feel left out. Can you explain it, so that I, a humble AI might understand?"

Then they sent Garbeaux off to the alien pavilion, and it took nearly two days for the AI to return. The third meeting was coming up in a few hours, the cook was waiting on cupcake orders, and the admiral was getting anxious. Fortunately, Garbeaux returned with a timely answer.

"It was a long story," the AI said, "Made all the more time-consuming that every species I spoke to directed me to the Frawn, a fungal hive mind, who spoke extremely slowly in a bizarre dialect I had difficulty translating, but I am certain I got the gist of the story, which I will distill for you in the time we have now before the next meeting."

"Before you begin, Garbeaux," the cultural minister said, "shall we instruct the cook to make more cupcakes?"

"It couldn't hurt," Garbeaux said. "Somebody will always eat cupcakes."

The story went like this:

In the early days of the Outer Scutum-Centaurus Federation, one of the founding members was a race of dog-like, highly-intelligent creatures called the Daglion. They were much loved in that corner of the galaxy for their many good qualities. They were pack animals, hard-working, tough, jovial, and extremely loyal to their allies. Over tens of thousands of years, they made allies of hundreds of races, and truly, it was their diplomatic nature and skill that brought the earliest forms of the federation into being, cementing the shaky alliance whenever the federation began to fray.

Several hundred years into the federation's earliest days, the small group of allies brought a new race into the fold, though it wasn't without reservations. The newcomers, the Barraxa, were a race of gangly, mean-looking, reptilian-mammal hybrids, bipedal, horned, and possessing a most serious and stern disposition. When the Barraxa were confronted with any type of friendly gesture, their response was almost always suspicion, as though friendship itself was a foreign concept. Trade was trade, but anything beyond that made the Barraxa wary.

Among the most disagreeable of the Barraxa's many irksome traits was their absolute certainty of their reading of others' motives. They were decidedly untelepathic, yet, at the same time, they were utterly convinced that they always knew what others were up to, and it was always some form of maliciousness directed against the Barraxa. When the Daglion gave them a deal on bauxite, they knew it must be an attempt at misdirection so that they'd miss another way the Daglion were screwing them over. When the Passca commissioned a statue of their leaders as a gesture of goodwill, the Barraxa were certain it was a way to portray them before the rest of the federation as uglier than they actually were in person, and they were ugly in person. About the only gesture the Barraxa would accept at face value was the offering of sweets, for as hideous as they appeared, and as nasty as their disposition was, the Barraxa had a soft spot for sweet foods that, once discovered, began to serve as the preferred manner of smoothing over any business transaction with them. It was about the only way to deal with the Barraxa and not be accused of insulting, bullying, or oppressing them in some uncharitable way. The cost of doing business with the Barraxa became the market cost plus some form of special sweets, which always went unreciprocated. As the federation expanded, it became a cultural guideline that was passed on to all new species: Always give a Barraxa sweets.

In the middle of the third century after the Barraxa joined the federation, a new species made the mistake of conducting a territorial negotiation with the Barraxa without bringing cakes, cookies, or candy to sweeten the deal, and the Daglion were called to mediate the uproar that followed. The misunderstanding threatened to develop into a full-fledged territorial war that was certain to disrupt a key interstellar trade channel. The crab-like species, the Haatat, who hailed from a sea-covered world, had no idea what a sweet-tooth was, nor did they have any means of producing any such foodstuffs underwater. Yet the Barraxa were incensed and threatened war for the insult. The Daglion promised the crabs they'd take care of it and sent the Barraxa a freight container filled with cupcakes and a greeting card that read:

Dear Barraxa,

You guys need to relax, like a lot. Anyway, enjoy the cupcakes and don't start wars for no good reason.

Your friends,

The Daglion.

The Barraxa ate the peace offering, but they took the gesture as an insult to their honor. They responded by launching a sneak attack against the Daglion to avenge the perceived slight. In the military sense, the Barraxa's attack was devastating, crippling the shipyards of the Daglion home system, irradiating about half their homeworld, and killing an uncountable number of the friendly Daglion civilians, which some estimates placed at nearly half the species. What the Barraxa didn't account for, being the self-involved and short-sighted species that they were, was that the Daglions' loyalty to their friends and allies meant far more than the Barraxa could have calculated. Rather than turning on the bested and weakened Daglion, as the Barraxa expected and would have done themselves, federation members rallied to the Daglion cause, blockading the Barraxa from access to resources and cutting their warships to pieces at every opportunity. The Barraxa found themselves isolated, beleaguered, and besieged by every race in the federation, who'd all had enough of the Barraxa and their obnoxious ways.

Within five years, there was almost nothing left of the Barraxa's fleet, and their home world was little more than a ball of smoldering ash. They hadn't a friend left in the galaxy. The final intelligence report from the Horry, an outlying species on the very edge of the Scutum-Centaurus Arm of the galaxy, was that what remained of the Barraxa fleet was seen fleeing into the intergalactic void, a plume of smoke trailing ignominiously behind them.

The federation left it up to the Daglion to decide whether they should be pursued and eliminated. The Daglion, being the decent sort everyone knew them to be, unsurprisingly, insisted they be let go in the hopes that the Barraxa might quietly reflect on the mistakes they'd made and change their ways, or at least screw off for good.

For a while, it became a common expression when one species or other was being disagreeable in negotiations that they were "acting like a Barraxa" or would tell others "we don't want to be a Barraxa here, but that price is outrageous!" But mention of the Barraxa left such a sour taste that the word was used infrequently, and then, over the years, all mention of them fell out of favor and they were forgotten by living beings, and would have been entirely forgotten if not for the files of federation history, where the Barraxa were but a footnote in what became known as the Horrific Cupcake War.

That wasn't the funny part.

What became of the Barraxa was unknown for nearly thirteen thousand years until a strange looking traveler appeared in the Daglion system in a junker of a ship claiming to have vital information of the gravest nature. The stranger claimed to be Barraxa and was perplexed when the response he got to that statement was, "You're who?"

"I'm of the Barraxa," he said. "Your mortal enemies."

The odd-looking, malodorous fellow was brought before the Daglion chancellor.

"I didn't know we had any mortal enemies," Fabian, Chancellor of the Daglion, responded. "But thanks for stopping by. We're not really that concerned."

"You should be," the stranger said. "If only you'd allow me to tell you of the ungodly wrath headed your way, you might be inclined to take precautions."

"Very well," Fabian said. "Pull up a chair and help yourself to some tea and scones, friend. I like a good story."

The stranger claimed to be a Barraxa named Siro. He only wished to prevent another ill-fated war with the Daglion, which he suspected wouldn't end well for either species.

"Why would your species want to make war on ours?" Fabian asked.

The stranger went on to explain the history between their species, which, the chancellor's historian was able to corroborate in a thirteen-thousand-year-old entry that mentioned something about cupcakes and a nasty race of fellows that looked an awful lot like this mysterious stranger.

"Go on then," Fabian said. "Tell us why you guys are angry at us now."

Angry, apparently didn't begin to touch the way the Barraxa felt about the Daglion. They had retreated into interstellar space following their defeat in the Horrific Cupcake War. The defeat had left them in dire conditions. The remaining Barraxa had managed to cobble together enough antimatter from their warships to power a modest-sized stealth habitat. They'd been unsure whether the federation would pursue them, so they had prioritized stealth. Their habitat gave off no light, no energy signatures, and was undetectable in the dark of intergalactic space, where they attempted to lie low for long enough to escape the pursuit of the Daglion and their allies. Then, once forgotten, they planned to strike at the heart of the federation and have their revenge. The plan, according to Siro the stranger, was to unleash an energy weapon that disrupts the bonds in carbon atoms, which, theoretically would dissolve all living creatures in the beam's wake. Siro stated the weapon had already been developed and was en route to the Daglion system as they were speaking.

"You guys are still mad over something that happened thirteen thousand years ago?" Fabian asked the stranger.

Siro explained that the Barraxa weren't just upset about the war. No. The malodorous stranger described the conditions the Barraxa had been forced to endure on their intergalactic sanctuary. Things had not been pretty for the Barraxa.

First off, their hawkish and aggressive posture at the start of the war with the Daglion had taken a great toll on their home planet's ecosystem even before the federation allies besieged it. By the time it became necessary for the Barraxa to flee to interstellar space, there was hardly enough life remaining to sustain a food cycle. What was left consisted of three species that were hastily crammed into a cargo cruiser when the Barraxa fled.

The Barraxa retreated into the black of intergalactic space, several light years from the outer star systems of the galaxy, where they disassembled their fleet and reconstituted it as a moon-sized habitat invisible to the EM spectrum. They didn't lack for the technology to sustain themselves in the deep of space. What they lacked was biological matter beyond what they carried with them into the deep.

The conditions on their habitat were as follows. Their primary food source were eggs from the toxxi, a large bird-like species that was preserved because their egg's nutritional profile was one of the only complete sources of nutrition the Barraxa could digest. The eggs themselves consisted of a chalky, bitter substance that revolted the taste buds, the nose, and the eyeballs all at once. Each meal became a solitary gag-inducing ritual, because if two Barraxa gathered together to eat, the sight of the other consuming the vile eggs would induce an endless, self-reinforcing cycle of retching, hacking, and cursing as they struggled to hork down the toxxi eggs' disgusting, chalky-white phlegm.

The bird-ish toxxi that produced the eggs were a peculiar species that alternated sleep between the two hemispheres of their brains, such that the toxxi seemed to never fully sleep, but a truer description would be that they were always half awake. With half their brains switched off, they relied on cries and signals from their packmates for group safety. They produced a constant stream of outlandish squawks that established a baseline, every ten seconds or so, each toxxi-bird emitting a deafening high honk that transmitted to their compatriots that all was well. In the early days on the Barraxa refuge, the few remaining biologists worked furiously to disable the incessant honking only to find that no matter the methodology, whether it was lobotomizing, genetic modification, surgical removal of the vocal cords, or deaf-ening the animals, in each case, the animals would simply lie down and die without the steady squawking assurance that all was well in the pack. Many of the Barraxa in those early years threw themselves into the antimatter chamber to escape the din of the egg-laying squawking toxxi-birds.

Nearly as awful as the toxxi themselves was their food source, which came from a vegetable misnamed jagfruit. The foul-smelling, reddish, gourd-like vegetable, once cracked open by the beaks of the lanky toxxi birds, emitted a foul cloud of stank that hung in the air of the habitat's decks for hours on end, such that within weeks of the habitat's completion, the stench was omnipresent and forever in-escapable. And if the toxxi neglected to crack open the jagfruit gourds on their own, the suppurating gourds would burst, spilling out their seedy guts to the deck of the habitat, leaving a long fetid stink that hung in the area for months before dissipating back to the noxious baseline.

The last of the three species that came with the Barraxa to the anti-matter globe was a type of feather flea that hitched a ride on the squawking toxxi-birds. The fleas, seemed to cause the toxxi no noticeable issues, as they'd co-evolved on the Barraxan homeworld. But lacking a natural predator on the extragalactic habitat, and in need of a further food source as their numbers flourished, the bird-fleas quickly evolved to feed on the Barraxa themselves, causing a piercing bite that incited an unstoppable, flaming itch that didn't abate for weeks on end.

The endless cycle of sleeplessness, the constant squawk-ing, the incessant itching, the persistent stench, and the putrid diet itself only served to heighten the Barraxa's already overblown sense that the universe was out to deal them an oversized dose of injustice. And the focus of their anger fell hard upon the Daglion, whom they blamed for their terrible plight. The only release from their torment was when they gathered each morning and evening to howl their anger in unison for ten minutes of daily wrath. They followed this ritualistic outburst of rage with an oath in which they swore on their species' existence that they would carry their anger with them every minute of every day until ultimate vengeance was delivered upon every last living Daglion no matter where they may go in the universe.

During these thirteen thousand years of seclusion in their self-induced intergalactic torture chamber, the Barraxa, inasmuch as they could focus on anything at all, focused all their energy on vengeance. Centuries were spent brainstorming, developing, and troubleshooting various technologies that would destroy the Daglion homeworld and every last living thing on it. Though for the first twelve millennia, the Barraxa found failure upon failure, which all of them chalked-up to their inability to focus amid the myriad distractions, squawking birds, flea bites, and nauseating stench which conspired to sap the concentration of the top Barraxa scientists for centuries on end.

Finally, Siro related to the Daglion Chancellor, that in recent years a breakthrough had been made on an antimatter weapon that could trigger a cascading wave of energy that disrupted the bonds of carbon atoms. It was a weapon that required a small payload to deliver and would result in the destruction of all life on the Daglion planet without warning.

"But you're warning us right now," Fabian, the Daglion Chancellor said to Siro. "Why exactly would you come to warn us, by the way?"

The Barraxa stranger paused and said solemnly, "For thirteen thousand years, my species lived under the dogma that we were wronged by the Daglion. I merely looked into the accounts of the actual events and found out that we started the war, and we did so over a type of food I had never heard of, some confectionary called cupcakes. In retrospect, it seemed to me like our ancestors had it coming, and instead of reflecting on that truth and mending our ways, we spent thirteen thousand years blaming you guys and plotting revenge in all kinds of hideous manners. Somehow, I suspect if we continue down this same path, it won't end well for us. But, Chancellor, I implore you not to underestimate the fury of the Barraxa. We have lived for millennia on end aboard a fetid, putrid, hate-filled, seething ball of rage. You may not have thought much of us for thousands of years, but for thousands of years all we have thought about was your destruction. Now that our species has the means to act, there is no doubt in my mind that we will."

"Well, fella," Fabian said, "we certainly appreciate the heads-up. If there's any way you can convince your fellow Barraxa to give up their assault, that would be better for everyone."

"I will try," the stranger said, "but I doubt there is any swaying the thousands of years of raw fury set against you."

"Good luck anyway, Siro, and for your troubles, before you go, I'll have my personal chef send you off with a token of our species' good will."

Fabian outfitted the Barraxa informant with a fine meal, complete with a box of cupcakes for the ride home and a thank you card. Then he tasked his best researchers with finding out the true history between the Daglion and the Barraxa so he and his defense secretary could set about defending their homeworld.

When the Barraxa attack came months later, the results were devastating. The bomb was delivered by a single stealth ship that snuck between the Daglion satellite network. The warhead set off a chain reaction in the atmosphere that took apart every carbon bond on the planet, including graphene structures, igniting a furious wave of heat and destruction that completely devastated the Daglion homeworld's eco-system. The loss was total, and no sign of the Daglion remained.

The Barraxa, exulting in their victory, waited patiently for the heat from the energy wave to dissipate. When the atmosphere finally cooled, the Barraxa donned space suits and began to search the ashen landscape. They celebrated their triumph. They danced on the flaming ruins of the Daglion civilization. They crowed about their triumph. Never had the Barraxa in their species history enjoyed a day as much as this one.

In the center square of the now-demolished Daglion capital city, the Barraxa found a gigantic tungsten cube. On the side facing the open city square, there was a button with an engraving beneath it that read: Dear Barraxa, push to open.

The Barraxa leader was summoned to the square. They were perplexed but not suspicious. After all, the Barraxa were so self-absorbed that they believed the Daglion had been as much obsessed about them as they had been with the Daglion. It made sense to them that their mortal enemies would have their name on a monument to a thirteen-thousand-year-old enemy. The Barraxan leader pushed the button, and the thick tungsten cube opened slowly, revealing a hollow room whose interior had been unaffected by the cascading heat wave.

The room was empty but for a podium with a small box, on top of which was a paper envelope with a greeting card inside. The Barraxa leader read the card aloud to the troops and civilian leaders who had crowded into the room to see what was inside. The card read:

Dear Barraxa.

We understand that you guys have had a tough run of luck over the last thirteen millennia. Way back when you first tried to incinerate our planet, we researched ways to prevent such a thing from ever happening again. We recently succeeded in transferring our consciousness to a higher plane. As such, we no longer have any use for our bodies, our star, or our beautiful home planet. Because you've suffered so much over the years, we figured the least we could do to alleviate your suffering was to leave our beloved home world for you to enjoy. We think you'll like it. Try not to make too much of a mess.

Your friend,

> Fabian, Chancellor of the
> Immortal Daglion of the
> Higher Planes of Existence

> P.S. As a final token of our good will, please enjoy
> a box of my personal chef's finest cupcakes.

The cupcakes were the final insult. It drove the Barraxa into such a fit of rage that they began to tear each other limb from limb, each blaming the other for the strategic failure that had led them into the folly of annihilating another perfectly good home world. Within hours, there were no Barraxa remaining in the galaxy save one.

The informant who had warned the Daglion of the impending attack had been aboard one of the hastily re-constituted warships when the Barraxa in-fighting had broken out on the planet below. When word spread of what had happened, the Barraxa on the ships began to spon-taneously tear each other apart with the same vigor they'd reserved for the Daglion. Siro the informant retreated to an escape pod, shaking his hideous head at the stupidity of his species, and he sat out the violence in the escape pod, his face firmly planted in his palms.

When he discerned that the fighting had finally stopped, he descended to the planet, walked to the main square in the capital city, and entered the tungsten cube. On the podium he left an encoded digital file, on which was a book titled: *A True Account of the Horrific Cupcake Wars of the Daglion and Barraxa Peoples, By Siro Farragna, Historian of the Barraxa.*

He also took the cupcakes and left a card behind that read:

> Dear Fabian,
>
> Thanks for the cupcakes. The last batch was superb. Looking forward to these. Turns out, you guys weren't so bad after all. Good luck in the higher plane.
>
> Siro

The last of the Barraxa, Siro the Historian, was never heard from again.

When Garbeaux, the humans' AI, had finished telling the tale, the cultural minister was perplexed. She needed repeated reassurance from Garbeaux that the story wasn't just a myth but, in fact, a recorded account in the federation's history. Indeed, they found Siro's book in the federation archives under the genre headings: Federation History, War, Daglion, Confectionary, and Comedy.

The cultural minister quickly assembled the six funniest crewmembers in the fleet to write a series of one-liners for the Admiral to unleash at the upcoming meeting. She also instructed the cook to frost the upcoming batch of cupcakes with themes from the Horrific Cupcake Wars of the Daglion and Barraxa Peoples—two of which were Jagfruit-Cherry and Daglion Carrot Cake.

In an unprecedented show of unanimity, the humans were admitted to the Outer Scutum-Centaurus Federation following the third session of the membership sub-committee. The special envoy cited unique circumstances in the history of the membership subcommittee, inscribing the highest possible compliment on the "reason for expedited admittance" line. It read: You humans are funny, funny bastards.

Empress of Shadow

It happened that in the sixteenth year of the reign of the House of Amuʺr, in a form most improbable, the Fifth Declan found peril come unto her reign. The Empire of Shadow, under the protection of the House of Amuʺr, was experiencing the longest stretch of prosperity in memory, due both to the enduring equilibrium established between the Shadow Empire of the Western continents and the Empire of Light in the East, and, most profitably, the riches that were now pouring in from distant solar systems by the gift of the Ihmetti drive. The pressures toward outward expansion had grown larger than even they were in the Age of Exploration in the historical epochs, when nations founded colonies in search of gold, spices, and fruits unknown in the heartland of the West. Once more, the Empress in the West leveraged as much capital and expertise as she could spare, only now, instead of sailing in ships to far off lands in search of returns, the treasure of nations was spent to support the Empire's rapid expanse into the cosmos, just as her counterpart in the East was compelled to do. For fear of being overtaken and overrun by the tireless ingenuity and industriousness of their expansive and eternal rivals was ever the driving force of empires. Such was the nature of the peace.

The most closely guarded but poorly-hidden information in that era were the locations of commissioned starships, for movement revealed strategy—allocated resources betrayed intention, which was almost always discovered by the other. What was found in the dark was brought to the light, and so too of lightness to dark. The most lucrative secret of all, though, yet discovered, was evidence of alien life, for if relationships could be forged early with a powerful and supportive ally, the House of Amuʺr, Declans of the Empire of Shadow, could definitively tip the balance of power and rule the planet in perpetuity.

This was the news the Declan was prepared to receive on the morning the ʹEttoʺr and her crew arrived unexpectedly in orbit, surprising both the Empress of Shadow, whose seat commanded that formidable vessel, and the Declan on the other side of the world, whose spies knew nothing of the ʹEttoʺr's return. The Empress closed the House to all visitors, and all but the most trusted staff were dismissed. There was no direct communication between the ground and ´Etto¨r's commander, who sent word through the military's back channels to expect himself and several members of their expedition. All the proper and furtive signs were given that what must be said must be said in strictest secrecy, thus few eyes were present to bear witness to the news of alien life in the cosmos arriving at the foot of the Fifth Declan of the House of Amu¨r in the Empire of Shadow.

The Empress of Shadow was donned in her most impressive regalia, for it was not lost on her that such a moment would be recorded by the House Archivist and captured for all time, a moment that could not be repeated in the history of the human race. Her face would be studied for generations unknowable. All preparations were made at her empty seat. The Declan was then sat, and the Declan's retinue, with the strictest adherence to highest ceremony, escorted in the commander of the ´Etto¨r along with a small group of his cosmonauts and a lone female civilian, whose unkempt appearance shocked the small audience in the Declan's chamber on such a monumental occasion.

"What news have you for the House of Amu¨r, Commander?" the Declan demanded in her regal, well-practiced tone.

"I cannot entirely say, Excellency. For our expedition's Archaeologist has informed myself and my command staff that she now has definitive proof of life beyond our world. But she swore that the gravity of the information she must convey is of such import that it should be revealed to thyself first, most honorable Declan, from her lips to your ears, and that the knowledge she bears would shake the foundations of our very world, light and dark, to the core of our being. Before she speaks, I would mention, Excellency, that despite her unsettling appearance, Maha Djech´n has always been regarded as among the most highly respected scientists in the rite of scholars. Though some on my crew have openly expressed concerns of her sanity to me. I do not hold that same concern, for I witnessed with my own eyes the structure wherein she and her group obtained this information. It was among the most wondrous sights I have beheld, and I but peered inside from the arch of the entryway. Maha Djech´n and but one other, her most trusted assistant, were the only people to enter the basilica, and neither has been quite the same since. My opinion, should your Excellency forgive my boldness in offering such, is that you consider Maha Djech´n's account with due consideration despite the distraction her disturbing appearance may impress on you, Excellency."

"This is the archeologist?" the Declan stated, facing Maha Djech´n.

"Yes, Excellency," she said, kneeling to reflect her station, for her origin was a base one, contrasting her lofty position, which she'd achieved through sheer force of will and a peerless record of competence.

"Is it true what the Commander stated? You have witnessed proof of alien life?"

"What I have witnessed, Excellency, is beyond the realm of belief—a set of circumstances none of our scholars could have predicted or accepted as true. But this truth will be neither easy to believe nor desirable, so be sure that in uttering it, I understand that one of my station takes considerable risks. When you understand what I now know, and what I now am, if you do anything but believe and heed what it is I say, you will understand that the Declan's wrath is a trifling matter in the face of what looms in our very galaxy, for the worst that you could do to me for my honesty, if you mistake such honesty for insolence, pales in comparison to what has already been done unto me and to my assistant Maha Az´hriin who has fared less well than myself in the ordeal. Furthermore, whether the Declan wishes it or likes it, what I must tell must be heard."

"Excellency," the commander said, sensing considerable tension at the Declan's seat, "please forgive Maha Djech´n her impudence, for we are led to believe she and her assistant have undergone considerable anguish of the mind by what happened on that distant planet. Such outlandish exhorttations as these are what prompted my crew to fear for her sanity."

"If I wish for your opinion further Commander, I shall ask it. Do not think your Declan so fragile as to be wounded by the mere words of a single archaeologist, well respected as she may be in the rite of scholars."

"My apologies, Excellency."

"You may continue, Maha Djech'n," the Empress said. "What evidence did you discover in the course of the expedition?"

"As Excellency knows," Maha Djech'n began, "I was dispatched to evaluate the nature of an artificial structure discovered in the caverns on the second planet orbiting i'Alsioun 18, a body quite similar in mass to our own world. And what I found there, initially, was a welcome sight."

"Rise," the Declan stated, accepting that Maha Djech'n's testimony would be heard with the consideration of the House of Amu"r.

"Thank you, Excellency," Maha Djech'n continued. "Deep in the caverns where the forward party had discovered a structure of architectural regularity, they held a perimeter, per protocol, and I was told that none had entered before my team's arrival. It seemed a nondescript corridor. But as I entered, I found that, to my surprise, the architecture seemed more familiar than alien. The walls, for lack of a better way of saying it, seemed to have been carved out of the rock with human sensibility."

"Human you say?"

"It seemed so in the moment, Excellency. And we were able to confirm as much when we came to the threshold of the basilica—the room at the lowest extreme of the corridor, which we named as such, because it seemed to take on the architectural significance of a sacred space. The eyes perceived it as such on first sight, and nothing disabused us of that initial impression.

"Yet on our first approach to the threshold, we did not enter. For there were pictographs carved in the stone that communicated to us in rather universal ways that we would be wise to pay heed to the markings on the wall before proceeding in haste.

"Just beyond the pictographs, on the two walls, the floor, and the ceiling there were carvings in four different scripts, all four of which seemed both unfamiliar and familiar at once to the eyes. Not one of the symbols save for the odd circle and cross was of any known script in the human lexicon. However, when we scanned the surfaces of the rock, we were quickly able to discern that on the ceiling was a script of a ten-digit numerical system inscribing the first hundred prime numbers, indicating the architect's numerical system, which they'd used to assign a digital reference for each letter in the three scripts on the walls and the floor. Our algorithmic intelligences, within hours, because of the cleverness of the carvers, was able to teach itself the three distinct languages, each of which conformed to universal principles embedded in our understanding of human linguistics: expressions of past, present, and future; verbs; subjects of actions; descriptors and compliments of those descriptors; pronouns; syntactical consistency. The carvings were human, yet of no human language known, and carved therein the walls conveyed a single message in these three unknown tongues: that this temple's flame must burn for all time; for, so soon as the flame was extinguished, soon after, too, would the human race's flame be extinguished. The three scripts exhorted all who enter to prepare and take heed, for the temple held visceral pain, but, through that pain, would we come to know the price of our continued survival. It was both an exciting discovery and a terrifying one, for it seemed that the flame burned no longer, and no sign remained of the creators of the wonderous room we beheld.

"By this time, Excellency, we could see from the threshold the majesty of the basilica therein. We, my assistant Maha Az´hriin and I, entered the room together. And truly the sight was one to behold.

Running along the entire length of the basilica floor was a pool of stars, a map of the cosmos that looked to the naked eye indistinguishable from the night sky itself. This star map shone with stars as truly as the stars of our night sky, and wondrously, the blackness of the pool seemed to have depth to it as infinite as the depths of the eternal cosmos. And floating in the space above this star map were cubes of a colorful translucent material that seemed to reflect the starlight and also generate such a pleasant glow as to be welcoming to the eye.

This miracle of ingenuity suggested a race technologically advanced enough that we already revered their brilliance. In and of themselves the cubes portrayed no symbolic significance. Yet as Maha Az´hriin and I stood marveling at the first cube, hovering above the night sky, we learned that the cubes were not symbolic themselves but were a mode of communication unlike any we have ever encountered, for we were swept into the consciousness of another, of a human woman who was of the people who had carved that temple out of the stone, and that each of the five cubes told a piece of the story that I will relate to you now, for as then, it holds significance for our survival, just as it did for them.

"But I must first warn you, Excellency, that as our consciousness was taken in by these mysterious cubes, we became this other person, both retaining our own identity and simultaneously possessing hers as faithfully as she did herself. The star map became familiar to us, presenting the locations of thousands of planets hosting an empire of trillions of human souls, an empire of which both the House of Shadow and the House of Light would be but footnotes in a history that would overwrite our own a thousand-fold.

"Excellency, we are but children to these people, our elders. You must understand this."

"I believe I understand this point, Maha Djech´n," the Empress of Shadow said. "Now convey to me the message these cubes conveyed unto you as faithfully as you can report it."

Cube 1:

The new setting, a large planet, came first to me as a feeling. And in this feeling, I must first express that as I relate this, I, Maha Djech´n, no longer exist in this tale. Nor does Maha Az´hriin, for even as I felt her there with me, present in those moments, we had both become this other, an explorer, a human female, Veral Kathon, she who would become the prophet, and it was Veral Kathon's feeling I felt as my own and now relate as my own. For her actions were my own as I experienced them, even to the extent that as she chose her actions, I was made to feel the agent of those actions, as though I had chosen them myself in the moment, just as such was it too with Maha Az´hriin in her experience. And Veral Kathon's feelings I felt with her depth. The first was aching, most prominently in my knees where the long bones of the legs met, and I knew from my depth of memory that it was the price of such an extended stay in such heavy gravity. Even with exoskeletal support and conditioning to the

114

planet, my bones ached. I also felt as though I was drowning in the fetid odor of sulfur and doubly detested the stench, for I was there in service not of humanity but of the hideous others.

This vast community of human colonies in the stars, to which I – Veral Kathon – belonged, counted planetary colonies numbering in the thousands, each with tens of billions of inhabitants belonging to an empire in the midst of an age of prosperity and genius such as our wildest storytellers would not even dare to imagine. Their technology and understanding of the nature of both themselves and the universe outstripped ours by millennia, yet they seemed all too familiar, for just as we have struggled for centuries with the Empire of Light, these humans had met other races in the stars and had endured wars that lasted for tens of thousands of years.

Their chief rival were a race of monstrous creatures they knew as the Taul-al-ghal, an insect-like species whose genetic imperative was expansion. They bred at alarming rates and were short-lived compared to us, and they were asexual, living lives of ten to twenty years in service of their collective and then dying in the act of giving birth to their offspring, which often numbered in the teens, who were then left to the collective to be raised in compassionless, loveless servitude of the progression of the group.

The Taul-al-ghal plagued humanity at every opportunity, so much so, that our history was not of ships or cities destroyed in battles but of entire planets annihilated in conflagrations at scales that cannot be imagined if not witnessed first-hand. Such desperate exposure to the Taul left those people at the outer reaches of our empire so battle-hardened that they became much more warlike and compassionless than the more peaceful peoples of the inner planets.

The Taul, though a persistent menace, could never make meaningful gains against us, for they had but one strategy—overwhelm with numbers. Meanwhile, the humans, who won nearly every battle in the Endless War, ingenious as our commanders were, could never definitively push the Taul back, for a million would appear to take the place of each million destroyed.

Then, several hundred years before my birth on the planet of Madiera, one of the most beautiful of the inner worlds of the empire, the Taul-al-ghal, reeling from a string of terrible defeats, shocked our empire by suing for peace, something thought impossible by all human experience. We were cautious but pressed forward to negotiation, for any possibility of peace needed to be investigated. The Taul demanded terms. We presented counterdemands. The negotiations, through intermittent returns to battle, lasted a generation. Territory was distinguished, as were strict rules. The Taul would push forward no more into human systems, and in exchange, the humans, masters of technologies the Taul lacked, would terraform planets for the Taul-al-ghal at the far extremes of their empire, removing the need for them to expand into human space. We agreed but only if human terms were followed, which meant all life-bearing planets were off-limits, just as we humans forbade the destruction of alien ecosystems for our own benefit. And strict measures were put in place, just as with human exploration of new bodies, that rigorous tests must show no potential for natural life on worlds where the Taul hoped to terraform.

This was my task on that heavy planet at the far end of Taul territory, running tests in obscure pools of chemicals, searching for branching chains of proteins and peptides that could, given millions of years, spring to life. For days upon days, with aching knees and weary hands, exhausted by the monotony of the labor, the loneliness of my isolation, and the relentless presence of the sulfuric odor, I performed my duty faithfully.

Gifted with all this new knowledge, and settled as I had become in my new body, it came as the harshest shock of my lifetime when I was suddenly released and returned to the Basilica of the Prophet Veral Kathon. I found myself back in the darkness, staring absently at the floating cube, standing once more in my own body beside Maha Az´hriin, whose shock was as pronounced as my own. And as we reflected on the wonder of the experience and knowledge bestowed to us in what we learned was but a mere moment of absence, we both turned instinctually toward the second cube.

Cube 2:

I was settled aboard my cruiser when I returned to that awful sulfuric planet. I had just divested of my eternally noxious suit after the second ten-hour spell outside testing plots in grid 4271 in the northern hemisphere, one of many thousands of locations selected for closer scrutiny by the geospatial profiling program for its potential to host proteins. I had long been established on that nameless rock, nearly fifteen hundred days, and I refused to name the planet, for it would never be my home. We—I and my artificial assistant Trieste—hadn't found so much as a complex protein, and then on that day, we discovered after all that time, in a single obscure pool, peptides that seemed so far out of place we immediately suspected contamination by either myself or Trieste. We tested three times, and to our dismay, found the initial readings, improbable as they were, to be accurate. Peptides. On this day of all days.

The Taul overseer, who seemed a domineering and spiteful creature, was scheduled for a quarterly visit per treaty bylaws. I detested its presence in my ship even more than I resented the stench of my helmet and suit, and I feared its presence in ideal circumstances, when I could report that the survey was ahead of schedule. I knew immediately that I would need to deceive the creature, for to tell it of our findings would certainly send it into a violent paroxysm. The only question would be how dangerous its fury would be for Trieste and me.

I was wrestling more substantively with how deep the deception would go. I was duty bound, under the letter of the treaty, to report our findings to the human oversight board, but here was a single pool with a single chain of peptides on an enormous planetary body, perhaps a billion years before any possibility of evolutionary progression.

When the Taul overseer arrived, per usual, I instructed Trieste what to relate in their disgusting guttural, clicky language. And though they were unfamiliar with human emotion and behavior, it was somehow able to distinguish that there was a difference between our usual behavior and our behavior that day—a hesitation on Trieste's part to relate faithfully the words I conveyed to him to translate to the creature.

The beast kicked Trieste across the room and seemed to threaten to crush his head in its claw-like hand. It accused us of deception because of our irregular behavior.

I told the creature that it must not harm Trieste, for if he was damaged and could not communicate with the Taul, I would need to return to human territory to find a replacement, which would delay the project much further than any previous complication we'd encountered.

It set its eyes on me and released Trieste. It now glared at me menacingly.

"If you kill me," I told Trieste to tell it, "that may end the project altogether, perhaps even the treaty."

This was the ultimate threat, for in the centuries since the treaty was struck, the Taul came to rely on the letter of treaty law almost as though it was an instinctive rule written into the behavior of the species.

"Human would never destroy the law for the body of one," it said.

"That is the difference between us," I had Trieste convey. "We value the one."

"You value nothing," it said. "Disgusting, deceitful creatures."

But it seemed to forget what had sent it into the violent outburst to begin with. I told it everything was on schedule, and that it was welcome to collect our data for review, as was their right under law, and I hadn't yet transferred the day's files into the permanent record, so the Taul would have no knowledge of the peptides we'd found.

When it finally departed and I had composed myself from the fear and the trauma Trieste and I had endured, we discussed our way forward, for Trieste was insistent that the peptides be reported to the human oversight commission, yet I had a powerful sense of temptation governing my actions. For it was not only my duty to humanity and to our empire that I was out on that planet. There was a motivation beyond all others that drove me to that horrible place.

Servants of the empire who did this field work, the jobs least desired of all humankind, were rewarded highest. The highest reward of all was citizenship on the home world,

Ashtu. Even Madiera, my home planet, one of the inner worlds revered for its beauty, was no comparison for Ashtu, the seat of our empire, a world whose natural beauty was unsurpassed and unsurpassable, according to any human who'd set foot there. Few humans had, for in the generations of war with the Taul, all information about Ashtu became a tightly guarded secret, especially its location. It was our most precious gem, and we guarded it as such with wartime protocols, and in the thousands of years of conflict, Ashtu remained untouched. But the impact of this on humanity through the generations was that humans in the outer worlds lost any sense of their home world. And because pictures of Ashtu were forbidden, lest they somehow fall into the Taul's possession, stories of her beauty were all that spread, until the world itself became but a legend for the trillions of people on the worlds outside Ashtu, including myself Veral Kathon. From the earliest age, my mind had been captured by the legend of Ashtu's beauty. It was the sole reason for my servitude—the hope that one day, I might witness it with my own eyes.

It was this I struggled to convey to Trieste, whose programming was conflicted between loyalty to me after so long and loyalty to the letter of the treaty. Over several days, we discussed our way forward, for Trieste was troubled by my equivocation, and he could not understand my hesitation to report our findings exactly as we recorded them. But my mind was equally troubled, for I knew that for all the powers superior to us, both human and Taul-al-ghal, it was clearly in their interest to find nothing on the planet, no hindrances, no threats to the peace, no conflicts, and certainly in the case of my direct superiors—whose authority shaped my future—no peptides.

Ultimately, after many days of discussion, we decided to file a formal complaint to the human oversight committee over the mis-treatment the Taul inspector was guilty of toward myself and Trieste. This would give me an opportunity to report both the abuse and, if I so chose, our true findings to a human board, even though it likely meant an end to my hopes to one day see Ashtu.

And after this long time embodied as Veral Kathon in my tiny ship on this putrid world with my only friend an artificial being, I found myself returned again to the basilica in the darkness beside Maha Az´hriin. Thus engrossed in the life of Veral Kathon then, far more than even our own lives, which now felt foreign and distant to us, I and Maha Az´hriin both made for the third cube.

Cube 3:

I returned to the universe of Veral Kathon, still abord my cruiser, only instead of sitting parked on the hideous yellow planet of the Taul's expansion, Trieste and I were in hyper-space, on the way to the planet we called Acchi, one of the border worlds of the Taul-al-ghal. It was there the treaty outlined safe haven to meet with our human oversight, and even though I felt the experience of the months that had elapsed, the tireless hours of internal debate with my own mind, the external debate I continued with Trieste, the periods of certainty and wavering, still, I had yet to decide whether I would report the peptides.

Trieste brought the cruiser out of hyperspace outside the Acchi system, or at least where the Acchi system was supposed to be. Yet it wasn't. Not the planets, not the moons, not even the star.

Trieste checked the star charts and rechecked navi-gational data. It seemed an anomaly, but all our readings were consistent with us being where we were supposed to be. Acchi wasn't.

I suggested to Trieste that we approach the space where Acchi itself should have been, and we could discern no reason not to investigate further, so we proceeded to that location with caution.

As we arrived in the planet's space, it was just as we had observed before, empty space. An entire star system had vanished without a trace. Both Trieste and I doubted what we saw, but all our instrumentation and the stars themselves confirmed and reconfirmed.

Then, I observed with the naked eye, a tiny, odd refraction of light in the darkness, and as Trieste brought us closer to investigate, I Maha Djech´n saw something I recognized, only I realized, quite separately from the consciousness of Veral Kathon, that she had never seen the odd cube before. She instructed Trieste to bring the cruiser close to the object, and just as I and Maha Az'hriin had been drawn to its alluring light in the basilica, Veral Kathon stared deeply into the cube's glow and I was suddenly back in a place I very much recognized—the Tzokin pine forest outside my home city of Annoris on Madiera.

After five long years on that sulfuric rock, the smell of the air and the pines and the moisture in the air overtook my senses. I skipped right through the shock of being transported home in this sudden unaccountable way and my emotions overcame all. I wept. I dropped to my knees and touched the dirt. I took up pine needles in my hands and inhaled their heavenly scent. It was only after several minutes of relishing my homecoming before I began to question how it was I had come to be there. That's when I noticed the observer.

"You enjoyed that far more than I had anticipated," he said, or at least he seemed a he, for he appeared to me as a pleasant young man.

I somehow knew he was responsible for all of it.

"How?" I said, and then, "Who?"

"There will be more questions than I can answer, and truly more to the answers than you can possibly understand."

"Why have you brought me here?" I asked him.

"You brought you here, Veral Kathon. All your choices, your actions, those were yours. I'd like to know what you've decided."

And I somehow knew he was asking me about the planet, about the peptides, and I also knew I could not lie to him, for he knew my mind, my memories, had forged the world of Madiera for me from the fabric of my mind and brought me there. To lie to him would have been folly.

"I do not truly know," I said. "I suppose I came to see, and I was prepared to make the decision in the moment."

"That moment is now, Veral Kathon."

"I feel deeply that it is wrong to work with these creatures, to create for them, and even worse to destroy—even the dumb rocks they occupy are corrupted by their very presence. But to ignore the treaty is to ignore the peace, to welcome a perpetual state of war to the human experience. Everything I learned from my earliest childhood of the cost

121

of the Endless War, though, leads me to believe almost any action that could prevent it from happening again should be taken. If the cost of preventing such unspeakable carnage is a pool of peptides, I struggle to do what I feel and know to be right."

"Yet you know what is right, for you understand the essence of it. I ask you now to tell me why."

"The proteins," I said, still kneeling in the dirt. I breathed in deep, bathing in the glory of Madiera's fresh air. "What I do today may stop a billion years of evolution that I have no right to halt."

"This is so," he said. "We have been watching, and you are very much like the rest of your kind. You understand today, forget tomorrow, and remember again if it suits your purpose. I am here to tell you that you are not to forget again. In ages long past, your ancestors understood what was important. They knew what you were and what you were not, and they lived their lives by edicts. We give you this one final edict now and exhort you to heed it, for we do not caution you lightly, and we shall not warn you again."

And his kind eyes grew very grave. He stepped forward and stood above me there as I knelt on the forest floor.

"Thou shalt not take that which is not yours."

And I knew exactly what he meant. He meant everything. Not another planet, not another moon, not another asteroid. Not for us. Not to keep the peace with the Taul. Nothing.

"Return and tell them all, even at the cost of all you hold dear," he said.

And in that moment, I made the costliest mistake of my life. I feared what others would think when I told them this story. I thought of the ridicule and doubt, the cost of my reputation, my chances of seeing Ashtu.

He glared at me, and simply said, "You have heard what I said. Behave, monkey."

I cannot describe what happened then except to say that far beyond the cells of my body, through the last fiber of my existence, every ounce of my essence was scorched with the most excruciating and inexhaustible pain I imagined could exist, and I felt myself being held there in the clutches of this other eternal being's consciousness. I was made to feel the extent of its power and wrath. And I hung there in that moment for an eternity, for longer than I had been on that sulfuric rock, for every day I'd spent on Madiera dreaming of Ashtu, for the weeks in hyperspace. It was longer than my life. Pure agony, deeper than the reaches of space itself. And then, long after a time when I had forgotten anything but hopelessness and despair, there was I, Maha Djech´n, returned to the temple of Veral Kathon, reeling in the darkness with Maha Az´hriin, who shrank back from the starlit pool in horror. And we two collapsed into a heap in the dark shadows of the temple, holding each other to be certain our deliverance was real, that we had been released from damnation by the being that had never had us but had taken Veral Kathon. Yet it haunts us both still, for we experienced it as surely and as deeply as if it had been us, for it was our experience, just as it was hers. And looming there, as horrible as the experience had been, were the two final cubes.

"No, mistress, I beg you, please. Do not make me go back," Maha Az´hriin said to me, for she noticed that after some time I had begun to look at the star pool in the direction of the fourth cube.

I felt, though, a powerful pull toward the cubes, not just for the knowledge of what became of Veral Kathon, nor for the remainder of the story, but because I knew that just as much as the being had commanded her, he had commanded all of us: "Thou shalt not!" And we needed to know. The etchings at the mouth of the basilica had told us as much. The flame must be kept burning, and extinguished as it had been, it was our duty to once again light the flame, or I knew we would meet him in the darkness. So, I alone went forth to the rim of the star pool and gazed into the fourth cube.

Cube 4:

I was then returned, in body and in consciousness, to the existence of Veral Kathon in the moment she too was returned to her body in the cruiser. I found myself seated beside Trieste, for whom the near eternity of hellish suffering I, Veral Kathon, had endured seemed but a brief moment of absence while I stared at the cube. This was one of the few moments in the entire experience that I, Maha Djech´n, felt somewhat disconnected from Veral Kathon, for

I had spent considerable time in the basilica in the arms of Maha Az'hriin, where we two had held each other for comfort, reclaiming our sanity as best we could from the terrors of hell. I returned to Veral Kathon's consciousness at the selfsame moment as she, who was justifiably hysterical, physically agitated, and mentally tormented to the same degree as myself and Maha Az'hriin had been. Having gone through this anguish once before, I now had to endure it again but, unlike Veral Kathon, I had the benefit of the knowledge that the terror would eventually pass, and I'd had the comfort of Maha Az'hriin's commiseration to quell my spirit. Veral Kathon had no such comfort, only an artificial being who was quite perplexed by his mistress's inexplicable exhortations of horror. I was made to feel her terror as I had felt my own, and there was nothing I could do to explain it to Trieste or Veral Kathon herself. I writhed in her skin for hours. I wept till my chest and my cheeks ached. I mourned. And then I breathed deep the release from damnation, as I had done once already, and then I began to process the experience.

Through the moments of terror, I noticed that the cube, which had previously been floating in the depths of space was now beside me on the floor of the cruiser, the sudden appearance of which Trieste, having no understanding of my true experience, mistook as the source of my sudden insanity. I recoiled from it out of instinct, for I recalled it as the source of that horror, but as I began to regain my senses, I knew it was not bestowed on me as a source of torment, but a sign, and something much deeper, but I knew not what yet.

After several hours of quiet reflection once the hysteria had passed, I instructed Trieste to set a course for Madiera. I knew not the exact course I was to set for my life with my new knowledge, but I knew the bearing. I prepared myself to endure the ridicule. I prepared to be ignored, outcast, reviled. I prepared for my voice to grow hoarse from shouting the new truth of human existence, and to do it with the urgency of a civilization whose foundation was imperiled existentially. I prepared to be seen as the maddest woman who had ever beheld the depths of space and had the abyss reach back into her soul, for if there had been one true thing that had ever happened to me, Veral Kathon, it had been that.

I arrived at Madiera to the shock of my friends, family, and even the conveyors of the news of the empire, for I was thought to have perished in the depths of space, either by some horrific accident or, what was seen as more likely, some treachery of the Taul-al-ghal. I had expected some moment of quiet reflection with my family before my mission began, but no such grace blessed me. I was given a pulpit immediately, not just to the people of Madiera but to the surrounding worlds as well. Everyone wanted to know what I had experienced in that lost time. And to the horror of my family, I told the tale as truly as I could recount. I exhorted all people to repress every instinct to expand, to shun the Taul-al-ghal and make no further effort to help their empire expand as well. I told them there were beings powerful enough to destroy star systems, just as they had made Acchi to vanish from the realm of existence. And I was immediately accounted a madwoman, for unbeknownst to me it had been Acchi that had reported my disappearance. To everyone but myself and Trieste, Acchi hadn't disappeared at all. We were the ones who'd gone missing.

The powerful force of disbelief, bolstered by the faces of all who beheld me, the whispers, the depth of concern from my family, from Trieste even—all this made me doubt my own sanity. But then, there was the cube.

My family wanted to place me in a hospital against my own wishes, and indeed, for a time, they prevailed upon the state to make this happen. But before they took me away, I gave Trieste one final mission as his charge—to bring the cube to a professor of mine at the academy—a peerless scientific mind—for I knew it would pique his curiosity enough to investigate its powers and purposes, and indeed we came to know them well.

I spent nearly a year in the hospital learning the story I needed to tell for them to believe me sane once more. I spat out their medicine furtively. I mouthed their words as a forced non-believer. I falsely worshipped in the cult of conformity, yet through it, I saw the wave of hellfire rolling across the stars toward us. And then one day, when I had recited the words convincingly enough, I was released.

My colleague, the professor, had made some startling discoveries about the cube's properties. It transmitted signals by the trillions so precisely that he determined it could have only been tuned precisely for the human mind. And by his own genius, he was able to design a process whereby we could replicate the advanced materials composing the cube.

When I was reunited with him, his work progressed far more rapidly, for he was able to determine the answer to many questions he'd had about the device—that it captured consciousness, transferred memories, conveyed experiences. And though I feared the cube terribly, he prevailed upon me to approach it again, to see if it might react to my presence.

Over several months, we learned that the cube could imprint an experience and bestow that experience on others just as the imprinter had endured it. It was the most powerful form of communication any human had ever beheld. But when I finally successfully imprinted on the device, we found that the amount of information was so voluminous, we would need to replicate the device at least three times over to share my experience with others. So, over several months, we perfected the process of replicating the device.

I was beginning to understand the wisdom of the being's gift. For my words alone would never be enough to sway even my family and friends to believe the truth of my story. To strangers, I would never be more than a madwoman. But when the cubes finally enabled me to fully share my tribulations with my collaborator, who claimed previously to have believed me, all doubt vanished. He became my greatest adherent. We then knew the path forward, painful as it would be.

We set out across Madiera, spreading the word and exhorting any who would dare to share in my experiences. And those who did so gaze into the cubes, being so greatly affected, either became dedicated adherents and believers or vehement deniers of the truth they had seen, for such an awful truth was unpleasant to believe, and this life we had been living on Madiera, even in the darkest days of the Endless War, it was a pleasant dream. My truth was reality.

As our numbers grew, we became pariahs, for many were seen to be driven to madness instantaneously by simply gazing into the third cube. And we preached, as was the truth, that we should go no further out into the stars and take nothing that was not already ours. It countermanded the curiosity ingrained in our genetic imperative. It was a heresy against our very biology. Yet it was our only pathway to survival.

Pariahs all, we set out from Madiera, cubes in hand, to spread the word to the thousands of worlds of the empire in the hopes of reaching as many minds as we could before it was too late.

For years it went like this. We would arrive at a new world attempting to spread our message. Violence and strife would ensue. I was branded an enemy of the peace. A shaman terrorist. A lunatic. An apocalypticist. And of all the messages I spread the furthest and loudest it was this, if we did not heed the one edict, we would be wiped from existence, just as the Taul-al-ghal would be. And for those who had not seen, had not been in the grasp of the cubes, the message seemed absurd.

Nearly a decade passed thus for my followers, hiding our identities, sneaking the cubes in cargo, sleeping in back rooms and safehouses. All the while our doubters wondered how anyone could believe a truth so ridiculous, until one day, the skirmishes that had once again erupted between ourselves and the Taul suddenly stopped. The Taul-al-ghal simply were no more.

Against the howling of my adherents, the empire sent scouts to investigate. Ships ventured cautiously into space that for thousands of years no human had dared to tread. Yet as exhaustively as our starships searched, for months on end, not so much as the smallest artifact of their entire civilization—hundreds of thousands of years of empire across reaches of the galaxy that rivalled our own—in all that space, nothing was ever found.

I found myself, once more, back at the star pool, Maha Az´hriin still behind me in the shadows weeping, and I knew that Veral Kathon had decided, in the wisdom that had come with her many tribulations, to record that fourth cube to convey her whole story. For there was wisdom in it, and knowing what I knew now from that fourth piece of her trials, I stepped forward toward the fifth.

Cube 5:

The first thing I noticed when I returned to my body yet again was that I was suddenly now much older. My hands were the most prominent and shocking change. Wrinkles and creases, callouses, spots.

I was now, after many years, finally on my way to Ashtu. I and my closest circle of adherents had been summoned to advise the leaders of the home world on the perspective of the Evangelists, as my believers had come to be called. And it was as true a name as one could have chosen. For, as was now fully known to me, we had spread our message over the entire outer empire, and we had held the line, politically whenever possible, but, in extreme times when particularly bold expansionists challenged our hegemony, we were left no choice but to resort to forceful measures, first imprisonment and then, only when all else had failed, violence. The home world understood little of our motives, for the discussion to them was an abstract one. The residents of such a paradise had no cause or desire to travel elsewhere, nor could they understand the gravity of a threat on their border, because for generations immemorial there had been none.

I was asked to brief the leaders, because I, Veral Kathon, Prophet of the Evangelists, understood their motives and could predict their actions, and because, after so long— decades of struggle to be heard by the establishment, followed by decades of hegemonic political and cultural dominance—with the Taul a distant memory, the empire's political environment had become entirely unaccountable to the leaders on Ashtu.

I believed I could explain it to them coherently, but I feared that no matter how well it was explained to them, they would not be able to understand, for the one special con- dition of my visa as dictated by the guardians of their world was that I was forbidden from bringing the cubes, now num- bering four, onto the home world of Ashtu. It was even said, both there and in other wealthy inner worlds, that I possessed technology that could bewitch and twist the minds of any I wished to convert. Again, a certain limited kind of truth.

I prepared for many hours over many days during our journey. I rehearsed my speech for my acolytes. I explained that the problems erupting along the outer worlds were unavoidable, for the young could not themselves remember the Taul-al-ghal. For them, the Taul were a frightful bedtime story. And so too, for many in our society, whose lives knew no strife, just like the people of Ashtu had been for millennia, true peril itself became a fairy tale—a plotline we used to entertain ourselves when we tired of the regularity of our secure and happy homes and communities. The danger that had once been existential was now only mythological, and in my heart, as much as I wished to believe that vigilance, wisdom, and the power of the cubes would be enough, I knew that inevitably, over time, it must certainly fail. Of all the countless trillions, some contrarians would spring forth somewhere, defying the wisdom of the ages, pulled by the curiosity embedded in our cellular makeup. Someone would slip through.

Of Ashtu, all I can say now, was that after all those years— pining, longing, imagining, hoping—her beauty surprised in ways I could never have predicted. The plants and the trees seemed to call out to my heart. The landscape embraced me with its familiarity and wonder. The colors brought tears to my eyes. It was, as had always been said, by far the most beautiful place I had ever been in the universe, which seemed fitting, because all of us out there, even arriving for the first time after a life lived in the stars, were returning home.

I delivered my speech to the leaders of Ashtu, word for word as I had practiced in transit. And, as I'd anticipated, for them the sentiments seemed peculiar. I felt the sensations deep within me, a hope because the leaders of Ashtu were trying to understand, and a deeper regret that it would take more; because always, beneath everything, there was a nagging terror at the bottom of my soul, that he was still out there in the darkness of the infinite, watching. "Thou shalt not take." His words still haunted me in my bones, in my aching knees. "Behave, monkey."

Then at last, I found myself returned to the Basilica of Veral Kathon.

"And now you have truly become her, Maha Djech´n," the Empress of Shadow said unto the archaeologist, sensing that her tale was complete, "for your story is so peculiar as to make all who hear it question your sanity, just as the crew of my starship ´Etto¨r did. I am left with questions innumerable, and, as much as your tale is compelling and your telling of it powerful, Maha Djech´n, I freely admit I have doubts."

"This too is familiar, Excellency," Maha Djech´n said, "for I lived the whole life of Veral Kathon in the hours I and Maha Az´hriin beheld the cubes within the basilica. In that lifetime, I experienced the doubts of a thousand worlds as well as their scorn, contempt, and disdain. Doubt me you may, but believe me you must. For he is still out there, and the edict still stands."

"Let's say I believed you Maha Djech´n—that I trusted in your expertise and relied upon your honesty and bravery, and I staked the fate of the entire Empire on the truth of your tale—even if I did as such, I wonder, what would you have me do? Abandon the stars? Watch idly while the House of Light went forth to the richness of the cosmos and passed us by, subjugated us, denigrated our traditions, culture, and language until we were but a colony of theirs?"

"No, Excellency, you cannot do this, for the House of Light must be made to understand as well. The edict is not just for those who have heard it. It is for all."

"The question stands, Maha Djech´n. What would you have me do with this information?"

"I would have you use every power at your disposal to bring the Empire of Light to the table, to convince them of this necessary truth, revealing it in every detail to the Eastern Declans. And as painful an experience as it has been for me, Excellency, I propose that you and your counterpart travel to the second planet orbiting the star we have designated i´Alsioun 18. I recommend that you descend together to the Basilica of Veral Kathon and you receive the truth together. For if you do not, all will be lost once more."

"Once more you say, Maha Djech´n?"

"Yes, excellency, for Veral Kathon's final truth was one she could not have known when she recorded her life. It was something only we could have known."

"That her civilization was doomed?"

"Yes, true, Excellency," Maha Djech'n said, and as she said this she knelt at the foot of the Empress of Shadow, and looking up into her monarch's eyes she said, "I do not kneel as a supplicant, for surely, I am not that. I kneel as your ancestor, begging you to take heed, for all was as I said, Excellency.

"The final truth in the Basilica of Veral Kathon was in the stars, in the pool on the floor, when I was returned to my body, I knew them still from her knowledge, by name and by sight, star after star, constellation after constellation. And the one location I wondered about all that time ensconced in Veral Kathon's consciousness was where, oh, where was my beloved home? Where was Madiera? And I knew it the moment I finally returned to the Basilica, in the same manner I knew all that I knew from the consciousness of Veral Kathon herself, I simply felt her knowledge as my own. And as I stooped to bring Maha Az'hriin with me, out from that room to the lifeless, barren rock of a planet above, suffused still in those final few moments with the wisdom of the ages, I knew in my soul that it was there. Planet two of i'Alsioun 18 was Madiera. I was finally home again, but it was home no longer."

The Empress now beheld the sincerity of Maha Djech'n's face. She pitied the poor woman for the depth of her sadness, her face now awash in tears. Yet the Empress stood first, as always, to her duty.

"Sad as that may be, Maha Djech'n," the Empress of Shadow said. "I fail to see how this changes our understanding of the situation, for we all knew at the outset that their civilization had come to ruin. Such is the labor of an archeologist, is it not?"

"There is more, Excellency," Maha Djech'n said, wiping tears from her eyes. "I knew the names of the stars and planets in the pool on the basilica's star map just as surely as she did. I remembered those places. But I did not remember that which I did not know was there. Not until the end, for she never went there until the end. And its beauty, I thought, as Veral Kathon did, was in her familiarity. But that, Empress, was not Veral Kathon's feeling but my own, for I had been there. She could not have known, and because she did not know, I did not know either, not until I left, that it was here.

Home. They used another name than we use now, but the House of Light, the House of Shadow, all this, your very seat, our nation, this planet, Excellency; it is Ashtu.

"Ashtu is here."

To Geddes

Julian Hartsock. "To Geddes." *Precipice: The Autobiographical Ramblings of Julian Hartsock.* (Chapter) A & A Publications, 2123.

OPENNESS (Proper)—(Hartsock, Julian Q.) 97th Percentile:

Openness—i.e. Openness Proper—(OP) is the psychometric score assigned to an individual's proclivity to seek out new experiences or ideas. People exceptionally high in Openness tend to be creative thinkers who are immediately capable of generating numerous new ideas or solutions to problems; however, people high in Openness often struggle with routine work that does not involve creativity or problem solving and can also struggle choosing from among the diverse ideas they generate. They also gravitate toward art and representations of beauty, whether in stories, music, architecture, or all of the above. Open people crave change and can be radical thinkers likely to upset pre-existing states of order or equilibrium.

A score in the (97th) percentile, coupled with the distribution profile of psychometric measures herein, suggests an extremely creative introvert, perhaps even a savant, prone to spending time alone developing new ideas or solutions to new problems. Professions where serious and necessarily solitary intellectual work would be ideal. The exceedingly rare constellation of Conscientiousness (Industriousness), Openness (Intellect), and G, all measuring above the 96th percentile, coupled with an OP in the 97th percentile suggests the subject should seek professional engagement in an environment where idea generation is highly valued (such as a think tank, a university, or an entrepreneurial enterprise).

Yes, Openness both describes and explains quite a lot about my personality, especially as MM[3] described the trait in their literature. I couldn't help but generate new ideas. My struggle was implementing them all. And Beauty is a God to me. Gladstone et al. rated me even higher on their scale (99), but their narrative (as usual) was scant; their feedback read as follows: Exceptionally high OP contributes to unique grouping of factors.

The future began with a story.

It sounds too ridiculous to be true, but it is, and I never told anyone the story behind the story at the time, because they wouldn't have believed me. They'd already dismissed it as false. The story may seem familiar to some, but what's unfamiliar for anyone who's heard it, is that it wasn't a fabrication, a hoax, or an exaggeration as everyone assumed. The story was true. For those unfamiliar, it went like this.

A group of American backpackers were hiking in the Andes on a post-college graduation trip in 2058. They were a group of friends from California with wealthy parents, and in exchange for their permission (and funding) for the trip, one of the stipulations was that the group hire a guide for the duration, both to ensure the routes they hiked were safe from dangerous weather conditions or alpine hazards and from kidnappers, the cartels, or otherwise unsavory types who could get a group of reveling young Americans into undue trouble in short order. The guide they hired was an Argentine outdoorsman about ten years their senior named Jorge Domani-Acuña, whom they referred to as JDA in their pre-trip correspondence, and they continued to call him JDA in person when they arrived in Chile.

On the second week of their trip, the group took an afternoon hike outside the small mountain town of Pisco Elqui. It was an overcast day. The hike was a mild, three-mile walk to an overlook above a spectacular river basin in the valley. About halfway to the overlook, JDA calmly turned to the Americans and told them to stand back from him because he was about to be struck by lightning.

The Americans didn't know how to react, because JDA hadn't shown any signs of being a practical joker, and of course, how could he know he was about to be struck by lightning, especially on an overcast day with no rain and no thunder? Then suddenly, the American graduates began to step back from JDA, as they themselves began to feel "an electricity in the air." Over the course of the next thirty seconds, JDA's hair began to spark and stand on end, before suddenly, the Argentine guide began to levitate. He hovered in the air about ten feet above the trail hyperventilating for nearly a minute before finally, the young man was struck with a bolt of lightning so fierce that it ruptured the eardrums of the two Americans standing closest to JDA.

When the Americans had recovered from the shock of the blast, they found JDA unconscious and pulseless on the trail. They tried for fifteen minutes to revive him to no avail, nor could they call for help, because the electricity in the air had fried all of their electronic devices, phones included.

When the authorities investigated, all four of the American hikers told the same congruent, uniform story, and the autopsy was consistent with a lightning strike and no other trauma. Even though the story was unbelievable, the most powerful corroborating evidence was the sudden simultaneous overload of so many electronic devices. Without video, the world was left with only the accounts of the hikers, and though it became a given that JDA died by lightning strike, the consensus was that the recent graduates were lying about everything else, most especially JDA's premonition and the levitation. They were ridiculed and denounced for making a spectacle out of the poor Argentine's death, presumably for attention. It was the simplest explanation.

I hadn't heard the story until about thirty years after it happened, when, by chance I bumped into one of the hikers at a hotel in D.C. She had changed her name after marriage and had built a respectable career as a lawyer in the political sphere. And she'd learned the hard way thirty years earlier to run from the story and never mention it again, but after hearing about it from a third party, I brought it up to her, assuring her that I truly wanted to hear her perspective. It took a tremendous amount of convincing to even get her to acknowledge the event had happened or that she had in fact been there, but I was surprised, when she finally did talk about it, that she stuck to the original story, said she would swear by it till the grave. I was so surprised, that I sought out the other three hikers, and all three behaved the same way when I met them—reluctance to talk and then confirmation of the story. They had every reason to recant at the time and didn't, and after thirty years, they still hadn't.

JDA had predicted the strike and levitated for nearly a minute. Even now, you probably don't believe it happened, and no matter how I tell you the story, you still won't believe it. Even when I tell you that this is what makes me different, more than intelligence, more than the incredibly vast resources and wealth I've compiled over my lifetime, more than the risks I am willing to take. This. People didn't believe the hikers then, and they still don't now. But why?

Most would probably say that they don't believe the story, because it's impossible, such a thing violates the laws of physics. But that's simply not true. Nothing can violate the laws of physics, definitionally. So that didn't happen. But in order to even say something like "that violates the laws of physics," you have to believe a few things that amount to gigantic intractable barriers to understanding JDA's story, the most prominent of which is that we "understand" the laws of physics. And we may have some understanding, yes. But when 99.999% of people hear this story and say, "What these people say happened couldn't have happened," I say, "If that happened, which is possible, however unlikely, then there is a gap in our understanding of the laws of physics," which is not only a plausible proposition, it is a certainty.

I went to Yanagisawa with a story of a gap in our understanding, and the lunatic changed everything forever.

This was in the third year of the Osaka project, and we were just starting to understand the data we'd been collecting from the Florida Space Ladder, and there was a strange anomaly none of the physicists could really explain. I didn't initially connect what was going on with our lift data and the story of the hikers, but both these things were bubbling up in my consciousness around this time. The data anomaly was something everyone at A & A ignored, because it wasn't costing us any money, but it bothered me not knowing. We kept meticulous records of the cargo, up and down, mass, weight, size, destinations, origins. And it turned out that over the course of each of the first three years of the space ladder's operation, we'd used less energy getting objects into orbit than we'd calculated was necessary. And it was consistent over all three years. We'd moved roughly the same amount of cargo, and though it was a tiny discrepancy no one would have noticed per lift, over the course of a year, it became quite a discrepancy—one of the physicists calculated it was about the weight of two standard sized bank vaults, a rather interesting unit of measure. It was a drop in the bucket when placed in relief with the total weight of yearly cargo, but I couldn't get over it. Bank safes don't just leap into orbit. So how did that happen if the laws of physics hadn't been violated?

I didn't hear about Susumu Yanagisawa until we started working in Japan. All the Japanese physicists knew of him and joked about him. He was a kind of living folk tale among the deeply academic—the fable of the student who studied too much turning into a crazy, reclusive troll who lived under a bridge. Don't stare at the sun. Don't share your data with strangers. Don't study for too long or you'll end up like Yanagisawa. I had to track this guy down.

It turned out he was in Osaka, just across the city. He wasn't living under a bridge after all. He'd just given up on physics. He'd taken a modest job as a high school math teacher and played chess in the local park on weekends on a board he drew out in chalk on the concrete. Often, when there was no opponent, he'd play both sides of the board. Hell, I thought, I was no grandmaster, but why not go see about a game?

He destroyed me. Embarrassingly so. Multiple times. Ten, fourteen, and twenty-one move mates. I couldn't decide whether it was more important to level-up my chess or my Japanese at that point, because as much as the Japanese engineers on the project had laughed when I told them I'd played chess with Yanagisawa in the park, I didn't need to talk to the guy to know there was a crazy serious mind there. I could see it in his eyes.

I opted for chess.

Yanagisawa didn't know who I was. He might have been the only person in Osaka who didn't, but it was clear that to him, I was just the crazy *gaijin* from the previous Saturday who'd come back for more punishment. And I kept coming.

After a month or so of constant reading, playing bots, and thinking about strategy, I was beginning to understand the game a little. I can't put it another way than to say I started to get a feel for the board. Strategies became sensations and intuitions. Little by little each weekend, the mates that had once come in double-digit moves turned into drawn out battles.

The fifth week I was there, I was playing him to a stalemate for a good half hour, which I'm sure he eventually would have figured a way through. But during a long pause in play while he was considering his next move, I uncrossed my legs, got up, picked up the chalk, and on the sidewalk I wrote out a calculation for the energy gained per lift on the Florida Space Ladder. The equation was just descriptive, and nobody outside of our development team in Clearwater could have known a thing about the context for that calculation, but I knew a physicist of his caliber would see something interesting there.

He got angry.

"*Nani sore*," he grumbled, and he started to make the stereotypical Japanese noises of exasperation that I always found slightly amusing.

After a few minutes splitting his attention between the board and the equation, he began to sweat. Then he tipped over his king and walked out of the park. It wasn't the result I'd been hoping for.

The following weekend, I went to the park hoping he'd be back, but he wasn't. But all over the sidewalk, there were smudges of chalked out equations that people had trodden into incoherence, and I knew the seed I'd planted was growing and gnawing at him.

I didn't see him at all over the following year when I was splitting time between Clearwater and Osaka, and I thought I'd never hear anything about it again.

I couldn't figure out the mystery. The physics was beyond me, even though I knew enough to know there was something mysterious going on between electricity, magnetism, gravity, and even time.

Then in the fourth year of the Osaka project, Yanagisawa published the hyperspace paper online. It dropped like a bomb in the physics community. And to be in Japan when it happened was interesting. My Japanese was still not great, but I could tell all our engineers were talking about it—in comes the child prodigy turned hermit and drops out of thin air like a wizard, destroying everyone's conceptions of almost everything, and as it played out, characterizing the problem as "almost everything" wasn't hyperbolic, wasn't exaggeration, if anything it sold his theory short.

Yanagisawa's treatise rambled from black holes to magnetism to the center of suns to fusion reactors and artificial gravity. I had to read the thing five times to be confident I understood the outline. Then, on a hunch, I went down to the park and drew a chessboard on the sidewalk. The following Saturday, he was there with a chess set ready to go. He'd been waiting.

"Jurian Hartasaku," he said when he saw me approach, and then he gestured for me to sit.

His English was bad, but my Japanese was good enough to speak with him a little. I think he was trying to figure out what my endgame was, and not on the chessboard, mind you; I had no endgame against a master of Yanagisawa's caliber and never would. We played two fairly competitive games that he won before I picked up the chalk. I'd been thinking about the magnetics in particle colliders for decades by that point, and he knew immediately what I meant when I'd finished.

He asked for the chalk, and when I handed it to him, he stroked his chin for a minute and wrote the following on the sidewalk:

X > 27km

Meaning the accelerator had to be at least twenty-seven kilometers to finally answer that question posed by our space elevator and by the unfortunate demise of the young Argentine mountain guide.

Then Yanagisawa pointed to the sky, and I think he meant that the only place to practically construct a particle accelerator that big would be space. I took the chalk and wrote:

$ = ?

Then I took my opportunity to knock over my king and walk off theatrically to talk to some actuaries at A & A who could turn that question mark into a number.

It's important to note, at this point, with the clarity of history, all this was so speculative that even to Yanagisawa and me, it amounted to a curiosity. It just happened that the curiosity was a billion times more significant than Columbus wondering about whether the Earth was round. We weren't thinking on those terms. We were just looking at shadows and thinking that they weren't standing exactly where they were supposed to be, and it was interesting. And getting an answer to that curiosity? The actuaries at A & A told me the floor was a trillion dollars.

Well, there went that bright idea.

At that point, A & A was still going to be paying for Clearwater for about six more years before making our first dollar, and even with the Japanese government going all-in on the massive Osaka Space Lift, A & A wouldn't gross a trillion dollars total for another five years if everything on the ground and in space went perfectly. A trillion dollars for a particle accelerator, and the ring drive wasn't even an idea at that point—this was just to answer an odd point in theoretical physics. A trillion dollars.

But...

Now I had a gnawing feeling in the same way Yanagisawa did when I drew that first equation on the sidewalk. There was something about that missing energy, the story of JDA and the levitation, and intuition told me to do something about it.

I couldn't throw a trillion dollars at the project, but I could throw a little money at a team of theoretical physicists to sit in a room and toss the idea around for a few years. And I could loan them some engineers on occasion. I had more than a few of these secret projects that very few people knew anything about. What was one more? I could even drop in from time to time to participate in the discussion.

I offered Yanagisawa himself a seat at the table. He turned me down.

By this point I had been blustering behind the scenes for about five years about Apogee and the Florida Space Ladder being a gateway to the heavens, but realistically, I'd never truly thought I'd live to see humans in other solar systems, not unless aliens stopped by and picked us up on their way home. There were beautiful images of exoplanets coming in from NASA and the Europeans. The new data coming out of L2 was enticing, sure, but I found it difficult to believe we'd ever do anything other than see clearer and clearer images of an unreachable place, much like the early opticians of the renaissance trying to get a better look at the moon. At best we could migrate out into our solar system and build a few mega-cylinders orbiting the moons of the gas giants. That was all.

Then came the images of Geddes.

She was like a mirror image of Earth. Her spectroscopy had intrigued the Indians enough to point *Surya Kaanch* at her for over two months. Sure, they were composites of data and CGI, but it was the image. The oceans, the puffy white clouds, the green!

Humans had to go to Geddes, trillion dollars be damned. Enter Florence Tolland.

There are several extant accounts of the Osaka meeting that brought Flor into the fray. It is probably true that this was a turning point in history, and the story gets told as though I turned it. For whatever reason, I've been given credit, I think, perhaps because the narrative is simpler that way, or perhaps the various narrators have told the story that way to somehow curry future favor with me or my organization by portraying me as an effective leader. Here's what really happened.

A & A's board in the first fifteen years was a country club. Its members were lawyers and business leaders with weight on their resumes and a desire to sign off on as sure a deal as could be found on Earth. A & A was that. We had a clear, executable plan, and we hit every benchmark, largely because our goals were attainable and our logisticians the best we could recruit from everywhere in the world, and they all wanted to come, because it was the biggest, most important project ever. Hands down. The board just had to sit back and watch a winning idea happen and wait for the money to roll in. As sure a bet as you can have in business.

Flor was placed on the board at the recommendation of my Ohio legal team, and quite frankly, I'd never liked her all that much. She hardly talked to me, and most of the time had a sour look on her face every time I opened my mouth, and at the Osaka meeting, she looked openly hostile and didn't say a word. I thought the presentation had gone well enough, in that I hadn't gotten nearly the level of pushback I'd been anticipating setting a rather aggressive and exciting new direction. Flor pulled me aside afterward, handed me a card with an address, date, and time on it, and said, "If you're a minute late for that meeting, Julian, I'll murder you."

Well, okay then, I thought. Say two words to me in a decade, scowl at me, and threaten to murder me? Doesn't get much better than that.

The address on the card was for a Korean barbecue restaurant, so at the very least, I was getting a decent meal out of it, or so I thought.

When I arrived, I was seated in a private room and kept waiting for about a half hour drinking tea before Flor finally showed up. And when she showed up, I immediately understood why she'd taken the meeting outside A & A's Japanese offices. That level of dissent couldn't be seen in that building. She hadn't even sat before she started tearing into me. It went largely like this, and believe me, I remember this almost verbatim, because I don't think I'd been spoken to like that ever—certainly not since I'd become the world's richest space tycoon.

"If you ever," she began, "and I mean *ever* go into another board meeting without clearing your agenda with me again, I will destroy you. The only reason you get to be this hot young international business magnate is because the people in that board room let you wear the hat, and thus far, you've been content to sit in the chair like a good boy and just wear the hat. You are a scientist, and a brilliant one, sure, but you're not a businessman and you're not qualified to run a corporation the size of A & A if you can walk into a board meeting like today's without a clue as to what was going on in that room. You probably thought that went well, didn't you?"

"Certainly not the travesty you're making it out to be, Florence," I told her. "I thought I would get a bit more pushback, honestly."

"That's because they're keeping their intentions hidden and their powder dry."

"And you?" I asked her.

"Oh, you'll know when I come for you, mister. All those friendly faces in that board room kissing your ass for the last ten years? Sharks, absolute cutthroat bastards. Mark my words, Julian, after today, the only question on their minds now is *when* they're going to cut your throat. You just told them your intention is to transition the safest trillion-dollar

142

bet anyone has ever made into a multi-trillion-dollar long shot that you'd have to be insane to think is a good idea.

"Right now, I'm the only friend you've got in that room."

I had never been that wrong about anything so consequential, and to be fair, time proved that I wasn't wrong about the substance of it. How I handled the matter was the problem. And it took me a while to believe it. I actually went back to my lawyer in Ohio who'd recommended Flor in the first place. I was contemplating firing her.

"Have you lost your mind, Julian?"

I explained the situation and how she'd spoken to me and how she'd never said a useful thing to me in over a decade.

"She just said the most useful thing she could possibly say to you right when you needed it. We put her on the board to keep you from going off the rails. Let her do her damn job or you'll find yourself cut out of your own company faster than even you'll know what happened."

The data points were starting to add up.

I asked Flor for another lunch meeting, and I explained where I was coming from—the legitimate potential for interstellar travel, scientific exploration, mining—who knows—even colonization someday. She'd already understood all that. What I didn't understand was that the board was playing a different game than the one I was. I wanted to spearhead those benchmarks of human progress and they wanted three things: money, power, and more money. And, their game was in maneuvering to get those three things. I only existed in their world insofar as I could provide those things, and I damn well wasn't going to do it by taking a company that had been the smoothest of sailing for a decade and setting a course downwind toward rocks, reefs, and raging weather; I found metaphorical over-simplifications to be a feature of Flor's communication style. When she finally did speak, she made sure she was understood, metaphorically if not literally.

I asked her if she played chess.

"What, outside the board room?"

I laughed. She didn't.

"That's your biggest problem, Julian. You don't even know what game you're playing. And yes, I play chess."

So I took her to meet Yanagisawa. She turned out to be a demon. We showed up about an hour before the Japanese master did, and she easily bested me in three games before I got a decent enough foothold to even offer a challenge in the fourth. Yanagisawa showed up toward the end to observe. Then she offered to play him. Her Japanese, which she'd learned in the five years since A & A's Osaka Project was announced, was nearly as expert as her chess. And, as luck had it, Yanagisawa was a bit smitten. I couldn't blame him. She was a better player and better looking than I was. They played a match that lasted nearly two hours before Yanagisawa finally got the edge.

When we got up to leave, I left him an equation on the sidewalk.

"Have you tried to get him on the payroll?" she asked me.

"Yeah, but he's a firm no. If he does anything, though, he'll just publish it. We'll see it when everyone else does."

The next paper came about six months later: "Black Holes, Hyperdensity, and the Physics of Sub-Space." That was the one that changed the game.

In the board room, with Flor's coaching, I managed to pull the hat back down over my head and go sit in the corner. All that crazy talk of trillion-dollar space supercolliders was just a bit of "scientific over-exuberance"—she literally made me say those words. It wasn't though. We just couldn't say the quiet part out loud until I had a realistic course to put in front of them that made the bet palatable to the other board members.

Flor also helped me to realize that being chair of A & A's board was a bit like being a king on the chess board. Only make a move when necessary, never arbitrarily, and never more than one space at a time. Let the queen make the real moves, smile like the rest of them, and just wear the hat.

When I look back on that Osaka meeting, with the knowledge I've learned since, it's so embarrassing it's sickening. But I talk about it in gut-churning honesty because in so many of the stories of history-making in geopolitics or business or science, we don't talk about the times the figures we lionize happenstance their way out of becoming absolute donkeys by way of sheer luck or the sound advice of others.

Better to own being a donkey for a day than to deny it and become one on a permanent basis.

After Yanagisawa's black hole paper, Flor and I spent every Saturday in the park playing chess with the master. I finally got him to open up about the physics while we were playing, speculating about theoretical ways to generate hyperdense materials and what we could do with them if we could ever stabilize them reliably. The energy requirement to do so would be outrageous, but I re-envisioned the supercollider project to start following the Osaka Space Lift's inauguration. That move alone cut the prospective price nearly in half. A little bit of patience got us nearly halfway there. We also started a foundation to fund projects in academia that made use of the Earth-based colliders that could start piecing smaller elements of the puzzle together. That served the dual purpose of getting some of the science off the ground and figuring out which minds in the field were worth a damn. When the time came, we'd have a list of what we needed done and by whom.

In the background, Flor was slowly and methodically chopping off the heads of the backstabbers who were truly coming for me, all the while building alliances with the board members willing to let the bet ride. I wore the hat; she was the player. That's the reality of everything that happened at A & A after year fourteen. But just as at the outset, I saw something that others didn't. I had an intuition about the physics Yanagisawa was revealing. I knew we could build something with it, and as luck had it, when the solution came to us, it happened to be magnetics. It was going to take a decade, but I knew I'd see it in my lifetime, far sooner than anyone would have predicted. Unfortunately, we don't always know how long we have, for a lifetime may be guaranteed but its length is another matter.

When Yanagisawa disappeared, I didn't think too much of it, because it was like him. He'd done it several times before. He'd get so deep into an idea that he'd disappear for six months and reappear several weeks after the paper was published online. So I waited and kept an eye on his portal. I started to worry around the five-month mark. No paper. No chess. No word from Yanagisawa himself. Flor contacted his school and found out that he'd died following a protracted seizure that was one of the many medical issues he'd never spoken about with us. We found out from his journals that the main reason he didn't take my offer to do physics at A & A was the stress. He put so much pressure on himself when it came to theoretical ideas that it was detrimental to his health. That was what everyone had missed about him, what he'd never told anyone. Apparently, though, he really enjoyed being around the kids, found it relaxing somehow. There was no pressure in it.

Flor and I had to go to his school to finally track his family down. No one at his school had any idea who he really was. He'd never told anyone about me, so they were dumbfounded when I came looking for him.

"Yanagisawa Susumu San?" the principal said. "Heh? Jurian Hartasaku? *Honto ni?*"

He couldn't believe it when I told him the caliber of physicist his tenth-grade math teacher had been. I put it to him like this.

"I'll give you a complete list of the physicists I think were probably more important than Susumu Yanagisawa," I said, "Albert Einstein and Sir Isaac Newton. End of list."

"What did he do that was so important?" the principal asked.

"You'll find out in about ten years," I told him.

He gave us Yanagisawa's mother's address. She lived, in all places, in a small city in Shizuoka Prefecture called Hamamatsu. You couldn't make this stuff up, really.

It took Flor and I a couple hours to get up there by shinkansen, the old line. It was an idyllic ride up the countryside—mountainous, lush green landscape, and when we got up to Shizuoka, terraces upon terraces of sculpted tea crops in linear hedges lining hillsides for as far as the eye could see. A remarkably beautiful place.

The city itself, though, was much like any other Japanese city. Clean streets, concrete buildings, busy intersections.

His mother was a sweet older woman who had no idea who we were, even after I told her our names and our business. He hadn't even told her he'd been working again, and when I told her everything we'd been working on, I detected a poorly repressed sense of resentment, sort of like I might have been the bad influence that had led Susumu astray after he'd finally kicked his bad physics habit. And maybe that was true. The thought had certainly occurred to me now that he was gone. I'd never really considered how unwelcome it may have been for me to waltz into his life and casually drop an equation in his lap, never pausing to ponder why he'd taken a job as a high school math teacher in the first place. I kept trying to impress upon his mother the gravity of his work without telling her exactly what he'd done, but it was clear that between my being vague and Flor's translating, it just wasn't getting through.

"What was so important? All these equations he would do?" his mother said.

Finally, Flor and I agreed that we owed her the truth.

"Your son provided the theoretical basis for interstellar space travel. If people ever end up on planets around other stars, it will be because Susumu Yanagisawa provided the foundation."

"Eh," she said, and shrugged. "We cannot even manage one planet."

I asked her if I could have his journals.

"What would you want with Susumu's journals?" she asked.

"To read them, study them, put them in a museum in the future."

"If you publish anything," she insisted, "publish it for free and for everyone. I know he believed it should all be this way."

"We wouldn't have it any other way," Flor told her.

Long before Susumu Yanagisawa became a household name worldwide, about eight years before the ring drive's maiden voyage, I commissioned a statue of him in front of the main entrance to A & A's Japanese headquarters. It was him, in bronze, seated cross-legged on the sidewalk, his face fixed on a chess board, opponentless and deep in concentration. I insisted that Flor position the board. I went back and forth for weeks considering whether we should inscribe one of his equations beside the board to signify who and what Yanagisawa was. Ultimately, knowing the stress the physics had caused him, I thought it better to leave him in peace, just the great thinker, his chess board, and the only opponent worthy of Susumu Yanagisawa's uniquely creative mind.

I came back to the statue to pay my respects whenever something happened that mattered: when we first fired the collider; when we began to fabricate hyperdense materials; when we completed the first ring; when the *Ake* flew from lunar orbit to Jupiter in six minutes. It was a ritual of sorts, even if we were in Clearwater at the time. We'd take a shuttle from Apogee to *Uchukaigan* and then take the lift down to A & A headquarters in Osaka. Flor and I would sit across from him and usually we'd talk about how little we knew of him, and usually that would get me talking about how little we actually knew about anything.

Now at the dawn of hyperspace travel, the main barrier to taking the drive interstellar had been the question of the hazard to a human crew. It would be years still before the effects of sub-space exposure to biological matter—or any matter—were well understood. All the ships would be piloted by AI, which meant they'd have to make all the decisions about the exploration of a system. Even then, after fourteen decades of electronic computation it was still a challenge to teach AI what to value and prioritize in exploring a solar system. So we sent out the *Ake* and subsequent ships to the edge of our own solar system, again and again, each time wiping their memory clean, and using our solar system as a model, developing algorithms for locating planetary bodies based on size, composition, moons, likelihood of metals, hydrocarbons, liquid water, and other ingredients for life. We'd restart the AIs at different distances, different approach vectors. At times, they got confused and couldn't find Earth for weeks, especially if we instructed them to ignore EM signals. But after a few months training, they'd figured it out. Then it was off to see the neighborhood.

By the time we were ready for extra-stellar missions, we had five ships ready to go. We didn't expect to see anything new. What we expected to see, though, was a new type of staggering resolution of our closest star systems: Alpha Centauri, Procyon, 61 Cygni, Epsilon Indi, and Tau Ceti. When they all came back within weeks, we made the decision at A & A to publish all the data, including images and video, open source for all of humanity to explore and discover. It was enough data to keep every astrophysicist on Earth busy for their lifetimes and then some, and its public release was a fitting tribute to Yanagisawa San.

Both Flor and I were on Apogee a year later when *Ake* returned from Geddes. The first of our automated fleet of ring ships had spent the bulk of its two-month exploration time surveying the second planet of the Geddes system. Geddes II was an interstellar oasis whose surface was half covered in liquid water, was ninety-eight percent the mass of Earth, held an atmosphere that wasn't just breathable but nearly identical to our own, and hosted an abundance of plant life. She was breathtaking. Beautiful. As green as the Garden of Eden. It was a staggering and emotional day—the culmination of a thousand years of science and ingenuity and seeking and new ideas. It was a surreal honor to bear witness to it with hundreds of other scientists and engineers who had made it happen. I spent the entire day suppressing the powerful urge to shed tears of joy for everything humanity had accomplished.

After all that, Flor and I ended up at Susumu's statue again. For us Floridians it was nearly midnight, but when we arrived in Osaka the sun was high overhead, early afternoon. I kept glancing over at his statue as it reflected the sunlight so brightly I eventually had to put up my hand to shield my eyes. I so wished Yanagisawa could have been with us that day. It was clear and hot, too hot to be out in the open sun. But Flor went out there from under the shade, crossed her legs, and sat across from him on the scalding pavement, and the sight of those two—Florence the warrior and Susumu the mind—staring each other down again in friendly competition from across a chess board, it was too much to take in. I couldn't keep my emotions in check anymore, doubling over in tears right in front of my own building. I hadn't wept like that since my mother left. It was the weight of it all, the pain and unknowing howl of a child being born. Our eyes were opening. A miracle of a story every bit as unbelievable as levitation. Out there was a second Earth. We had pictures. Soon everyone would see it and believe in Geddes as though it had never not been a fact as certain as gravity. One day, we would go.

The future began with a story.

With an OP in the 97th percentile, even when I couldn't see how it ended, regardless of the struggles along the way, I always believed that our story would end well.

Dark Station

By the time Lee Hriniak arrived back at Apogee from the L2 Outstation, she was feeling the dread of cycling down again. She hadn't spoken to anyone about the heavy anxiety she had on returning to Earth, as it wasn't a smart way forward on her career track to admit such a strong psychological barrier directly related to her chosen profession. To jeopardize what little hope she had of digging out of the deep hole she and her family were in by admitting weakness wasn't a winning play. So few people ever had a chance to win at all that to let her phobia become an issue seemed to Lee like she'd be tapping out before the weight was even on her.

She'd been out at L2 for nearly three months, which put her weightless time almost two weeks over limit for the year, and if her bone density check came up short, she'd be on-world for the foreseeable future, which meant back to cranes and cargo planes for at least the next six months, which meant treading water on bills, as long as interest rates didn't rise.

It wasn't that Lee hated gravity, as much as she didn't like the feeling of weight on top of her, literally or metaphorically. And if she could open up and speak to a psychologist about it, she knew exactly where she'd begin, because whenever Lee came back to Apogee, every time she got on the elevator down to Clearwater the same incident popped into her mind.

Combat training.

Sheila Dunfee had outweighed Lee by forty pounds, and in Lee's mind, they never should have been paired together, but you can't opt out of combat training if you want to stay in the military. Sheila had body slammed Lee hard enough to knock the wind out of her lungs, and at that point, Sheila Dunfee could have done anything to Lee—a blood choke, an armbar—anything. Sheila had Lee clinched around the shoulder and neck, and she arched up with her body weight pressing down on Lee's chest. Lee was too weak to even move her arms to tap out. She was limp and breathless with nearly two hundred pounds of Sheila Dunfee keeping her lungs from inflating, and Dunfee kept driving Lee's body across the mat so that even though Lee had gone limp, it seemed like she was still resisting. It went on for nearly a minute before the sergeant called time. That weight on her, the heavy sensation, the breathlessness, it kept coming. Gravity. Debt. Cycling back to Earth. It usually took Lee a drink or two at Star Gallery to work up the nerve to get on the elevator and go down. If it hadn't been for the Space Force's strict regulations on time in low-G, Lee would've been tempted to stay off world indefinitely, even if intellectually she knew it would eat her bones outside in and her kidneys inside out.

The Star Gallery was oddly empty for the time—mid-afternoon Eastern Standard. There would usually be officers or commercial pilots or private captains in the lounge, but it was almost empty, so Lee took up a coveted spot at the outward glass wall with a perfect view of the rounding sapphire globe curving into the pitch-black backdrop of space. There was a small team of walkers clipped into a table behind her, but other than that and the waiter and the bartender, no one. The weather was clear below, so the Gulf Coast beneath her looked a pristine, bejeweled blue all the way to the Texas Coast. A good scene for the cold margarita Lee was nursing. Her first drink in three months, since deploying to the L2 Outstation.

Lee was scrolling through the JABR app on her glasses, which had quite a few more options here on Apogee than she could view out at the L2. There were the usual commercial crane shifts in the dockyards, and all the commercial cargo flights were off-limits for at least two weeks while she acclimated, which meant that at best she might be able to inch ahead in the four weeks before redeploying if her bone density scans came out okay.

Then, more out of curiosity than intent, she cleared out the zero-G filter to see what she'd be missing out on. And there it was, the jackpot.

Lee's first impulse was to look deeper into the specifics to see why the cap was so high on the contract. Mercury was part of the answer, sure, and, the diverse array of necessary skills was pretty specialized. But she wasn't the only space jockey who checked all those boxes, and two million for a twenty-day turnaround was insanely high. There had to be a complication. Did that matter though? Two million was enough to erase her dad's medical debt and get her brother Damon back on level ground. And if the Space Force grounded her on the zero-G violation? It wouldn't matter if she could pull three years' salary in three weeks. It wasn't just tempting, it was stupid not to look into it.

"Who's it through?" Lee asked the assistant.

"J. Heller through Fallon Galaxie."

"Who are they, Frenchies?"

"Industrial metallurgy and mining, ground-based in Antigua."

"Antigua? Tax haven?"

The app bonked in her ear, as though she'd gotten the wrong answer on a quiz show.

"Okay then, who are the principals?"

The app ran down a list of finance firms and board members, and it was a pretty diverse group of multinational individuals and financial backers. What it looked like to Lee after a little investigation was that they'd poached a division of Hatton Solaris as a way to get a foothold in the mining game without staking the capital out front to build from scratch, a bit like a budget airline buying older planes from the big boys and trying to squeeze as many operating years out of them as they could. It didn't explain the two million cap, but the job seemed legit.

"Put a line in for me," Lee told the app. "I'll talk to them from Clearwater if they're interested."

Lee finished up the margarita and began to think about getting on the next lift down. She felt better about heading down planetside with a drink in her system and a major score to daydream about on the ride down.

By the time Lee got back on base outside Clearwater it was early evening. Her mother had cooked, and Damon was in. He looked heavier but decent, all things considered. He'd shattered his tibial plateau so severely on a jump that the Army doctors had nearly opted to amputate his leg. It led to a knee replacement that had gone terribly wrong. Between his back and knee, he'd been at Walter Reed for nearly four months, and if that wasn't tough enough luck, the drone fleet pilot qualification Lee had taken out a loan to put Damon through had become all but obsolete when the Squadfire AI took over all but the most specialized commercial opportunities.

These days, just seeing Damon off the sofa was a welcome sight, even if he didn't quite know what to do with himself.

"You look frail, Lee," Damon said about halfway through dinner.

"First day's tough, D," she said.

"I mean in general. Not that we need to see any more of you around here, but you should take some more ground shifts."

Lee smiled. "You'd get sick of me in a week."

Lee was so tired she was nodding in and out for much of the meal. As much as she hated the transition back to gravity, it was always worth it to see her family.

By the time she'd finished eating, Lee didn't have much strength to move. She needed help from Damon to get up the stairs to her bed.

"You've lost twenty pounds," he said, all but carrying her up the stairwell.

"You're just getting stronger," Lee said.

"Both can be true," Damon said. "Earthside."

That word was the last thing she remembered on her first night back. That, and the subtle heat of the headaches setting in.

Jean-D'Arte Heller called at 7:30 the following morning. Lee's head was pounding, and her bones were aching. She put on her buzzing glasses and hit the audio switch.

"Who is this?" Lee said, and as she said it, she could hear that her voice sounded like hell.

"J.D. Heller with Fallon Galaxie."

"Oh," Lee said. "The Mercury thing."

"I beg your pardon but I cannot pronounce your name."

"It's Hriniak," Lee said. "But call me Lee. I'm off duty."

"Okay, Lee. I'm Jean, and we were very interested in your CV. You seem to have all the qualifications, which is somewhat rare."

"Two million dollars rare? Not that I'm arguing, but it's more than I usually get paid on a single contract."

"It is a complicated job, and we've had some trouble filling it."

"At that cap? I'm sure you could have your pick or hire a team for that matter."

"We did, and that was the problem—getting a team to coordinate, and then when they failed, we decided to look for one person who could do everything."

Lee was beginning to wake up. She sat up in bed.

"I don't even know what it is," Lee said. "I know it's Mercury, which is tight on time, but doable if we get things in motion."

"I'd need you to sign an NDA before getting into the details."

"That's not exactly standard," Lee said.

"Nor is the cap, nor the work," Jean said. "But you can evaluate that for yourself, when you get the details."

"I'll take a look at it as soon as I have a cup of coffee. It's my first day down."

"We'd like to get you out again as soon as tonight if that's possible."

"Really? No interviews or anything?"

"We looked into your commercial record yesterday, Lee. My superiors only had one concern, or I guess it's a logistical question."

"Shoot."

"You were three months on L2, so I presume it's better the Air Force doesn't find out about an unsanctioned contract like this?"

"That's correct."

"So, logistically, we want to be clearing through Osaka then?"

Lee sighed. "I don't exactly want to sit on a plane for fourteen hours, but yeah."

"Okay. We understand each other," Jean said. "I will forward the paperwork."

"I have a med check this afternoon," Lee said. "I can move it up if it's a problem."

"My job is to make the problems go away, Lee. I'll check in with you later today. Once we get your commitment, then we'll talk about all that."

"Really," Lee said. "I mean, great. I'll get back to you shortly."

Lee switched off her glasses and rolled out of bed. She'd have to put on a brave face for the docs at the base, but again, the prospect of a job that could make five years' worth of financial problems evaporate? That was worth rolling out of bed and suffering a headache for.

It was almost like there wasn't a decision in it at all, at least one that Lee seemed to make consciously. Her checkup didn't go well. In addition to being underweight and weak, she had an untimely nosebleed that the doctor made a big deal of and demanded to see Lee again in four weeks. She wasn't grounded yet, but Lee could feel it coming.

Jean booked her out of Miami that evening on a hypersonic to Osaka. Lee mixed a painkiller and a couple glasses of prosecco before takeoff, slept the whole way to Japan, and when she regained her senses again, she was already halfway up the Space Lift. Had she even looked at the file? She couldn't remember for sure but probably, yes. She figured she could get deep enough into the details on the way. There was a last call on forty minutes to *Uchukaigan*, and Lee called for some warm *sake* to hopefully calm her nerves. She realized it wasn't just the drawdown and the stress catching up with her, she was still on L2 time, which was Greenwich, and she'd been trying to transition to Florida time, and now she was in Osaka, heading to the Moon, then to Mercury. *Sake* couldn't possibly confuse the issue any further, especially with four more dry weeks awaiting.

Lee slept for the first sixteen hours of the transit. Then, after two cups of coffee she felt good enough to dive into the Fallon files. Near as she could tell, Fallon's crawlers—really their entire mining operation—had been reliant on Hatton Solaris's and A & A's arrays to supply them with power. That arrangement had been sufficient to keep Fallon operating, but it had always come at a premium cost and was a limiting factor on the size of their fleet. So Fallon's first major investment in capital on Mercury was on their own array so they'd no longer have to pay for power or rely on others for it. Four months into operating, though, Fallon's Amity Array had gone down. Now they were not only reliant on Hatton Solaris again, but Solaris was no longer contractually obligated to service Fallon under the original agreement, so Fallon was getting bled dry on energy costs by their competitors. They'd save the two million they were paying Lee in a week if she could get their array up again.

According to the files, the original shielding on the array's control unit had a manufacturing flaw, which caused its hardware to gradually fail—processors, transceivers, memory. Mama needed a whole new brain.

Lee could see why the job had been such a challenge to coordinate. The array was in a stable orbit for the time being, but it basically sat in a stream of solar wind at the outer edge of the sun's corona—more or less. The more Lee read about the problem, the more she likened it to trying to change clothes in a downpour while staying dry.

After looking at the problem for a couple days en route, Lee was confident she could fix it. She kept her nose in the files, kept to herself and her quarters, read, studied the systems, and developed five distinct operations, ranging from lower likelihood of success and lower risk, to higher likelihood of success and higher risk. She only had a six-day window aboard Mercury Horizon once she got there, so Lee was going to make every last minute of the transit count.

By the time the *Striker* arrived at the common station at Mercera, Lee was feeling downright sanguine about life. Apart from the minor nagging feeling that she might get caught off-world and grounded, she was hopeful. One of her five fixes would work, and in the meantime, there was nothing she enjoyed more than floating in space, working on a challenging problem, and operating specialized gear in ways no one else could. As a kid, she'd raced drones as a hobby, and this work was like an extension of that with the difficulty level hyped-up by a factor of ten and a coolness factor of fifty.

The airlock disembarking at Mercera was cramped, but out this far everyone knew how to handle themselves in zero-G, so there wasn't nearly the long wait in the bunch-up that there usually was at Luna, Apogee, or *Uchukaigan*. The second her head protruded into the causeway proper, a man with an eastern European accent began talking to her.

"You're military, yes? Here for Fallon, yes?"

"Yes," Lee said. "You're with them?"

"Let me show you down to short shuttle. I am Dodek. I tell you some things."

"I'm Lee," she said.

As anxious as she was to get started, Lee was grateful to have the guide, even on a station as small as Mercera.

"I have wait for you here, Lee."

"I appreciate it."

Dodek pulled his way down the hallway to an area that seemed to be away from the main causeway. Lee hadn't been to Mercury before, but she had a good enough sense of stations that she felt like Dodek was leading her the wrong way. He kept looking around and then finally back over his shoulder.

He began to talk softly. "The sound carries in the causeway, you see. If you sign same papers I sign before coming, you cannot talk much and I cannot talk much, Lee, no?"

"I think I'm understanding you."

"You must understand this. Two things. First is nothing here works as rated. Range is hundred thousand kilometers, you can count on ten thousand, no more. Solar wind is bitch out there. Screw all work. Second is that you have right," and he pulled Lee by the shoulder closer to him and looked her dead in the eyes and pointed to her chest; "you have obligation and right to return to your family. That is most important. I cannot say specific," he said now looking over his shoulder both ways, "but they do not respect that. Be safe. Be so safe, Lee. Go home to your family. Is first thing. Is only thing."

"Okay," she said. "I don't have any intention of doing otherwise."

"You are military," he said. "So you know safety. Is no different in private work. Do not let them say otherwise."

"I won't," she said.

"I wish you best of luck, Lee and safety. Safety. Short shuttle is this way. And you have never seen me, yes?"

"Seen who?" Lee said.

"Very good," Dodek said. "I never see you too."

Lee found the encounter more than a little unsettling. She'd never had an experience even approaching it. Something had rattled Dodek, but she hadn't talked to him for long enough to take a measure of him. All she knew was that he had seemed sincere.

Javier, the pilot for the short shuttle was much friendlier. He jokingly asked Lee if she wanted to fly, assuming she wasn't a pilot herself.

"You can take a nap if you like," she joked back, gesturing toward the controls. "I wouldn't mind taking us on a little detour to the array. Never hurts to have a closer look."

"Oh, mama. You want to cook us alive? I'd like to have kids someday, you know. Shielding's not so good on this bucket."

"No?"

"No, no, no. I'm going to take the controls."

Javier flew the hop out to the dark little deadstation the Fallon Galaxie files had referred to as Mercury Horizon. The tiny station amounted to a small cluster of pre-fab space pods with an airlock on either side and a bundle of antennae on both top and bottom, a modest worksite that reminded Lee of the replica of the old ISS at the Museum of Space Flight on Apogee.

Javier docked the short shuttle like he'd flown the route a thousand times.

"You get to know Pierce real fast," he said. "I'll be seeing you, but I got a few supply runs down to the surface from all what the *Striker* brung with it. Good luck with the work."

Lee thanked him and hopped into the airlock. Before long, she was aboard Mercury Horizon with no way off and a difficult task ahead.

Once inside, she tried to introduce herself to Pierce, who wore an indifferent gaze on his face and a Canadian patch on his jumpsuit. It was a first for Lee to meet a Canadian who was both impolite and seemingly completely devoid of a personality. When she said, "I'm Lee," he just said, "I've read your CV." And when she asked if there were quarters, he told her that Fallon didn't bring her to Mercury to sleep. She shrugged and got to work inspecting the gear.

There were twelve decent IE drones, and there was a diverse collection of transceivers and repeaters. The inventory looked pretty similar to what she'd seen in the files, so she told Pierce that she was going to test the gear, unless he had more accurate range data he wanted to report to her.

"Do you have reason to doubt the specs?" he asked.

She was tempted to say she'd bumped into Dodek at Mercera.

"Just my instincts," she said, "And the solar wind."

"The sooner you get that out of the way, the sooner you can get to work," he said.

So, within the first hour of arriving, Lee was testing the drones in teams of three with a repeater in trail position in case she lost the signals, and true almost exactly to Dodek's warning, the signals got wonky at about a tenth their rated range. It wasn't that they didn't respond, it was just that the interference corrupted the signal, delaying the controls.

Scenario One collapsed before Lee even had a chance to attempt it. Lee had drawn up the first attempt for how the repair should unfold in a perfect world. The drones would attach magnetically to the shield, and Lee would run the swarm downstream behind the shield, carrying the quarter arm and the new hardware. Then she would open the array and replace the hardware using the shielded quarter arm.

None of that turned out to be realistic. As the drones periodically lost signal, they fell out of sync, which meant Lee risked the shield getting ahead of the hardware and the quarter arm, frying both the new parts and the only tool she could use to install them. Lee spent her whole first day just mapping out where in the process equipment became unreliable or failed altogether.

Scenario Two involved an innovation Lee had picked up from a clever engineer on Allegis, who liked to have all his tools at hand. He used to use an assortment of conventional magnets and a loose sheet of hull plating to lay out everything. Lee figured she could do something similar to shield the two repeaters and generate a steadier signal, even in the heavy solar wind. That didn't fail so much in principle as in practice. The signals got through, but again, when she began to test the quarter arm, the signal was patchy. It would cut in and out, and replacing hardware required a smooth, delicate touch on the arm.

By the end of day two, Lee decided she'd need to skip Scenario Three altogether. And whenever Pierce came to get updates on her progress, she got the sense that he was just waiting for her to wind up at a place further down the road that he already knew and she had yet to discover. Like she was retreading the work of the previous teams and possibly

Dodek, and things would be so much easier if she were just told what the hell she was dealing with.

"I'm going to need the short shuttle," she told Pierce. "I can't run these instruments from here."

"It's not rated," he said.

"I'm not taking it all the way out there. I don't particularly have a death wish, but I would actually like to fix the array."

Pierce shrugged. "Can you fly it?"

"I can fly just about anything."

"Javier won't be back for another six hours. So be prepared for the moment he arrives. You're down to three days, Hriniak."

"I'm well aware," Lee said.

The ugliness of the scenario was beginning to set in for Lee. She could only see one real scenario that would end with a functioning array, and that involved moving the Amity Array into the penumbra behind Mercury, repairing it, and then repositioning it afterward. Given the delicate nature of the solar panels and the catchment structure, that would take weeks if not months and would cost millions in lost operating revenue and contracting flight specialists to execute a rescue at that scale.

Lee insisted to Pierce that she needed Javier to fly the short shuttle while she operated the quarter arm. She guessed that Pierce allowed it because it was an aggressive step forward.

Lee flew the hop out to the edge of the penumbra, stopping the shuttle just outside the leading edge of the solar wind.

"Ever been out there yourself?" she asked Javier, "to the array?"

"I shouldn't say."

"With Dodek? Or with the team before him?"

"You trying to get me fired?"

"I'm trying to fix the array. How far did Dodek get? He went out there with the shuttle, didn't he? You don't have to say anything," Lee said. "You can blink once for yes and twice for no."

Javier laughed. "What are we doing out here if it seems like you know?"

161

"I need to know a few more things about this situation," Lee said.

"I can't tell you anything. I've been told."

"I know, but you can speculate, like if I was to ask you, Javier, what do you think my odds are of getting the quarter arm to be functional from this distance?"

"I see, I see. You mean functional or useful?"

"I need it useful."

"Then I speculate you'd need to get closer. A lot closer."

"And what would you speculate my chances would be, say, situating the shuttle in front of the array?"

Javier shrugged.

"That good, huh?"

Lee examined Javier's eyes.

"Dodek was a capable operator?" Lee said. "As good or better than me?"

"I don't really know you, ma'am, and I don't know nobody named Dodek."

"Please, don't call me ma'am, Javier. It's Lee. And the only thing I can't figure out is why the secrecy. If Fallon is losing money every day, why waste two days letting me spin my wheels instead of telling me what the situation really is?"

"I really couldn't say, Lee," Javier said.

"You're really uncomfortable with this," Lee said. "I can tell you don't much like what's going on here. What the hell am I missing?" she said to herself more than Javier.

"He got it open, didn't he? That's the only thing I can figure. I'll bet that quarter arm couldn't get the old hardware out without torquing the array out of position."

"I can't say nothing. Didn't say nothing."

Lee sighed. "I know it's not you, but Jesus, this is some cold-blooded shit right here."

"I don't want nothing to do with this. I just fly supplies, fly people. That's all I wanna do."

"I understand," Lee said. "It's okay. We're going to stay out here for a while, make a show of it."

From then on, Lee went through the motions, executing the scenario she'd laid out for Pierce, getting to know Javier, and expecting the failure that ultimately came several hours later. She'd pieced it together, thought it all through. Poor Javier had been told to keep his mouth shut while Pierce had been running what amounted to a psy-op on Lee. There was one way to fix the array, and she could see it plain as day now—a spacewalk, out there in the solar wind, using the additional shielding as an umbrella. She could do it too, she thought. That's what Dodek had been talking about, and if he'd never waited around for her, she'd likely have come to the same conclusion in another day or so. Then, with the clock ticking and the pressure on, she would have considered it organically.

Everything made sense now. The absurdly high cap, the NDA, the secrecy. Fallon Galaxie couldn't advertise that job, but financially, this move versus the hundreds of millions they were losing by having a dead array lying derelict in the solar wind? So, what did they think she'd gamble her life on? Two million dollars. It was a good number. Some actuary somewhere had chosen it well. Two million was just small enough to be plausible and just large enough to gamble a life on, and Fallon had doubtless looked as much into Lee's family's debt profile as her CV and knew not only that Lee could do the walk, that she probably would do the walk. And if she died, they could say it was her crazy idea anyway. Fallon would report that Pierce advised her against such a risky proposition. Lee couldn't imagine a human being had thought up the scenario, but as much as she wanted to believe that some diabolical AI was at the bottom of it, there were enough humans down the line who'd set it in motion that absolution went barely as far as Javier by her reckoning.

When they got back to the station, Pierce wanted a report, the next step, Lee's plan of action. She told him she had to think.

She did think. Two million dollars was still two million dollars. Business was still business, even if it was an evil bastard of a corporation shelling out the money. Lee figured she owed it to herself to spend the rest of the day planning out the walk as meticulously as though she'd already opted to do it, and then she could weigh the pros and cons and sleep on it.

After several hours of consideration, Lee was convinced she could pull it off. In her mind, it was a go. But still, she told Pierce she'd update him after a few hours' sleep, and after sleeping on it, she'd changed her mind.

She couldn't get the thought of Damon, half-crippled and in constant pain, pulling her up the stairs to her bedroom. What would he do if it went wrong? He and mom would get thrown off base. There'd be no benefits paid out on a death that happened on some unsanctioned contract off-world against regulations. Then her thoughts spiraled downward. Ninety percent, Lee kept telling herself, but what about the ten? What happens then?

"I'm not doing it," she told Pierce. "I've figured this whole thing out, and I don't appreciate it."

He played dumb. "Figured out what?"

"You want me to do a spacewalk and fix it. I'm not doing it. It's too damn risky."

"You are contracted to fix the array, Sergeant Hriniak. No one said anything about a spacewalk, though, except you."

"Look. I told you, I know what you're up to, and I don't appreciate it. We're done here."

"We could be done. Fine. That's your decision. But Fallon Galaxie has incurred considerable expense bringing you out here, and you've failed to deliver on your end of the contract. If you fail to make a good-faith effort, we may be left with little choice but to try to recover those expenses. That's not to speak of the added cost in delays to a return to full operating capacity."

"Are you threatening to sue me?"

"That's not a decision for me to make," Pierce said. "But our legal division has been known to be aggressive in circumstances like this."

"You people are evil, my God!"

"Let's not be overly contentious about this. This is a business contract, and we expect you to fulfill it. Far be it from me to offer advice to an intelligent person such as yourself, but at this point there are simply two pathways forward for you, sergeant: the first, where you fulfill the contract and get paid in full for your services; the second, where you risk litigation, legal expenses, and tarnishing a promising military career in the process. I know what I would choose if I were in your position."

Lee took a deep breath. "You need to get me off this station right now, Pierce. Call Javier and get me out of here now."

Lee shut the hatch to the third pod, and she focused on controlling the building anger that was boiling inside her.

The shuttle ride over to Mercera was quiet. Javier kept shaking his head. He told her he was sorry.

"It's not you," Lee said. "I know it's not you. I wish you better than this, Javier. I really do."

On Mercera, Lee didn't have any idea what to do with herself. *Striker* wasn't due back till the following day. She paid for treadmill time, put on some music and walked as much as she could tolerate. She'd need to get as strong as possible for when she got back. She found a quiet corner at the far end of the causeway and did her best to remain inconspicuous through the night. She had the sense that everyone must know what a sucker she'd been to get dragged out here by those evil hucksters.

In the evening, Lee received a text from Aeris letting her know that her return ticket aboard *Striker* had been canceled. It was the first salvo meant to rattle her cage. She still had twenty-four hours to go down the other path. She could fix the array in six. Or, she could put another thirty thousand dollars on credit to get back to *Uchukaigan* and figure out how to get back to Florida on her own from there. A lump in her throat began to build and the thought of the cost of her ticket had her angry and terrified, stuck, hungry, powerless, and waiting. She spent a long, cold, sleepless night of doubt in the causeway aboard Mercera.

In the morning, she pulled together enough credit to get back home and spent the rest of the morning on the treadmill until *Striker* arrived.

Lee did her best on the way back to Earth to exercise as much as she could tolerate. She got in as much treadmill time as she was allowed and did band work and stretching. But all that, she knew, was a poor substitute for four weeks on the ground. Even if she got back in time, she knew she was going to fail her physical. That was out of her control, though. All Lee could do was put her head down and work.

As bad as everything had gone on Mercury, on the way back Lee did everything she could think to get her head right. She knew a reckoning was coming, and she'd prepared herself to take her lumps like an adult and own it. She still had skills, and she still had her life to live. Yes, she still had all that debt to deal with, but there's a way back from debt. There's no way back from dead. It had been too risky, and damn them for putting her in that position.

It was a long eleven days getting right with herself.

When the shuttle from Luna finally docked at *Uchukaigan*, Lee should have been expecting something. She was so focused on figuring out how to get home, though, and once again dreading cycling down to gravity, that Fallon Galaxie was the last thing on her mind. A young Japanese woman with a perfect American accent was waiting for her at the gate, saying simply, "Technical Sargent Lee Hriniak?"

And Lee said yes.

"You've been served."

And the filings came through to her glasses. It was a blow, yes, but Lee told herself that she'd known it was coming. Get home. Get home, Lee, she told herself. One thing at a time. She resolved not to even open the files until after she reported for duty, but the ride down got the better of her. She could feel the weight again. The debt, the gravity, the sense of loss for the terrible Mercury fiasco. Lee's anxiety overcame her resolve. She had to look.

She figured she was looking at about double her ticket price. She'd fight it, but that would cost legal fees too. When she opened the files, she couldn't believe her eyes. It wasn't just the thirty thousand one-way trip to Mercury or the hypersonic to Osaka and the trip up to *Uchukaigan*. Those costs were in there, of course, but they were the sugar on top. Fallon Galaxie was suing her for thirteen-point-five million dollars for "failing to provide contracted services, resulting in the delay of business operations," and "over-representing her ability to complete necessary contracted technical deep-space operations."

Thirteen million dollars.

Lee's first reaction was to laugh. It was a laughable amount of money for a military brat. That was tycoon money. Socialite money. Tech mogul money. Lee would have to live to two hundred to ever be able to pay that back, and she'd be damned if she paid Fallon Galaxie a dollar. She was angry, tired, and more than anything, she felt heavy. She needed a helping hand from the porter getting to her feet once the space lift had settled at ground level.

Lee walked out of the Grand Concourse at the OSL and was overcome by gravity. Lee felt her chest get heavy and her legs beginning to fail her. She happened to be just outside a private lounge, and she made a line for the nearest chair. She didn't care who the chairs belonged to. It felt again like she had a big bully on her chest pressing the life out of her, and there was no tapping out, no referee to save her, no drill sergeant to call time.

A moment after Lee sat, several people approached her and began to speak to her in Japanese. She didn't understand, but she knew what they were saying. She knew that wherever she was, she wasn't supposed to be sitting there. One woman asking nicely turned into three women pointing and telling her she had to get up. One of them even tried to take her by the wrist and pull her out of the big leather chair. Then two Japanese men in suitcoats came over.

"Just leave me alone," Lee said, and it was the sound of her own voice that set her off, the weakness of it. She sounded utterly defeated. She had this bizarre, rather meta moment of clarity in which she realized that this was truly the lowest point in her life, and she had the sense that it didn't really matter what they did to her, she couldn't possibly feel any worse even if the Japanese police dragged her out of that lounge kicking and screaming.

Lee Hriniak decided she wasn't moving.

The five people surrounding her began to try to pull her up.

"Don't touch me!" Lee stated. "Do not touch me. Get your hands off me."

She didn't have the strength to fight them, but she decided to fight nonetheless. The alternative was to turn into a blubbering mess, and she'd be damned if she let Fallon Galaxie do that to her. Lee was preparing to kick the man closest to her in the kneecap.

"*Kanojo o hanatte oite!*" she heard a voice shout. "Stand back from her."

The five people surrounding her froze.

"*Ima!*" the woman speaking said, and the lounge attendants and the security guards scattered.

"You're American," the woman stated as though she knew it as fact. "Military, right?"

"How could you tell?"

"Backed into a corner and you're still fighting."

"Lost battle," Lee said. "Better to go down with the ship."

"Where you coming back from, let me guess, Lieutenant?"

Lee took a deep breath. "Tech Sergeant, on my way back to Florida by way of Mercury."

"You came down the wrong lift?"

Lee shrugged.

The woman, who looked about fifteen years Lee's senior, was dressed like an executive and carried herself like she owned the place. The moment Lee said Mercury, she shook her head.

"Tell me about Mercury, sergeant," she said. "And don't skimp on the details."

"I'm not sure I can," Lee said. "I signed an NDA, I'm getting sued, and I don't have a lawyer."

"You happen to be looking at a damn good lawyer," the executive said. "I want the details."

Lee took a deep breath, looked the woman in the eyes, and nodded. She started from the beginning and told the executive the whole story, from her service to her family's debt to the jackpot contract, the situation on Mercury, the psy-op they'd run on her—everything. At some point while she was talking, Lee began to take in her surroundings and realized that she was seated in the front-facing executive lounge of A & A's Astronautics division, and she was sharing trade secrets with one of Fallon Galaxie's direct competitors in a way that probably constituted industrial espionage. At that point, Lee didn't care, though. Fallon could go to hell.

The executive sat there, shaking her head at points in Lee's story, seemingly holding back anger. Lee punctuated the narrative with the magnitude of the lawsuit and the fact that she had less than six hours to report for her medical in Clearwater and that she barely had the strength to stand.

"Well, I'll say this for you, sergeant, you can take one on the chin," the woman said. "If I were in your shoes, I'm not sure I'd be handling it as well as you are."

"I don't feel like I'm handling it all that well."

"I'm glad you stopped by," the woman said. "I'm sure you're aware of where you are, and I know you're experienced enough up there to realize it's a real small world out there right now. I know exactly who put you in that position—apart from you, of course—and I know why they did it. Fallon is actually in litigation because one of the subcontractors for the Amity Array screwed up on manufacturing the shielding, and it wasn't Fallon's mistake. That doesn't give them license to treat you like disposable inventory, but it explains the motivation anyway.

"I can't make most of your problems go away, Lee. Your family debt, your physical condition—I mean, you're going to fail your physical. That's why I came over in the first place. I saw you walking up and I didn't think you'd even make it to the chair.

"I can however make a couple of your bigger problems go away. Fallon will continue to be dependent on our array until they pony-up the money to fix that power supply properly, and quite frankly, we're under no obligation to sell energy to our competitors—you get my meaning?"

"I'm not sure."

"I'll kill the lawsuit, Lee, and I'll get you back to Clearwater."

"Really?" Lee said. "Why would you do that for me?"

"Because it's a small world up there still, at least for the time being, and you strike me as a better friend to have than not."

Lee couldn't help it and began to cover her eyes with her hands.

"Stop that," the executive said. "This isn't the time or the place. Keep that private, sergeant."

Lee took a deep breath and composed herself. "What can I do to repay you?"

"I'm going to call you someday, Lee. Someday soon. I want you to take the call."

The woman sent her credentials through to Lee's glasses.

"Oh, and I want you to have a drink with me on the day I cut Vivienne Heitmeier's throat, in the business sense, of course. Hell, I'll fly you out."

Lee was about to ask who Vivienne Heitmeier was, but then she realized. She'd been the mastermind at Fallon Galaxie—the one who'd set Lee's life's worth at two million dollars.

"Thank you, Florence," Lee said.

"It's Flor," the executive said. "Thank you for your service, sergeant. I'm a military brat myself, and I'll be damned if I let some German Frenchie get away scot-free after treating an American servicewoman like she treated you.

"It's coming."

Lee shook Flor's hand gratefully.

A few minutes after Flor left Lee sitting in that big leather chair, a cart pulled up and a very polite porter helped Lee aboard his cart. She rode first class back up to *Uchukaigan*, was ferried in a private shuttle over to Apogee, and rode down to Clearwater, where, at the base of the Florida Space Ladder, there was a limousine waiting to take Lee to her doctor's appointment on the base.

Per doctor's orders, Sergeant Lee Hriniak would be grounded for the next six months. Nearly simultaneous to the issuance of the orders, Lee received notice of payment for twenty-two days contract work, a reimbursement for her return leg of the Mercury voyage, and notice that the lawsuit against her had been dropped. Shortly after that she received a carefully worded apology that admitted no fault, categorizing the Mercury affair as a "dreadful misunderstanding" in the legal department. The note was signed Vivienne Heitmeier, Fallon Galaxie.

A small, small world up there, Lee thought, with some good people still in it, and she went home to her mother and brother grateful, exhausted, and for the moment ever so slightly lighter.

Refuge

I'm sorry, love, but you cannot teach wisdom. You're going to have to walk it. I can only impart a sense of what you need to know. You're going to need to experience the rest. What I can tell you is how I learned that difficult lesson, and maybe that will help you keep an open mind about your own ignorance. That's an important thing to understand as you grow.

Right now, you are two years old. Your favorite food is pureed bananas. You adore Red, your guardian, who is helping you improve your vocabulary each day. You also named your stuffed dog Inira, after yourself. I can't imagine what goes on in that miraculous little head of yours. I see you now, and I want to teach you what I've learned over the past few months. It's so important yet so far beyond you. Red told me to set a date, asked me, "When do you think she would be ready? I can store this lesson and impart it to her when she comes of age." And just like he is helping you with your vocabulary, he has helped me craft this narrative. I was never much of a writer. I thought it would also be fun for you, as a young adult, when you get this, to come to know me for who I was then. I am twenty-seven now, a few years older than the age I told Red you would be ready to learn about war. At least, I hope you will not have to know anything about war before then.

What I knew about war before I met Devian Gilbert I learned in history lessons. I never understood why people would fight one another to the death. The idea seems insane as I write it. And to do so programmatically, almost as part of an encoded manner of being in our makeup, it makes no sense to a person who has lived in a society that has not seen war erupt directly in their presence. War is the most abstract concept until it isn't. And when it does happen, from what I've been told by the survivors, is that it's almost unbelievable that it is actually happening, actually real.

Devian Gilbert was real, though. I could see him, treat him, touch him, be touched by him. He was my patient, a boy whose family was living on a mining outpost called Reveen, a small nothing moon of metal being stripped for its resources, so far from any zone of conflict that the people there hadn't the slightest worry that the war would ever come to touch them. They were an independent colony near Etteran space that sold wholesale metals to the Etterans, but Reveen's people were not Etterans themselves.

When the war arrived, it was devastating. The miners were defenseless. The Trasps demanded that they abandon their home, which they refused to do. They knew the Trasps wouldn't try to hold such a small mining outpost so close to Etteran territory, and it had not been the Trasps' way to do harm to neutral non-military targets. The people of Reveen would have sold their metal to the Trasps just as readily as to the Etterans. But war, above all else, is unpredictable. The Trasps razed the outpost, rendering the mining colony in-operable, and for good measure, they nuked the moon, ensuring that the fallout would prevent the Etterans from mining the moon in the future. Devian Gilbert was on that moon when they nuked it. He survived the blast. His family did not.

Devian would have died if not for the Semmistratum, a cultural order Devian's people traded with. They found the colony smoldering and located stranded survivors, extri-cated them to off-world hospital ships that served refugees of the Etteran war. Devian Gilbert was in such rough shape he was nearly left for dead. There was debate among the medics about whether he was even treatable. Had he been older, they'd probably have left him, but even in war there are rules, and one of those rules is that people value children more than they value adults. The Semmistratum gave Devian a fighting chance, and he fought, which was how, eventually, he came to me, four weeks before your second birthday.

When I first set eyes on him, he had already been through nearly eighteen months of treatment, most of it thought to be pointless. Even with the most aggressive gene therapy and armies of nanotech coursing through his bloodstream, the boy didn't regain consciousness. He was with the best doctors the Semmistratum had on their medical ships, and when he did not improve, they asked if someone in Carrol's system could take him when they stopped here to resupply. Thousands of light years from Reveen, tens of thousands of light years from Etterus or Trasp, the war brought us an orphan, right here to Hellenia, and he'd slept through the whole journey.

Our medical intelligence set to work saving him, and in the early days, the consensus was the same as the doctors from the Semmistratum. There was little indication he would ever regain consciousness. I never would have met him if not for the miracle that he did. They'd re-grown and transplanted nearly every major organ, rebuilt legs that had been stripped of their tissues and broken to bits, encouraged skin regeneration that had failed and desquamated over and over. He was on artificial respiration and functionally braindead. Yet somehow, the algorithms always turned away from the red line, always pointed to one more attempt, one more procedure, until one day, Devian finally woke. And he said no more. When he finally spoke, that's what he said. No.

That was when the machines called me.

Their protocol demanded a human guardian. He was a minor, and without a legal guardian of his own, one needed to be appointed. With his complicated medical history, the state appointed both a legal guardian and a physician as a medical proxy. That was how I came to meet Devian Gilbert.

He was a wisp of bones and pale skin. He had scar tissue all up and down his body. There'd been more skin grafts than I'd ever seen on a single person, and on such a small young person. I found myself struggling to keep my emotions in check during that first exam. His face was bandaged, covering over his right eye, the socket of which had been reconstructed completely, with heavy scarification running down his right cheek all the way to the jaw. Yet when I turned his head the other way, I could see him, see what he'd looked like before his body had been so decimated by trauma, by radiation, by heat and then neglect and inactivity. Still there was radiance in his being that told me there was a reason this child had not died.

He did not speak much, but he listened. I told him that I was there to help him, was his guardian, would make decisions for him, to help him recover. I asked him if he understood.

"No," he said. "No nanotech. Nothing invasive. No genetech."

173

"But if it had not been for all of those things, Devian, you'd have died long ago," I told him.

"That was beyond my control, doctor," he said. "I was unaware. Now I know. My family and I, we are Purists."

"There is much we could do now that you're recovering. Your eye for instance. The optic nerve is still somewhat intact and can be recovered. You could see again."

"I see enough," he said. "I'm very tired. Please no more today."

"I'll leave you to your rest, Devian. It was great to meet you. We can discuss this more later."

He didn't answer but seemed to tail off in attention, or perhaps he fell asleep. I walked out slowly in case he might say more. He didn't that day.

That night I cried my eyes out for that boy. What those Trasps had done to him and his people was an abomination. I kept wondering why, why? With all the places in the universe we can get metal? Devian's people would have mined it for them. Why kill them over resources?

When he found me crying, your father had a different take, eternal economist that he is. People don't usually fight to protect resources they haven't already invested in. You fight and die for your home because it's yours, because you've spent years living there, improving it, cherishing it. Even a metal pile like Reveen meant something to Devian Gilbert's people, because they'd spent years living off it.

To nuke it, though? No one could explain that away.

When I saw Devian later that week, he was far more alert. He apologized.

"I h- haad no idea who you were, Dr. Lee. You must understand h- how many doctors I've seen. It's difficult to tell the important ones."

"Why do you think I'm so important?"

"They say you'll make decisions for me."

"I can, yes."

"So you can stop them. I don't want a new eye."

"I'm happy to talk about it, Devian. I'd like to know why you've told the medtechs to stop using genetech and nano-tech."

"I told you," he said. "We're Purists."

"We were all Purists at one point in our history or we'd most likely have been uploaded by now."

"Or we wouldn't exist at all," he said.

"Or, yes, maybe we wouldn't exist, at least as biological beings."

"My people on Reveen, we were religious. I still am."

"Would God be angry at you for accepting a new eye, perhaps one that wasn't his?"

Devian recoiled, shaking his head. "God is not a child, Dr. Lee, and neither am I. At least...we were miners. That doesn't mean we were unsophisticated people. I'm educated. I like philosophy. I read."

"How old are you?"

"I'm fifteen now. I was thirteen when Reveen was attacked."

"And you've been unconscious for almost two years, which means you were very much a child when this happened to you."

"No. Not out there. We were serious people. It takes serious people to live where we lived, and if any one of us failed in our responsibilities, people died. I know what serious decisions are. I should be allowed to make them for myself. If you give me an eye, I would be compelled to remove it."

"Remove it?"

"No more genetech. No more nanotech."

"But you will be blind."

"My body will repair itself as much as it will, and my mind will make up the difference."

"Perhaps if you explained to me, helped me to understand."

"Did you not read about this, your h- hi-history?"

"I have, but there have been so many perspectives on Purism and biological integrity over the centuries. I'd like to hear you explain where you come down on the matter. It will help me to understand you better, Devian."

"Somewhere between Nena Gilberto and your namesake, doctor, Abe Lee. Gilberto wrote about the slaves of Rome. Some men spent their entire lives chained in the belly of a trireme, powering the war engine of the machine that enslaved them. Some toiled in mines, long before machines did such labor.

"Lee said, if you are stuck living in one place, you can either lament your limitations and spend your life in misery, or you can embrace the beauty of the small place you inh- ha- habit. And you can live a ha- happy life wherever you are. My philosophy is something of the two. If I am blind, I will see what I will. My life will h- ha- have the same value seeing what little I can."

"I've noticed you have an aphasia, a difficulty speaking."

"Yes," he said, "a problem with the eighth letter of the alphabet, but only at the beginning of words it seems. I am trying to adapt, but some very useful words start with that letter. I am trying to decide whether to learn synonyms or whether the problem will be permanent."

"Our speech therapists and neurologists can help you with that."

"H- he- help is one of those useful words. Aid. Support. Um... Guidance, maybe."

"I've heard from the other doctors that you have another rather unique symptom, Devian."

"The colors?"

"Yes, the colors. Can you tell me about them?"

"I've been seeing colors, Dr. Lee. In my dead eye. The medtechs think it h- had something to do with the radiation and the treatments."

"It's very interesting."

"They told me it sometimes h- happens to hel- healthy people, with music or numbers. Something about sensory signals getting mixed up."

"We're going to take very good care of you, Devian. We want you to feel at home here now."

"H- have you decided that I'm capable of making my own decisions?"

"About your eye?"

"About everything?"

I smiled. "We don't need to make any decisions today, Devian. For now, let's just take it one day at a time, okay?"

"Thank you for coming, Dr. Lee." he said.

My focus then, as I began to get to know Devian, was to steer him toward the course I thought best for him. I believed

176

I could convince him to accept implantation of a new eye, whether it was re-grown for him from his own genetic material or a neurotech implant mattered very little to me. But I thought I could convince him that he needed to see. That first real substantive meeting convinced me only that it would be a greater challenge than I had anticipated.

Over the following weeks, he didn't move off his position, and to gain his trust, I acceded to his request to keep him off nanotech and genetech interventions. He was progressing well enough in other areas without pressing the issue, and he seemed to be adjusting well to the realities of his new life. His mood according to the grief counselor seeing him was about as upbeat as one could have expected. He ranged from profound sadness for the loss of his family and his home to one of gratitude for a second chance at life. Nothing about it seemed performative. Devian, more than anything, was genuine.

It was nearly two months after he regained consciousness that Devian walked out of the medical center. His vision was seriously impaired in his left eye and absent in the right. The optics technicians had fitted him with a set of glasses that maximized his limited vision, flashing different warning lights in his left eye that helped him to discern approaching objects and the outlines of walkways and doors. He also wore a camera on a necklace that vocalized and vibrated in certain situations. All of these external technological interventions made me wonder why Devian was so hesitant to accept similar technological interventions that were smoother and better integrated with his neurology. An eye would be all but unnoticeable to both him and others. The only barrier to it was Devian himself.

His story had gained enough attention in Hellenia that Devian had many families offering to take him in. I and his counselor discussed it with him and his legal guardian, and we all agreed that even though we could set him up on his own with his guardian and counselors checking in on him, it would be healthy for him to be a part of a family. He chose a family situated in a lower density neighborhood in Mentor, just outside the capitol of Gracia.

I saw him again at my office about a week after he'd moved to Mentor. He didn't want to talk about his medical status, more about how he was adjusting to life on Hellenia.

"I'd known of Dreeson's Star," he told me, "but never Carrol's, and not this planet."

"It's the rings," I said. "Dreeson's rings are much flashier than our humble little planet."

"With the rings I could at least visualize where I am. In this city, if it weren't for the directions from my glasses, I wouldn't know where I am most of the time, just some point on a matrix."

"Have you done anything interesting since you've moved to Mentor?"

"I met a girl," he said.

"A girl?"

"A neighbor. She's very sweet."

"A girlfriend?"

Devian shrugged. "We'll see."

"What's her name?"

"Tally. Tally Compans."

"I knew you were a charmer," I said, "but you work fast."

"Two years in a coma puts things in perspective, Dr. Lee. Nothing promised and all that."

"Fair enough," I said. "Have you given much thought to what we talked about last time."

"None at all. I know what I think. It's up to you to respect my feelings or not respect them."

"I'm not sure I would look at it quite that way, Devian. I don't want to force anything on you."

"But I can tell, you'd like it if I let the medtechs build me a new eye."

"It would certainly make your adjustment and your life here easier."

"Maybe," Devian said. "But my glasses were the reason Tally came to talk to me in the first place. She saw me struggling across a busy walkway and then we spent the afternoon together. Could be that never occurred if I could see."

"What did you two do together that day?"

"I was on my way to the AgScreen, and she came with me. All our food on Reveen was imported. I've never been anywhere like He- Hellenia before where they grow food. It

178

smelled incredible in there. Fresh, like where the air was born. The technicians love me there now."

"Why is that?"

"I asked them if I could try everything. By the time all the food got to us at the mines, all the flavor's gone out, just salt and sugar. At the AgScreen, you can smell things for what they are, taste things the way they were meant to taste. They gave me a carrot, and I'd eaten soups with carrots or dried salad, but I didn't really know what a carrot tasted like until three days ago. It was incredible."

"Carrots?"

"Yeah. You don't know these things and maybe I'm the blind one, but maybe there's also things I can see that are right before everyone in this place, and they miss them."

"Are you worried that might change if you could see again?"

"I'm worried about that regardless. You can only taste a cherry for the first time once."

I smiled. "I love cherries," I said. "I could eat a million of them and never grow tired of the taste."

"I know," he said. "I'm grateful. I really am. I told them I'd like to volunteer there, learn ways I can be useful to them, maybe learn to grow fruit too someday."

"What if there were sights here you were missing too, Devian? Would you maybe want to see them? Like Tally, maybe? Maybe the greens at the AgScreen? The crossing in Gracia center has its own kind of spectacular beauty."

He paused before answering. "Is it difficult for you to choose, Dr. Lee? You seem to be struggling with this decision."

"I have a daughter. She's two. I make a lot of decisions for her and they're not very difficult decisions. I've gotten used to making the easy decisions for her. Bedtime is bedtime or she'll be cranky tomorrow. Two-year-olds would make a lot of bad choices if adults didn't step in."

"Maybe teenagers too," Devian said. "I certainly made mistakes on Reveen."

"Maybe teenagers need to make mistakes so they can learn from them."

"But I don't think conforming to a belief system that I'm willing to sacrifice for is a mistake."

"I know what I would do if you were my daughter," I said. "I would fix her eyes, Devian. I would want her to see."

"Even if it meant violating your daughter's most sincere beliefs?"

"I can't see her in you, Devian. All I can see is her sweet, two-year-old face. And I can't stand the thought of her face being...well—"

"Let's call it all banged up," Devian said. "I understand. The universe breaks every beautiful thing it makes. And she'll grow. The decisions, they get tougher too."

"Yes, they do."

I was so stunned by the staggering wisdom in this young philosopher that I was fooled by him, fooled by his stoic humor, by his composure, by his insistence on principle. I couldn't see past it because I was a child myself. I'd never known pain, not here on Hellenia, insulated kingdom of wonder and hope. I couldn't see it hidden there behind his wounded eyes, the facial muscles that had melted and been restructured only passably. I thought there was still a decision to be made.

That night, I talked to your father, Inira, about the thoughts I'd had speaking with Devian that day, about the possible world where you were the broken one, and your father held me as I cried tears of recreational emotion, playacting as we were. And I thought about fixing Devian, repairing those eyes so he could see the universe as whole once more. The taste of fruits and the colors of stained-glass windows. I dreamt of flowers and woke to the smell of coffee and toast.

When I saw him again two weeks later, I thought he would take the news as he'd taken everything else, like a young man wise beyond his years. I couldn't have expected how wrong I was or how foolish I had been, for I knew nothing of war or even of true grief.

He was silent when I spoke of our protocols and our charge, how fixing people was our duty, when in balance it is a greater good for the patient, when it will cause no harm to do so. I wasn't even sure that he was crying when I saw something small that looked like a teardrop fall from his chin. He had turned what gaze remained away from me, and his missing eye, the one facing me, could no longer produce tears. Still, he didn't speak.

"Devian, I can see you're disappointed. But I've discussed this with my team, your therapist Dr. Kern. We agree that long-term for you, it gives you the best chance of recovery."

It was the last thing I was expecting. He laughed. "Do with me what you will, doctor. Recovery."

And he shook his head.

"Devian, I'm here for you. I'm listening and I'd like to hear what you have to say, but I can't help you if you don't share what's bothering you with me. I get the sense that your unwillingness to let us treat you, your vision, that there's more there than you've been willing to say, that you don't want to see so you don't have to see, so you can hide in there, keep whatever you're hiding to yourself."

"What would you do, brave doctor Lee? Stick your h- head out? Pass judgement on me, though, because what? Some committee decided that because I haven't been alive eighteen years yet, I'm unfit to decide for myself? Better you decide then, right?"

"Devian, we only want what's best for you."

"You tell me then, the people who pulled me off the floor, did they do that because it was best for me, or did they do it because they didn't possess the courage to do what was best for me? And now you're going to make me look people in the eye and smile at them for the rest of my life because that's what's best for me now? If that's what makes you feel good about yourself, doctor."

I listened. I was trained to listen, to let the patient talk, to try and get him to speak through his trauma. And when he failed to speak, to try and help him to speak.

"Devian, do you wish the Semmistratum hadn't rescued you?" I said.

"Rescued me? Rescued me? Rescued me? Doctor, rescued me?"

"Devian, Dr. Kern said that you didn't remember what happened to you on Reveen, but that's not true is it?"

"Could you forget?"

"Can you tell me about it?"

"No, I cannot," he said. "And if I could, I still wouldn't. Not in a million years. Not to anyone. Doctor Lee, you h- have a

181

heart and a baby. There are things in this life you're better off not knowing."

"I'd like to know, Devian."

"I'd like to continue to see the world the way I do today."

"Can you try to tell me?"

"I wish you could see the way I see. If you could try to see what I see. I would rather try that. Maybe you could understand that."

I went home very confused. And I thought and thought about that discussion we'd had. I thought about the surgery, and I was still convinced that it was the right thing to do, but I knew we couldn't do it until he was ready. I still thought there was such a thing for him as ready. He was grieving. He was working on it. We'd get through it.

When you don't know, you don't know.

I thought of clever things I could do, ways to help. I spoke to high-minded people. I thought back then there were such things as saints. I imagined technological interpretations, devices that might go into my eyes to explain to me the colors of blindness and the feelings of war, the sadness of songs I could weep to, the boundless depths of darkness lurking in bones. Only the universe could open such doors for me. The child I couldn't see before my very eyes was howling with every exhaled breath, and I mistook him for blind. So I went to the opticians and the prostheticians. What could they tell from my scans of Devian? And they furrowed their brows at me and wondered. I ordered new eyes made for me, and I told that boy I would see the world through his eyes.

He seemed genuinely interested when I told him about the ocular prosthetics I'd had made to mimic his vision. He asked me questions about the contact lenses, how they would fit over my eyes, what I would see, distinctions between the left and the right, which was totally opaque but projected colors in concert with certain stimuli that activated Devian's synesthesia. I hadn't put them in yet. He told me I should wear them for long enough that it seemed normal to me. Days, weeks, he didn't know how long it would take. I told him I would try and see how it went. He wanted to be there with me when I tried them for the first time. I told him to meet me at my office in the evening, a Friday at the end of the work week. He showed up with Tally Compans, his girlfriend. I couldn't help but see the part of myself in her that had tied us there together that day, and I resented it in her. Vanity abhors the truths in mirrors.

I'd never had anything placed in my eye before. I needed to call the ophthalmologist to help insert the lenses. At first, the lenses themselves felt strange and oddly constricting, as though something physically was at odds with my vision. I had to close my eyes to relax enough that I might open them and see as he saw. Tally Compans said something as we were waiting, that it had been about ten minutes. A pink glow surrounded the left side of my face, the left hemisphere of the world.

"Is that pink for you?" I asked Devian. "I saw pink."

"You see it?" Devian said.

"Yes, what was it?"

"That was ten," he said. "Tally said ten. Numbers have colors."

"Incredible," I said, as the room erupted in a pink glow after he'd spoken the word ten twice more.

"Wait till you see music," Devian said.

He wanted to show me the crossing in Gracia. Tally had taken him the previous week as the evening took hold and revelers came out to celebrate the night. Most of the open spaces on this ball of urban heat reflected the ordinary, the needs of the people who lived off the ecumenopolis that was Hellenia—water, air, power, heat. But some spaces spoke to the longing we have in our hearts for beauty, the reverence we have for feeling small. Gracia Crossing was one of those places. I thought there could be no better place to see and not see through Devian's eyes.

I struggled to make it out of the medical office building adjacent the hospital. There was vertigo of some kind, dizziness that seemed to be set off by the flashing signals that somehow oriented Devian in the world. I had no idea how to interpret them, so he began to narrate as we progressed down the corridor toward the lift.

"The green line on your right side is actually on your left, so we can walk toward it about a meter before reaching the wall. The gaps are the doorways."

It was backwards, and I was trying to puzzle out where the damage had to be in the visual pathways for his vision to be experienced this way—optic nerve, primary, secondary, and tertiary visual cortices? But I had no time to think deeply about that neurological curiosity, navigation demanded my attention. I nearly fell. Tally Compans took me by the hand.

"Dr. Lee," she said. "It's okay. I won't let you stray."

As soon as I had that anchor, it was as though a spinning world became solid under foot. I walked straighter, stood taller. Tally walked me forward toward a wall and stopped me right at it so I could feel. She took me to the edge of a railing at the office's open walkway which I knew and could remember, and I compared it in my mind to what I saw now, something Devian had no chance to experience. This world was all lines, blurred light, and colors to him, no memories to fill in gaps. To say I was blind, though would have been a mischaracterization. I'd have called his vision low resolution, radically different, and dramatically impaired. But Devian could see. And I could see how well he navigated the world compared to me. He was encouraging and a good teacher. On the way over to the crossing, he helped to compare what I was experiencing with his vision, and occasionally, for amusement, he would call out numbers he thought were beautiful, like five hundred forty-seven. I preferred the symmetry of one thousand and one. Tally pretended to laugh as we did, as though she understood, but I could hear envy in her. I promised her she would have her turn. The perspective was a priceless learning experience. No one could understand the significance of the hazards and barriers until they stepped into the reality Devian lived each day.

It took us three nearly an hour to get down to the crossing. We walked around the shops and eateries and I took the kids to dinner. It was a strange experience to be unable to see my food but to need to feel for it with my utensils and then, when that failed, with my hands. It would take real time to adapt fully to eating that way. I couldn't imagine trying to prepare a meal with those eyes. It made me think of the limitations that would exist for Devian if he wanted to grow fruit. Systems would have to be adapted to communicate aspects of crop health to him, though I knew such algorithms already existed for harvesting software and hardware.

The most notable change I could discern in my perceptions was an overwhelming feeling of vulnerability. I knew there were no threats here on Hellenia, and the eyes on us were friendly eyes. Even with a small teenage girl as our protector, the eyes around us watching her, I knew, were ready to step in and support her in support of us at the first sign of trouble, whatever that trouble might be. But still, placing myself in such an un-known vulnerable position among strangers, even sympathetic strangers, it felt simultaneously stressful and oddly liberating. I knew they were there watching, yet I couldn't see them, and Devian, I knew was blissfully unaware of how many thousands of onlookers saw us as we approached Gracia Crossing. We walked, and the crowds parted. The footsteps, the hum, they surrounded us and spread around us like a cloud silently colliding with a mountain. The experience was going well enough that I asked Tally to let Devian and I walk alone together after dinner. I promised her that if we encountered any trouble I would remove the prosthetics and guide Devian home safely with my own sight. Tally was reluctant to go, but when it came to it, Tally was still a minor and did as I told her.

We made our way up to the crow's nest above the grand carousel, where the macro designers flew their birds in the open space and flashing lights over Gracia Crossing. The balcony eighteen stories up hummed now in blue, and I didn't know whether it was the thought of the number eighteen or the distant music floating up from the carousel, and my memory of the Genesis Building lit up in red, a blazing red that Devian said he saw too. We walked the length of that magnificent causeway, I with one hand on the railing, Devian a step before me remarking on the magnificence of the open space and the sparking presence of the drone pilots' arcing birds. And at ten o'clock the sound system in the plaza began playing music. I felt lines to my left and colors saturating the open spaces, a kaleidoscope of sounds and sensations, feelings. It was like my first time stepping out into space—that sensation of floating at the beginning of infinity and knowing how insignificant you are before it but that all hope of significance begins and ends with your own perception of it. I understood what Devian meant when he said he couldn't explain what had happened to him. This was happening to me now, and I had no hope of explaining it to others. I could see now where Devian was hiding.

We walked along those balconies for two hours listening to the music. We spoke very little that night. By the time we each headed home, I knew somehow I'd find my way without taking my new eyes out. I slept with the contacts in and looked on your father and on you, my daughter, with Devian Gilbert's eyes the following morning. You were both missing. Your voices, your scents, your warmth, they were present before me in the gaps, but I couldn't see you in those spaces and it felt to me that I had become invisible.

I wore the eyes every last second that I could. Three days after I put the contacts in, a few minutes before I had to step into my first appointment of the week, I removed the prosthetics again and saw with my own eyes. I hadn't yet written a word of my report on Devian, but I knew that to force him against his wishes back to a state we considered neurological and visual normalcy would be nothing short of the same kind of savagery that had destroyed that boy's life in the first place. I resolved to choke out my fear and say as much to my superiors in the language I knew in my heart best reflected my feelings. In those days I served as his physician, I'd have given up my career, possibly my life for that boy, and I'd only known him a handful of weeks. I thought of him now every time I savored a piece of fruit or the taste of a carrot.

My report was unequivocal. I held nothing back. I refused any operation Devian failed to consent to. I opposed any counseling that advocated positive medical intervention beyond stringent Purist parameters. I quoted philosophy and condemned hypothetical detractors. I'd never seen a document like it in medicine, and I expected it would be a controversy amongst the neurology board. I was correct.

I was called before the fellows and the administration staff to answer for my position. They couldn't fathom the idea that I would neglect to fix a fixable problem that a child knew no better than to suffer. In their minds, his psychological trauma brought on by the war rendered his judgement suspect. Dr. Kern testified that Devian was blocking any chance of recovery by taking refuge behind his disability. Their consensus was that Devian would never recover if he were allowed to block out the world and hide behind his glasses. They wanted me to concur.

I challenged them to wear the prosthetics. I told them I would resign.

"You've gotten too close to this," Dr. Kern said to the board. "Dr. Lee, with respect, that's the only way I can explain your behavior. The document you presented to this neuro board is the most unprofessional report I've read in my fifteen years as a clinical psychologist."

"I've written what I've written," I said, "and I stand by every word of it. If each of you can't understand why Devian of all people deserves to make his own decisions about his present and his future, not only are you not a doctor, you're not even a moral human being, you're just a child walking around with a hammer seeing a nail, completely incapable of resisting the urge to use the hammer, but neither the hammer nor the nail truly belongs to you. I won't be a part of victimizing this boy. I can't make you understand any more than he can tell us the first thing about war. Ignorance is forgivable, but only if we wear it with humility. I will fight this in the courts if need be."

They smiled at me politely and disagreed, but nobody wanted to fight me, not that day. Not on those grounds.

I didn't last much longer at the hospital after that. But Devian Gilbert was never forced into surgery.

I helped him apply for emancipation the following year. His foster family supported him financially through his school years, and the last I'd heard of him, he'd taken work on an Ag Cylinder in Dreeson's System. I suppose it was easier to start anew again when he was strong enough to do so, rather than to carry the memory of that identity, the boy refugee, the poor broken child we'd taken in. He saw what he saw and he walked.

Years later, I bumped into Tally Compans on the street in Gracia. She'd grown into a lovely young woman, a teacher of elementary Ag Sciences. She told me she still had the ocular prosthetics our neuro team had designed for me, and she asked me if I remembered them. "In so many ways, the things we don't know inevitably define us," I told her. "Devian opened my eyes by teaching me that."

May we always remain ignorant of the right things.

I wanted you to know all this, Inira Lee, my precious daughter, but still I am not sure why. What I did not have the courage back then to explore was the real truth of war. I did not seek out Devian's medical files from the Semmistratum. I never watched the recordings they had of Reveen. They were then, and I presume still are, an anti-war activist group, peaceful humanitarians. Their most powerful and convincing tool has always been the images, sounds, and accounts of war itself, but I never had the courage to seek out any of that material. Devian Gilbert was enough.

I sometimes still think of the man who gave the order, the Trasp Captain, there, safe in the security of his bridge in the tranquility and darkness of space, suspended in orbit above that tiny moon. That moment he gave the order. Just then.

What monsters live in our hearts, daughter? Where do they come from?

How to Disappear Completely

People don't just disappear, at least not in the real world. There's always a witness, a fact pattern, evidence, and failing all that, there's the imprint that the person leaves behind, on family, on the community, all the ripples from person to person that nobody sees. Those things can't be erased, Mikaela. I was thinking a lot about your father this week. Not just because he asked me to take you down here, to show you the city, the real dangers, but I was working a case this past week, it brought a lot of things back for me. There's a lot about me you don't know.

Like what, Uncle Mike?

Well, like that. You know me as your uncle, and just the face that I show you and what your dad and your mom tell you about me. You know what I do now, and probably when I was a postal inspector. Do you remember what I did when you were a kid?

I remember you were a cop.

Do you ever remember seeing me in uniform?

Actually, I don't remember seeing you much at all back then.

I was a homicide detective for eight years with the Boston Police. And when you do a job like that you tell kids very little about it, like, you know, I catch bad guys who hurt people, because that's about all a kid should see of that side of life. And your father and mother have done a good job of keeping you shielded from all that horrible...that side of life.

It's okay, Uncle Mike. You can swear. I'm eighteen. I know who you are, and I've seen enough movies to know, like violence and all that stuff in the world.

No. It's good for me to watch my mouth. I know you're growing up, but one of the things about being eighteen is that you think you know. I remember being your age. You think you know, but you don't know. It's like seeing a picture of something and thinking you've been there. Until you've been there, you haven't been there. In the picture you see the outline, the major features, but you miss everything else, the sounds, the smells, the feel of the air, and more than anything, when it comes to the scenes I worked, there's something missing from everyone's conception of it unless you've stood there, it's the feeling of awe. It's almost like there's a reverence for something unspoken. People get quieter. The energy changes. Nobody gets taught that like they do in church. It's like it happens to them. Normal people, when they witness a murder or stumble upon the scene, there's a reverence that comes over them. You don't see it in the movies. It's in the atmosphere. Bad things only happen to somebody else until you're there. Then there's no such thing as somebody else anymore. Somebody else becomes somebody. Right there. You see it and you feel it.

How many murders did you investigate?

Eighty-four. I mean with BPD it was eighty-four. As a private investigator, I stumbled across two, and the one I was going to tell you about, from this week, it started as a missing person's case.

That must have been hard, all that death.

Yeah. It was. That's why I started working for the Postal Service. It's ironic, how everything turned out.

How so?

I shouldn't...well, I guess that's what this is supposed to be all about, exposing you to the parts of the world we kept hidden from you because you were a kid, and you're not a kid anymore, maybe.

Uncle Mike, just spit it out.

I'm going to tell you something about your father he's probably never told you, and I swear, what we discuss in this car tonight better never get back to him.

Mike?

I'm sorry. Anyway, when he was your age, your father went through a real rough time. And it was hard for me to figure out, because, you know, he was my big brother. I looked up to him. But he got really depressed. I didn't know it at the time, but he was suicidal, started dying his hair black, started listening to just really depressing music. Did he ever tell you any of this?

No.

One of the bands he was listening to a lot was Radiohead. You ever heard of them?

I've heard the name, but I don't know any of their music.

It was really depressing, at least to me anyway, but your father was into them, and they had this one song he used to listen to constantly, and the part they kept singing over and over again—

The refrain?

Yeah, yeah, the refrain. The words were: "I'm not here. This isn't happening." And he used to listen to that all the time, and, Mikaela, it was ironic it stuck with me, because I used to get that refrain in my head, for years, I'd work a scene, see mothers, brothers, sisters, looking at these young men gunned down, family members just taken, and they'd get this look on their faces like, "I'm not here. This isn't happening." And I'd hear it. The dead of night. The middle of the day. Not here. Not happening. But at the same time, they all knew that it was real. They would feel it.

What was ironic about it?

What?

You said it was ironic, Uncle Mike.

Oh, well, your father, he grew out of it, but it was his music not mine. He probably listened to that song a thousand times. And probably because of my work, it ended up sticking with me, that song. Never left me. And I was thinking about that song and your father all week because of the case I've been working. Song was called "How to Disappear Completely," and since we're talking about the world, I thought maybe I'd tell you about the case while it's fresh in my mind, and we got some time before all the bars let out.

Sure. Is it like some true crime drama?

It's not drama, Mikaela. It's real, yeah, so true, I guess.

Okay, I'm listening.

So the guy's wife came to me, and I hadn't heard anything about the case, but I guess it'd been on the news, because he was a pretty prominent professor at BC, and apparently, he'd just vanished. And the police working the case had no idea how or why or where. This was six weeks ago. Just up and disappears. But people don't disappear, especially not nowadays. When I was younger, it was a lot easier for people to get lost or hide. Now, I can make a phone call, and ninety-nine percent of the time, I can get your location within about five feet of wherever you are on the Earth, and if I do a little work, I can trace that back to about any point for the last few years, just because everyone's trained now to carry their phone around with them.

But apparently this professor, he'd switched off his phone on a Tuesday, and by Thursday, nobody had seen the guy. Not at work, not at home, nowhere. And the cops out in Brookline where his wife reported him missing, they couldn't find anything in the phone records. Nobody saw anything suspicious.

Is he dead?

We'll get to that. Don't get ahead of the story.

Okay, so it's a proper murder mystery?

It's not that mysterious. Mrs. Kay—professor's name was Stephen Kay—so Mrs. Kay hired me to find him, because at that point, nobody knows what happened to the guy, and from everyone I talked to, he was one of the nicest guys, one of those people you would think nobody would ever want to hurt. So I say, sure, I'll do what I can to track him down. I have some tricks not every cop knows. And to be honest, it was an interesting case, or at least it seemed that way, because it didn't seem like I was going to find the guy hanging out off the grid in some rich widow's vacation home. It just—he wasn't that type of guy. So I started to talk to people—people in his department, his family, friends, neighbors, whoever. And at the same time, I'm waiting to get access to all his data. What I really wanted was his emails, because the cops had already gone over all his phone records, and professors, they all still live by email.

Anyway, I learned this professor is some kind of prominent computer scientist—I don't know, what would you call it, philosopher? Theorist? Something like that.

He was working with some top-secret group at Los Alamos studying simulation theory. You ever hear of it?

I'm not sure.

It's like, you ever see *The Matrix*?

What, like the movie?

Yeah.

No. I've heard of it, but I don't really watch that many old movies.

Well, that's kind of what this professor was studying, the idea that our world is actually a computer simulation.

I had a biology teacher who talked about that sometimes. He was into all kinds of wild theories like that.

Okay, so you know about it?

Sorta.

Well, this guy wrote a book about that. He and his group were studying the probability that we lived in a simulation, and he was working with people at Google and IBM to figure out how to design a real universe simulator on super-computers out at Los Alamos, all kinds of crazy stuff like that. And then he just vanishes.

So when I start talking to his colleagues, I hear one or two of them make the same comment about it, like maybe he got too close or he got unplugged from the matrix, and that's the thing, Mikaela, when I'm working a strange case like that, really more than anything, I'm just looking for something that's off. And I hear that comment again two more times, almost like it was a dark joke about him getting wiped out from the matrix because he'd figured out the world was a simulation. There was something about it that was too coincidental, that they'd all have the same comment, and that so many of the people around him would think it was okay or somehow clever to joke about their colleague who'd gone missing. So I went back to the Brookline Police and asked the detective there if he'd heard anything like that. And it turned out that one of the guy's graduate students had mentioned that to the cops, that she thought it was legitimately possible because of a theory he was about to publish, that because, according to her, this publication proved that we live in a simulation, and somehow he'd been disappeared before he could publish it.

Did she believe that?

Well, we'll get to her in a minute. But the cops just thought she was quirky, and she was just throwing out the idea because nobody had any better idea.

I think she's a suspect.

I did too, but it's only obvious because that's the way I'm telling you the story. You have to understand, the cops didn't interview all the people I did, because they didn't suspect anything really happened to the guy yet, and they'd only met this lady once, and she seemed harmless.

So was she harmless?

193

Well, I guess that's next isn't it. I was still waiting to meet with the IT people over at BC to get into his emails, and I had spoken with his colleagues, but after I heard this about Vanessa—that was the woman's name, Vanessa Badgely—then I decided I needed to meet with her. So I call her and try to set up a meeting, and she told me she was too busy, couldn't come to meet. So I offered to go to her, and she was really evasive for someone whose mentor just went missing. Finally, she agreed to meet me, and she sets up the meeting for a Saturday morning, and the address is right downtown. Turns out to be this fancy assisted living facility for wealthy old folks. She would go down there every now and again and play piano. Here's the thing, though, Mikaela, if you learn one thing as a cop it's reading people, and rule one of reading people is that they only ever show you what they want you to see, so what they choose to show you means something— the clothes people wear, the people they hang out with, the things they do, all that. So for her to choose that place and time to meet me, it was definitely strange.

She was a really good pianist, like I don't know classical music all that good, but she sounded professional, not an amateur at all, and I like to try and watch people to see them before they know they're being seen. And my first impression was that she was interested in the music, not the people in the room—very much in her own mind.

I watch her for a while, and then eventually I go up and talk to her. And she doesn't get up, just sits there at the keyboard as I lean in and talk to her over the piano—and that's a cue, keeping that big familiar object between us, almost like a barrier. The other thing was that she talked funny, not a speech impediment or nothing or even like an accent, 'cuz God knows we Bostonians are one to talk, right? But she put on this manner, almost from some kind of old timey movie, like Fred Astaire or Clark Gable was about to walk up to the piano and ask her to dance. I thought she was joking at first. And she had the nerve to make a crack about the stupid hat I wear when I'm doing PI work.

Why do you wear it if you think it's stupid, Uncle Mike?

It's a signifier, same as the way a cop wears a uniform to let you know who they are. It's sounds stupid, but people take you more seriously when you tell them you're a PI if you're wearing a fedora or something. It's ridiculous, but it's true.

What did she sound like?

Oh, God, I can't do the accent. Pretentious. Like, "How do you do, darling." Like she was talking how she thought you should talk if you were talking to the queen or something. And, just so you know, that's another red flag. Anybody who has to put on airs like that, who isn't comfortable with their authentic self to the point they adopt a mannerism like that unironically, they're hiding something they don't like about themselves. And it could be something harmless, like she grew up poor and hated being poor, so she adopted the fanciest accent she could manage, but she didn't do a good job of it. Came off as very artificial. So I get this vibe off her, and I start probing. And I like to poke people in ways they won't expect and don't know how to react to.

So I say to her, "Hey that's Beethoven, right? I'm pretty sure I recognize that song."

And I knew it would get a reaction out of her, because I know it probably isn't Beethoven and I know that classical music people don't like it when you call their music songs. "We call them pieces, you see," she starts telling me.

"Oh, oh," I say. "Sure. Sure."

"You aren't even in the correct century, inspector," she says. "This is a sonata from a modern composer, from the TV show *Battlestar Galactica*."

And I swear, Mikaela, to hear that woman say that collection of words in that put-on accent, I almost couldn't keep a straight face with her, and I think she could tell, because she got real flustered, and we hadn't even started talking about the professor yet.

So I toss her the topic of the professor as a lifeline, to get her comfortable again, and I tell her, "Look, Miss Badgely, the reason I wanted to talk to you is about this simulation theory. I know you're an expert and I'm not. I wanted to ask your advice on who to talk to about it, but I can't ask you, given as you're so close to Professor Kay's work. So who should I talk to about this? Because I can tell you the cops aren't taking the idea seriously at all, but I'd like to at least give the idea a fair hearing."

So she starts talking about it, and gives me a breakdown of the whole theory, which I already know, because it's my job to be prepared. But she keeps going on and on about it, and I'm acting like this is all new information, all, "Oh, wow, this stuff is blowing my mind."

And she talked for probably forty minutes before she says, "I can see you're really taking this seriously, inspector."

And again, I have to repress the urge to laugh and just say, "Please, call me Mike. And yes, it's a real possibility, Miss Badgely, I think. Because people don't just disappear, and nobody's ever prepared if they get murdered, so all of his data on his phone and all the other patterns of life would look just like a normal day, but his phone disappeared with him. So until I get into his emails, it looks like it's entirely possible he disappeared."

And when I said the word emails, she turns white, like that was the one loose end she forgot. And let me tell you, Mikaela, with smart people, a lot of them think that criminals are dumb, so they assume crime must be easy, or maybe there's an arrogance about it. Dumb people don't usually get away with crimes, but a lot of smart people do, just not the type of smart people like her. She, and anyone else for that matter, stood about as much chance of getting away with a crime as you would if you never knew nothing about plumbing and decided you were going to repair your own pipes over the weekend. Like no smart people ever tried to solve a crime before. It's perplexing that someone could be smart enough to write computer code for the theory of a simulated universe and also think that cops would know nothing about metadata.

Is that how you caught her?

You're so certain it's her, are you?

I think so.

So what would you have done next, Inspector Mikaela?

Can you read his emails yet?

No, not yet.

Can you track her phone?

Um, not closely enough to get answers, but that's not a bad play. We'll get there eventually, but not yet.

I guess, I think I would try to figure out what their relationship was like. Why would she want him to disappear?

That is a good question to ask, but I actually went a different direction. I talked to the two professors she asked me to talk to.

What could they tell you?

I wanted to know the value of his work. And I wanted to know what she could benefit by finishing it and taking credit after he was dead. And I also wanted to know what their perspective would be as the universe programmer, like what motive would you have for disappearing a person in your simulation, just really to see how these people tick, what they think about when they think about the simulation theory.

But you don't actually believe it's real, though?

No, but you don't have to believe what a person believes to catch them out in inconsistencies in their own way of thinking. Like if you caught a priest down here in one of these bars after hours, and then you could say, "Hey, Father, I saw you down the Cask 'n Flagon the other night, but you have to know the way they're supposed to act to know that you're catching them out. Something like that.

I see. So did they say anything interesting?

A lot of interesting things. It's really fascinating. The Swiss guy said they were years behind the Los Alamos group, but said the New Mexico team was only a couple decades or so from a realistic, and I mean real-life quality simulation of a universe every bit as complex as ours. So, in all probability, he said that Vanessa and Professor Kay were probably right about the idea that we do live in a simulation. And I asked them both what they knew about Kay and Vanessa.

Wouldn't she get pretty famous if she proved his theory, Uncle Mike? I would think that's an important motive, maybe.

Yeah. Exactly. Especially in that field, she would instantly become the superstar of that specialized little world. She could get any job she wanted. Good salary, plenty of accolades. All that.

You think that's a good enough motive for a murder, though?

I've seen people get murdered over a cab fare, Mikaela. The question isn't usually whether the motive is enough, but whether it's enough for that particular suspect to do it.

I think so.

197

Why?

Because of her accent, maybe. She wants to be someone important.

That's one possible reason. Or maybe she's in love with the guy and he doesn't love her back. Maybe something else. All that really matters is whether the guy is actually dead, whether she had something to do with making him dead, and most importantly, can the DA prove it. And at this point, none of those things are a certain yes.

What next then, Uncle Mike?

I go to BC to meet with their head IT guy. And this is just amazing. So I had spoken with them right off the bat, and I made sure that they'd archived his account back to before he disappeared. And I had them leave the account live, so if Professor Kay shows up, it'll record his log in and we can trace him through that computer, or if someone else tries to log in to his account, I've got a backup of his account to compare against any emails or documents they try to delete, as well as a record of that login, so if they're dumb enough to not hide their computer, we can figure out who they are and go see who they are and why they're in the professor's account.

So did she?

Oh, yeah. And as smart as this woman must be, she was smart enough to realize, maybe I shouldn't log in on my own computer, but she went to a university library, never realizing the library had video surveillance. And she's not thinking about getting caught altering his account, because she probably thinks I'm just going to look at his emails, when all I really care about is the metadata.

Wow.

People do really stupid stuff when they feel like they're cornered. So now she's on video trying to alter the guy's email account, and because I had them archive his entire account, all we had to do was compare the before and after, and we got a list of all the communications and documents she deleted. We didn't even have to look.

So you got her?

More or less, but she doesn't know it yet. So I wanted to talk to her again—see if I can get her to say something she shouldn't, maybe even crack altogether.

Did she agree to talk to you?

I showed up. Parking lot of the Stop & Shop in Chestnut Hill, just met her there at the trunk of her car.

What'd she say to that?

"Oh, inspector, this is highly irregular. Highly irregular, my goodness. Have you been following me? How did you know where to find me?"

And it's like, hello! Private investigator. That is exactly my job, lady. Literally. And she's all flustered. But then, you know it's like before, you do something to poke them a little and then you try to set them at ease, get them talking. So the first thing I tell her is that I just really had a question about what those simulation experts were telling me, because the emails were a dead-end. Scoured his account for hours and hours and there was nothing useful at all.

That's clever.

So I tell her I have this question I can't figure out about simulation theory, and it goes like this: if a programmer of this simulation was bothered enough by a single professor finding out the secret to the simulation, and they're powerful enough to make the professor disappear completely, why wouldn't they just make all trace of him vanish, like *It's a Wonderful Life* and he'd never been born. How much more difficult could it be to do that?

And what did she say?

She froze, like a deer in the headlights, for three solid seconds with her mouth hanging open, in shock. And then she starts in, "Oh, well the degree of difficulty would be orders of magnitude higher—many orders of magnitude higher, all the connections, all the memories, the physical interactions that Professor Kay played a part in." Mind you, I'm recording this the whole time. And she keeps talking and talking for, I don't know, maybe twenty minutes trying to explain away that simple point, which wasn't even the real question I wanted to ask her.

Finally, I ask her a very simple, very specifically worded question: "So Professor Kay disappeared on a Tuesday, as far as anyone can tell. Can you tell me, Vanessa, what's the average Tuesday look like for him?"

Why's that important?

It's not. It's how she answers that's important. I get her talking about when he usually gets to work, when she interacted with him, when he had his classes, and I ask follow-up questions without leading her in the verb tense, so instead of asking, "Did Professor Kay meet with students after class?" You leave them open like, "And after class? And that Tuesday? Lunch?" And about halfway through that conversation, she started referring to him in the past tense and never caught herself out on it. At that point it's pretty clear. Best part of all, was that after all that, as flustered as she got, and she got flustered—couldn't get out of that parking lot fast enough—the moment she turns on her car, I see her car's a hotspot, and I had already got make, year, model, license plate, VIN number, and now I got the name of her little hotspot network. So I put a call in to the homicide detective in Brookline and gave her all the email data, my notes, recordings, and all the info they'd need to subpoena her phone and car's transponder data. Pretty sure there'll be a nice little itinerary for her on the night he went missing that leads right to Professor Kay's body. And the other ironic thing is that she'll be the one who disappears completely— off to Framingham for thirty to life.

So how did she kill him?

I still don't know. The coroner will figure that all out when they find the body or the crime scene or both. Probably poison would be my guess, or shot him—something like that.

That's an interesting story and all, Uncle Mike, but...

But what?

Well, what's the point?

Yeah, you're full of good questions, I guess. I don't know. I'm not sure I can remember anymore why I started telling you all this.

You were talking about Radiohead and disappearing completely, something like that.

Oh, your father. Look, Mikaela, I think all I'm trying to say is that your mother and father they can only live in their perspective, just like you're not going to see theirs when you decide whether you want to come out like this, and as much of a total cluster it is watching these bars let out, all these drunk ass kids running around, I think he wanted me to come down here show you the danger, give you a lecture about safety or something so that you never come out here. But let's be realistic. I was eighteen. You probably already have a fake ID, maybe even been down here on a Friday or Saturday. Whatever. Thing is, I think I told you about the professor because no matter how hard you try to take yourself out of bad situations, which on balance is a good thing to do, you'll never be able to opt out of risk altogether. That poor bastard was statistically about the least likely person to get murdered you could ever find, and he gets offed by his whack job of a student.

So the moral of the story is that I should have a good time and what mom and dad don't know about, they don't need to know about?

Don't be a smart ass, Mikaela. You know what I'm saying.

I don't, Uncle Mike, I'm sorry.

I don't know. Don't be like me, I guess. You look at these kids down here and I see stupid, stupid things, and I think lucky, I hope she gets lucky. That dumbass kid'll be lucky if he don't get knocked out tonight for mouthing off to the wrong guy. And statistically, they're all going to wake up tomorrow, Mikaela. The odds of things going wrong in the ultimate sense are just so astronomically small. I don't care what your mom and dad want me to say. Don't live your life in fear. It's okay to be a kid, you know, just don't be a stupid one if you can help it. You know, don't you?

I know, Uncle Mike.

You're a good kid.

I know. And you're a good man. I know you can't see it. It's the one thing you can't see. You can see everyone else but yourself, but I wish you could. I wish you could see yourself the way I do, the way other people do, even with the stupid detective hat on, maybe even especially with the hat on.

What are you trying to do to me, kid?

I'm trying to help you.

Gawd, kiddo, when did you grow up right in front of my eyes?

I haven't, I'm just, you know, figuring things out.

Let's get you home. You're not going to learn anything down here you've never seen before. I think you already know this, but if you ever get into trouble, and I mean real trouble, don't call your mother or father, call me. Right away. Don't ever hesitate.

I will. And, Uncle Mike...

Yeah?

It's not true, the simulation. I don't care what any of those professors say. Even if they could prove it, what would that really prove, that it's not real? That Professor Kay wasn't real? That you're not real, all the cases you've worked, all the days we've lived? Nothing would feel any less real to anyone. I've thought about it and it doesn't matter. It doesn't matter, because we matter. We are here. It is happening.

You're right, Mikaela. Yes. That's what I was trying to say. All this is happening. Don't be afraid of it. Be in it. Be here.

The Light in Heavy Basin

The starfighter appeared on A-Station's passive detective systems a day before it met Denera's atmosphere. Two other deep-space sensors were able to triangulate its position and anticipate its course. There was no question as to its destination. It had dropped out and within minutes set a course to intercept the planet, and though the leaders on Denera had no particular reason to think the ship would be a threat, there was also no reason to think anyone knew they were there. But it was clear the pilot knew something about them. Why else would they be tracking straight for Denera?

Spiro Hanno was the Sheriff of Kalb County, the planet's largest outpost of about two hundred thousand citizens, and security fell to him. The Denerans were not militaristic people—that was why they were here. But they always had half an eye on the system in the chance that the more militaristic peoples within reach ever discovered their quiet, humble little planet. There'd been the occasional ship. A few had even poked around within a few million miles of the planet, but Denera didn't look all that inviting from that distance, and, by design, it didn't look occupied. Hanno had data coming in through the night from the Farside observation station and the Oceanic. They'd both confirmed: the starfighter was coming, and Spiro Hanno needed to know why.

Within hours of its approach, they'd narrowed down its trajectory to the western hemisphere. The question now was where the ship would head when it arrived. Hanno had six parties out covering the continent. It hadn't leaked to the citizenry yet, and he wanted to keep it that way until they knew what they were dealing with. Hanno had his best deputy out in the scablands where the craft was most likely to crack the atmosphere. He'd given orders to stay hidden and observe, which is just what Deacon Dawes was doing the morning the starfighter arrived. Dawes had hidden his hopper in a valley and climbed to a useful vantage point on the western cliffs facing the scablands' Heavy Basin.

The starfighter entered the atmosphere and didn't waste any time getting to the ground. The ship was smoking heavily as it descended.

"Looks like this thing got clipped pretty good, sheriff," Dawes said, staring up at the sky through his oculus. "But, damn, looks like a hawk of a starship. Never seen that make before, but definitely Etteran."

Spiro Hanno, on the eastern side of the hemisphere, was watching on his office's monitor. "Sure looks like it. Keep eyes on it, Deek."

Deacon Dawes saw the starfighter come down, smoking heavily and on a steep descent, hugging the cliffs dangerously when it got down close to ground level. Deacon watched from the rim of the basin as the ship blew right past him, smoke and fire spewing out the back end of the dorsal thruster. The atmosphere was doing that Etteran starfighter no favors. Deek gave it a fifty-fifty chance of quickly evolving into a fiery crater, but somehow at about ten meters above ground level, the thrusters blew back hard and took enough edge off to prevent a severe crash. The starfighter jolted to a stop. A few seconds later, Deek heard the soundwave from the harsh touchdown blast by.

"Best count your teeth, cowboy," Deek said.

He half expected to see the pilot come running out with his hair on fire, but the rear hatch stayed shut. Deek kept his oculus trained on the starfighter, but no one got out. It was a bit unusual for someone to land like that with the engines aflame and then hang out in the ship while it smoldered. He relayed the update to Hanno.

"Might be injured," Deacon Dawes said. "Want me to go have a look?"

"No, I do not," Hanno said. "Intervene as a last resort, Deek. Just let the situation develop."

"Roger, Kalb City. I'll let you know."

The doors stayed shut for so long Deacon Dawes figured the pilot had to be dead or unconscious. The engine smoked for hours and then began to peter out. As the evening began to set in, the rear hatch cracked open.

"Got movement here, Hanno," Deek said, and he was shocked to see who stepped out, and her state of being.

The woman was wearing a respirator—strange, because even wounded, the starfighter would have had readings on the atmosphere, if she'd bothered to read them or knew how.

"She sure don't look the part of a fighter pilot, Hanno," Deek said. "She's not even wearing a jump suit."

"Passenger?" Spiro Hanno said.

"Maybe the pilot's hurt or dead?"

"Could be. No sense speculating, Deek. Just keep your eyes on."

"Roger."

Deek watched as the young lady sat on the rear gate looking around the desolate valley. She gave off decidedly unmilitary vibes. For one, even flaming, any pilot beyond a rank novice would have circled around a bit to find a better place to set down—some shade, a source of water, something. Second, her behavior seemed undirected, objectiveless passivity and a distinct air of despair in her manner. He caught her crying as the sun went down.

"Don't that just yank at the heart, Hanno?" he said. "We're going to end up picking her up anyway, right? Might as well spare her the anguish."

"Negative, Deek," Hanno said. "Still a chance she can get herself sorted, or maybe she'll have got off a message on the way here. Could get picked up."

"And then what?"

"This is a problem we don't need. Let's see if it fixes itself before we go stuffing our noses in it."

"Okay, boss."

As the sun set, the young lady went back inside and the rear hatch closed. Deek spent the night on the cliff with his oculus trained on the starfighter.

Early the next morning, the woman climbed atop the ship with a scope and began to survey the landscape.

"Oh, hell," Deek said. "I think she's going to make a break for it."

Spiro Hanno watched from the station in Kalb City. He didn't like what he saw, but he had to agree.

"We gonna let her, boss?" Deek asked. "She's gonna fry down there. If help were coming, she sure as hell wouldn't be cutting out into the desert, at daybreak no less."

"Hell is right," Hanno said.

It was trouble. It'd been over sixty years since the Denerans had splintered off the Trasp colony. Hanno's father had spent over two years in space looking for a site like Denera. Spiro Hanno had heard all the stories, of the wars, of the exodus, and for the sake of the old-timers who'd lived through it all and his kids who shouldn't have to, Sheriff Hanno didn't want their position revealed after all this time. Not to Trasp, not to the Etterans, not to nobody.

"Do I get her?" Deek said.

"What's your timeframe to get to the basin floor?"

"Two hours tops, boss. Half hour if I fly out there in the hopper."

"Hell."

"She spent an awful long time eying up the canyon to the Hot Basin."

"Standby," Hanno said.

"You're not going to make me watch this disaster, boss? I know she's Etteran, but damn, she don't look like much of a threat."

"It's not her I'm worried about, Deek. Standby."

Deacon Dawes grumbled and framed his oculus's sights on the starfighter in the basin again. What he saw next changed the equation.

"Hell, Hanno. She's got a kid down there with her. Looks like eight, maybe nine. I ain't standing by no more."

Deacon hadn't seen the boy the previous day, probably because the mother had kept him in the ship out of an abundance of caution on the strange planet. Deacon started for the hopper double-time. The sun was rising fast.

Deek set out across the basin, and opted to set the hopper down in a crag where they wouldn't see him coming. He planned to approach on foot without it seeming like a ship was running them down. The mother and the boy were walking along a narrow canyon along the basin floor when Deek approached on foot, he thought, in plain enough sight that he wouldn't startle them. Apparently, though, they weren't even looking straight ahead.

Deek said hello and the woman screamed, recoiling and stooping to protect her son. She rushed to pull out what looked to be a charged Etteran bolt pistol and pointed it at Deek's head.

"Whoa, there, ma'am," he said, putting his hands up to calm the situation.

"Who are you, and what do you want?" she said.

He pulled the cloth mask away from his mouth so she could see his face.

"My name is Deacon," Deek said, "and I certainly don't mean you or your boy any harm. Fact, I came down to make sure harm didn't come to you."

"Is that so?"

Deek nodded. "Fact, if I wanted harm to come to you, I'da let you keep walking toward the canyon wall you was eying up from your ship. 'Bout a ten-mile walk, not a drop of water, and with the sun coming up, you'd both be dead by sundown."

"Is that so?" she said, seeming to trust there was truth to what Deek was saying.

"That's so," he said.

"Who are you?" she repeated. "This planet is meant to be deserted."

"There's more than a few of us disagree, and a lucky bit of business for you and your boy on that point."

"That would seem so," the woman conceded. "You have an outpost nearby?"

"Not nearby," Deek said. "We saw you coming. Your entry wasn't exactly inconspicuous, wouldn't you say?"

The woman nodded.

"What's your name, young man?" Deek asked the boy.

He looked at his mother, who shook her head at him. The boy didn't respond.

"All right," Deek said. "You folks want to die out here in the desert or would you prefer to come meet your new friends?" He smiled. "Come on."

He led the way to the hopper and the mother and son followed reluctantly, but it didn't take long for them to realize that Deek's courtesy was genuine. He stopped at the ship again while they waited for the davjet to come get Deek's hopper. Deek pulled the transponder and diagnostic data from the starfighter.

Neither the mother nor the boy opened up much on the two-hour ride back to Kalb City. They had the look of folks who recognized their fate now relied upon the charity of others, and, Deek recognized, that for Etterans, that had to be an uncomfortable proposition.

Hanno was at the port to meet all six deputies on the detail as well as the davjet pilot, and it was an uneasy meeting, because no one really knew what to do with their new guests. The presence of Etterans on Denera would certainly set off a charged debate about the fate of the mother and the boy, and Hanno was old enough to know that debate could go to some uncomfortable places awful fast. He ordered his deputies to strictest secrecy and set about interviewing the woman to figure out how she'd come to be on Denera.

She and Hanno had a long discussion in a quiet side-office in the port's admin wing. She wasn't as initially forthcoming as Hanno would've liked. But he came to believe it wasn't anything other than dumb luck that had brought her there. She'd rushed the boy into the starfighter when their home on Attis was hit. And when things got too hot to wait for her husband to get back to them, he'd told her to take off. They'd barely gotten out on autopilot, and not unscathed at that, and, according to the woman, who purported to be a Mrs. Keenan Stock of Etterus, it had been the autopilot and a random scan through reconnaissance logs that set them on a path to the safest uninhabited planet they could cruise to.

"Who are you people?" she said, after Hanno seemed satisfied that he wasn't going to get any better answers. "You're not flying any colours. Not of Trasp nor Etterus. What are you going to do with us?"

"That is complicated," Hanno said. "It would certainly have been less complicated for us if you hadn't found us here, ma'am, but it happens now that you have."

"I'd like to go home."

"That's interesting," Hanno said. "Seems to me like you fled home fast enough to smoke out your engines."

"You know what I mean, sheriff."

"We're rather isolated here. Only ship on the planet capable of getting you back to Etterus, if there is one, was the one you flew in on, which, I hear is in pretty rough shape."

"You wouldn't let us go if it could fly, would you?"

Hanno thought about whether he would be straight with Mrs. Stock.

"Right now? No. I couldn't let you go. Our stability here has relied upon no one knowing we existed. I'm hopeful we can come to an understanding. But Deek was left with a tough choice, ma'am, and he chose to save your lives. In return for that kindness, I suppose we're going to ask you for your patience and cooperation while we figure out what to do about you now that he did. It's not a straightforward situation you and your son are in exactly."

"Are we in danger, sheriff?"

"Relative to the Hot Basin without a canteen, ma'am? Your patience, please. We're civil people, but we too have cause to be cautious. Fair enough?"

Mrs. Stock nodded.

Deek was waiting in the hallway when the sheriff left the office. Hanno could see the young deputy was more invested in the situation than he cared for him to be.

"What are you going to do with her, Hanno?"

Spiro Hanno shook his head. "Do me a favor and call Pip," he said. "She's going to raise holy hell with me, but who better to trust when you need it than family?"

Hanno briefed the deputies, swearing them all to secrecy, and in the moment, it seemed the best of limited options. Kalb City was a small place, and her people had ample cause to be suspicious and even hostile to outsiders, especially Etteran ones. But as Sheriff Hanno put it, Mrs. Stock didn't need her day to get any worse, and being the focus of a planet-wide debate where her identity, liberty, safety, and even her life would be imperiled wasn't exactly the kind of welcome Spiro Hanno had in mind for a harmless young art teacher and her eight-year-old son.

"How long do you think you'll be able to keep this a secret, Dad?" Pippa asked when she got to the port. "She even sounds Etteran. What the hell do I tell the neighbors?"

"Tell them to mind their own damn business and come see me if they have a problem."

"And Mat?"

"I trusted him to look out for my daughter, didn't I? Now, I'm trusting him with her."

Pip shook her head. "This isn't going to end well, Dad."

"The longer she's among us, the softer the landing's going to be when she's found out, Pip. Just do your best."

"So, is this permanent or what?"

"Well, not in your house, but unless you know someone who can repair an Etteran starfighter, I'd prepare Mrs. Stock to settle in."

Pip sighed.

The day's problem quietly became the week's. And, to Deek and Hanno's surprise, after a month or so no one had raised any alarm at all. Pip convinced the neighbors that the woman was a childhood friend who had suddenly and contentiously split with her husband, and Mrs. Stock had quickly learned to say very little and to say it quietly enough that her accent wasn't so prominent or alarming. The boy, Ayrik, meanwhile, with the company of Pip's kids, seamlessly adapted to Deneran culture, which wasn't so different to Etteran life that he seemed foreign very long.

Within several months, Ayrik was sent to school, and Mrs. Stock herself went to work for the Kalb City maintenance department. Soon after she was given her own water truck and care of the trees in the southwest quadrant, which she cared for as diligently as any of Kalb City's own workers would.

In the months that followed, every several weeks or so, though, Mrs. Stock would approach Sheriff Hanno about the starfighter, and each time he would deflect, stating that he was working on it, trying to get someone qualified to look at it. But to her, Hanno didn't seem all that eager to help. After a while, she gave up on him and went to Deacon Dawes.

Deek tried his best to make sense of the diagnostics, and he often needed help from Mrs. Stock to read through the script in the obscure files of the Etteran diagnostics manual. A few months later, she told him to stop calling her Mrs. Stock. It was Keenan now. Just Keenan. And as helpful as Deek tried to be, he couldn't help but hope he never got the ship off the ground.

Hanno sanctioned two trips out to Heavy Basin the following year. The first with himself, Deek, and Keenan, which bore no fruit. The second, with Deek, Keenan, and a hopper mechanic Grayson, who was a friend of Deek's. Grayson was suspicious but seemed earnest in his efforts to get the starfighter powered up again. But it had spent months idle in the desert sun, and it hadn't been in flying shape to begin with. Between the heat, the wind, the sand, the sun, and the passage of time, the starfighter was looking less and less space worthy, and for Keenan and Ayrik, Denera was beginning to feel more and more like home.

One particularly hot afternoon in Kalb City several months after the most recent trip to Heavy Basin, Sheriff Hanno happened upon Keenan, he on his way to a council meeting, she on her usual route, lounging beneath one of her farroe oaks. She seemed pleasantly engaged in a respite from both the sun and her work. Hanno stopped his vehicle to say hello.

"Mrs. Stock," he said.

"Hello, sheriff," she said. "Keenan, please."

"Hot one," he said, noticing the sweat bleeding into her clothing.

She nodded.

"There was something I wanted to broach with you at some point, Keenan, if you're open to a conversation?"

"Sounds serious."

"Delicate," Hanno said. "Not easy, but probably not something an intelligent woman such as yourself couldn't have predicted."

"The ship?"

"Like I said," Hanno replied.

"Grayson's been asking me about it," she said, "and I was asking him about you folks—all the ships that got your parents here. Ever since, I've been noticing parts of the ships all over town."

"Yeah, the Starcatcher's got a bit of a theme in the lounge that probably makes a little more sense after that conversation."

"It's tough," she said. "I realized a while back that as earnest as Deek is, he's no mechanic, and even if he were, he's not a miracle worker. But if I give Grayson permission to go out there and husk the ship, it's almost like I'm giving up hope of ever going back. And the truth is that if I could snap my fingers and make it fly, I'm not certain I would anymore."

"If you'd like a second opinion to be sure you're getting a fair price for it, I'm happy to advocate on your behalf."

"Mat's actually been helping me with it, estimating price per kilogram and transport costs."

"That's good of him," Hanno said.

"Yes, but he's got ulterior motives. Pip too, I think, good as she's been to us. They want their house back."

"You ready, you think?"

"To move out?" she said, thinking. "Yeah. It'll be quieter without the little ones around, and I think Rik's ready for his own space."

"And you?"

Keenan smiled and shook her head. "Me and Rik got used to being alone together a long time ago." She shrugged. "It's peaceful here. It really is."

Hanno nodded. "Have yourself a fine afternoon, Keenan."

"You too, sheriff."

A month or so later, Spiro Hanno heard from Pip that Keenan had given Grayson permission to husk the starfighter. It turned out to be considerably heavier than expected, and Keenan was able to do better than a meager down payment on a modest place. She ended up purchasing outright a nice little townhouse down the street from Pip and Mat's. And just like that, Keenan Stock had become a regular Deneran from the Settler District of Kalb City. A short time later, Hanno learned, she and Deek were seeing quite a bit of each other. And not long after, they were engaged to be married.

It was in the weeks before Deacon Dawes and the former Mrs. Stock's wedding that the scandal finally broke. An ex of Deek's, more out of curiosity than jealousy tried to figure out who the mysterious woman he was marrying actually was. She found no childhood friends in the city, no school records, and no birth certificate for Keenan Stock. Like many others in Kalb City, she'd heard rumors of an Etteran starfighter that had crash landed on the other side of the continent. Between the sudden appearance of Mrs. Stock and her son, her strange accent, and her missing past, Deek's ex had put two and two together. Fortunately for Sheriff Hanno, she approached him first, which put him in a position to soften the blow. Hanno told the young woman he'd look into it and get back to her and prepared the Stocks and Pip's family, and then he called the Kalb News Bureau and granted an interview. Hanno calmly explained that, yes, there'd been an Etteran among them, and she'd been a welcome addition

212

to the city's work force who had voluntarily husked her ship, adding to the outpost's limited metal supplies and cutting herself off from any chance of returning home forever. He explained the choice that Deek had made that morning out in the Heavy Basin and that it was the only decision a decent people could have made. The only thing he'd have changed about his actions, if any, was keeping the secret from the community for so long, but he was glad it was now out in the open.

Sheriff Hanno expected there to be calls for his resignation, but the response to his interview was far more muted than he'd anticipated. It seemed as though he'd banked enough trust with the community over the years that, though it was a big withdrawal, he hadn't quite overdrawn his account. It helped that Mrs. Stock herself came forward to explain herself, and her graciousness and gratitude toward the Deneran people for their hospitality turned her from a source of concern to a sympathetic figure in the eyes of many Denerans.

This, Sheriff Hanno thought, would finally draw the incident from that morning in the Heavy Basin to a close. It was about the best outcome everyone could have hoped for under the circumstances. The Stocks were alive and happy. The outpost was still a secret to the Trasps and Etterans, and Deek and Keenan were getting married. Hanno didn't regret a thing. Over the years, he'd celebrated at their wedding, congratulated Deek and Keenan on the birth of two children, and had even gotten to know young Rik quite well as the boy grew into a teenager with an avid interest in scouting and law enforcement. He was such a personable kid, Hanno thought he'd make an excellent deputy, and he had a great example to look up to in his step-father. Both Hanno himself and Deek were looking forward to a day in the near future when they could pin a star on young Rik for the first time.

Hanno was counting down his final six months before retirement, on a morning much like the one eight years prior when Keenan and Rik had arrived, when the Oceanic picked up a signal from the passive monitors at the edge of the system. The ping was confirmed, triangulated, and followed over the following sixteen hours, and though they'd picked up passing ships often enough over the years, none of them had given him the sinking feeling in his stomach that this one did. They couldn't get a transponder lock on it, but Hanno almost didn't need technological confirmation to tell him what his gut told him. It was Etteran.

When it got close enough for a visual from Farside the night before it arrived, the picture on the scope was clear—a starfighter similar in make to the former Mrs. Stock's ship. Hanno suspected this ship, though, was neither damaged nor piloted by an amateur. He expected to be seeing the pilot soon, and tracking as it was, steadily for Denera, Hanno knew the time of arrival.

The following afternoon, just ahead of Hanno's expected time frame, the starfighter touched down at an inconspicuous distance from Kalb City. It made no flyover and kept low enough to the horizon so that few in the city were even aware of its presence beyond the city officials. It hadn't even made the news yet. Sheriff Hanno went out to greet the pilot, grateful for the uncharacteristically muted approach from the Etteran military craft.

He arrived at the scene to an opening rear hatch and a middle-aged man wearing the uniform of a high-ranking officer, though he couldn't tell what rank at distance. The sheriff approached alone.

The Etteran officer stood, back straight, his feet planted firmly on the dry Deneran plain, awaiting the sheriff's arrival.

"Welcome, sir," Hanno said, nodding at the officer.

"Am I?" he responded. "I encountered a powerful jamming signal as I entered the planet's space. A sign of welcome, no doubt?"

"Far more welcoming than the alternative, I think you'd agree," Hanno said. "We like our privacy here."

"I see," the pilot said. "Officer?"

"Sheriff Spiro Hanno, and I gather by your uniform and epaulettes you're an Etteran Colonel?"

"Commodore."

"Commodore? Oh, well, then sincerely, welcome, commodore. I'm going to take a stab in the dark here and guess you might go by Commodore Stock, then?"

The pilot's eyes cracked slightly wider despite the well-practiced composure of a veteran fighter pilot.

"I wouldn't have expected my reputation to precede me this far out."

Hanno shook his head. "Not your reputation, sir." He could see the commodore processing, struggling to keep his emotions hidden.

"What are you saying then, sir?"

"I suspect you've been traveling a while in your search, no? And given we have much to discuss, I'd consider it an act of good faith on your part if you powered down your weapons systems, your engines and your transponder and joined me at my daughter's table for dinner, Commodore Stock."

"We didn't pick up the starfighter anywhere on our approach, sheriff. Will you tell me, please, are they alive? Are they here?"

"Yes, and yes, commodore." Hanno said.

He watched the commodore work to contain a complex wave of emotions, from shock to disbelief to relief and who knows what else.

The commodore shook his head and spoke. "Derrian, please power everything down and join me outside. We've been invited to dinner."

There was a long pause. "What is this, Willem?" a woman's voice came back.

"I think we've found them," Commodore Stock said. "Please."

Sheriff Hanno nodded, as if to reassure the commodore. And the two men stood for some time looking at each other awkwardly, the sheriff unwilling to reveal more in that setting, and the commodore, having taken a measure of the sheriff, knew better than to ask.

The woman who stepped out the rear hatch of the starfighter also wore an Etteran officer's uniform, and Hanno watched as she assessed their surroundings, scanning the horizon for vessels and positions where fire could come from, exposed as they were out on the plain.

"You're safe here, ma'am," Hanno said.

"You wear no colors," she said, eying the sheriff suspiciously. "Are you Trasp?"

"I'm Spiro Hanno," the sheriff said. "And you're on neutral ground."

The commodore gave the woman a reassuring look that confirmed the sheriff's suspicion—she was more than a junior officer to him.

"Please," Hanno said, gesturing toward his vehicle.

Hanno took a roundabout route to Pip's house, trying to avoid the spectacle that would doubtless arise from two fully uniformed officers of the Etteran Guild riding with the sheriff of Kalb County through the heart of the city. In the vehicle, the silence was stark.

When he got them to Pip's house, she quickly ushered them inside.

"What'll you bring home next, Dad?" she said under her breath.

"You be good, Pippa," he said.

Mat greeted both guests as they entered the living room, offering a seat. He'd just got in from work, and was surely not expecting Etteran houseguests.

"It's going to take some time," Hanno said, advising them to sit. "We're just as shocked by your presence as you two must be yourselves. We'd ask you, please, for your patience."

"Certainly," the commodore said, gesturing for his companion to sit and following beside her.

"No chance for this to go sideways," Pip whispered to Spiro Hanno as they stepped into the kitchen. "What do you suppose Etterans would like for dinner, Dad?"

"Same as anyone else, I guess, Pip. I'm sure they'll be happy for a homecooked meal."

Before long, Hanno saw Deek's cruiser pull up. It was him and Keenan and Rik. Out of the corner of his eye, the Sheriff saw the commodore stand in anticipation. Hanno signaled for him to wait there and went to meet the Dawes family at the front door, conferring with Keenan and Rik to be sure Deek had properly prepared them for what was awaiting. He wanted to confirm that no matter what happened, if they chose to stay, he would defend that choice no matter the cost, and if they chose to leave, they would be free to. They were both unequivocal. "Our family is here, sheriff," Keenan said.

"So it is," Hanno agreed, and he stood aside as they entered the home.

When they finally stepped into the living room, it seemed to Hanno like there was some galaxy-wide record set for suppressed emotions. Though, eventually, Rik was the one to bridge the gap and embrace his father. Hanno stepped in to make introductions between Deek and Commodore Stock, who took the opportunity to introduce his wife, the new Mrs. Stock to the former Mrs. Stock, who were both gracious if a bit apprehensive.

"We thought you were dead," Rik said after an awkward silence.

They all sat, and the commodore leaned forward to talk to his eldest son. "I was deployed after the Attis attack. From that day for two straight years. It was the fiercest stretch of the war—"

"Was, you said?" Keenan interrupted. "Does that mean it's over?"

There was an apprehensive nod from the commodore and his spouse. "There's been an armistice. It has held for two years without violation. A tenuous peace," he said.

"All that time you were fighting?" Rik asked.

Commodore Stock nodded. "You were both declared dead," he said. "But I didn't want to believe it, not without confirmation—debris, a witness, DNA. Over time, I started wondering what kind of information might have been in that starfighter's navigation drives, and we discovered that the squadron had done some reconnaissance work in the year before the Attis attack. Derrian was able to track down in Archives the list of survey targets for that starfighter you took. This planet was site sixty-two."

"It's very gracious of you," Keenan said to Mrs. Stock. "To aid Willem in searching for us. It can't have been easy for you."

She smiled. "I didn't imagine we'd find a trace of you, and certainly not alive, and in such circumstances. But it was important for him to look."

"We're grateful," Keenan said.

"It's strange," Derrian said. "It's unexpected, but I am very glad to see you both alive. You know Willem says very little about such things, but I can tell it has worn on his heart."

"Ours too," Rik said. "Only we didn't have a way to search."

"You look well," Commodore Stock said to his son. "Healthy, strong—"

"Handsome," Mrs. Stock interjected. "I've only seen pictures of a boy, and here we find a young man nearly ready to don the colours of Etterus."

Rik smiled, and Keenan sat back ever so slightly in her chair.

"Shall we eat," Sheriff Hanno asked from the doorway. "Pip tells me dinner's about ready."

"Smells heavenly," Commodore Stock said, standing.

They adjourned to the dining room, and sat. For most of the meal, the silverware made more noise than the diners, clinking against plates as the eight people enjoyed the goodness of the meal in silence.

"You've been quite hospitable, ma'am" the commodore said to Pip. "And you as well, Sheriff, though I get the sense that our presence here is not entirely welcome."

The sheriff smiled. "My grandparents and your grandparents made quite the habit of killing the other. They did it for long enough my parents' generation thought it a better course of action to cut ties with their own parents for the sake of their kids. And they came here. There's been no colours and no war on Denera, so the sight of an Etteran starfighter outside Kalb City, well, it won't take long to raise the anxiety level, let's say."

"I see," Commodore Stock said. "What little we saw on the way here...seemed a peaceful place."

"I was of two minds that morning your wife appeared in the desert. The smart thing, I kept telling myself was to let the desert take care of the problem for us. Of course, I didn't know her name yet, but Keenan was in a bad spot, and then Rik appeared, and Deek went running out into that desert too fast for me to tell him otherwise. While they was in the air on the way back here, all I could think was what the hell I was going to do with them. And then I got a chance to look a pair of Etterans in the eyes that afternoon, and all I could think was who in all of creation would allow a harm to come upon a pair such as them. And to think our grandparents had deliberately been doing it to each other for decades, and for what?"

Hanno shook his head.

"I'm ashamed Deek acted before I told him to. Been so since I laid eyes on the both of them. And I tell you, commodore, I got hope that one day your grandchildren will meet each other in the depths of space and the thought will never cross their minds that it's even an option to blow the hell out of each other."

The commodore looked across the table at the sheriff, processing, taking in the implications of his statement. Keenan was here, settled, among family with these people, and here, his son, without the need to don colours. The years of war. His personal losses.

Mrs. Derrian Stock seemed to come to the understanding at that moment that Keenan and Ayrik's apprehension wasn't what she'd thought but more fear for their family and friends here, and the sheriff could see the second Mrs. Stock calculating.

"I don't suppose the Etteran Guild would write off a commodore and a Lt. colonel as lost in space in peacetime and not go looking if you didn't make it home?"

"Not a chance, sheriff," the commodore said.

"I figured as much, commodore, and to be honest, I'm happy to hear it. Takes any hard decisions off the table, at least on our end. All that leaves us is trust."

Sheriff Hanno pulled his bolt pistol from his belt and neutralized it, handing it to Deek and gesturing for him to pass it down the table.

"This is my grandfather's. I'd like you to have it, commodore."

Deek looked at Spiro Hanno doubtfully, and Hanno gestured for Deek to pass it down the table.

"I've had a lot of deputies over the years. None better than Deek, as it happens, but that's just an aside. I learned early on that authority wasn't in the weapon you wielded or even in the way that you wielded it. Real authority was in handing a weapon to your people and knowing that they'd wield it with the same care and considerations you would."

Mrs. Stock looked flabbergasted by the sheriff's gesture. She'd never seen a man do such a thing. The commodore took the weapon in his hand, gracefully accepted it and set it in his lap.

"I'm happy you found us, Willem," Keenan Dawes said.

The commodore reached across the table and took his son's hand, and then, after releasing it, found his wife Derrian's hand beside his, there to take it up again.

As the meal ended, word came to Deek and Hanno that the starfighter had been spotted outside Kalb City, and residents were beginning to congregate and ask questions of the deputies who'd gone out to investigate the call. It occurred to Hanno that the longer the Stocks remained, the greater the probability the situation would grow complicated enough that he alone wouldn't be able to control it. He suggested they say their goodbyes then and there.

"I had hoped..." Willem Stock began to say.

"I know, sir," Hanno said. "Circumstances, though."

Stock nodded.

Sheriff Hanno and Deek took the Stocks back out to the plain after Rik and Keenan had said their goodbyes. The only thing that was said in the vehicle was Hanno suggesting that, for the sake of appearances, Mr. and Mrs. Stock should visit a few more planets on the list instead of returning to Etterus directly, and both seemed amenable.

The scene at the starfighter was more than Hanno and Deek were expecting. A crowd of hundreds had gathered at the ship, many armed, with firearms, wrenches, long metal poles, and though they'd been listening on their earpieces en route, neither Deacon Dawes nor the sheriff himself had a sense for the tension that the starfighter's presence had stirred in the community. The sight of the crowd and their hand-lights encircling the base of the Stocks' starfighter caused a sudden palpable tension in the sheriff's vehicle as they approached.

"Cut us a path, Deek," Hanno said as the vehicle came to a stop.

Deek got out and summoned two of the deputies that had been trying unsuccessfully to keep onlookers back from the ship. Deek ushered the deputies to the sheriff's vehicle, which prompted a large portion of the crowd to follow.

"Rest assured," Hanno told the Stocks. "No harm will come to anyone tonight." And he got out of the vehicle, opened their door and placed his hand over Mrs. Derrian Stock's shoulder, and they all walked behind Deek as the other two deputies cleared a path to the back hatch of the starfighter.

"Where's your wife, Deek?" a voice in the crowd shouted.

"She's home," Deacon Dawes shouted back.

And the crowd parted, looking on as the Etterans were escorted to their ship, some in disbelief, some angry, most merely observing the unusual occurrence. But no one raised a hand toward the outsiders.

As they entered the back hatch, Commodore Stock gestured to the old bolt pistol he had tucked into his belt and nodded. Sheriff Hanno returned the nod and stepped out the back hatch, wishing them luck on their journey home.

The sheriff and his deputies cleared a safe perimeter around the base of the starfighter. Concerned citizens demanded to know about the interlopers.

"You're just letting them go?" someone shouted.

And before any of the deputies or the sheriff had a meaningful chance to answer, the starfighter's engines hummed to life and a puff of hot air compelled the onlookers to step further back. Moments later, the dark plain lit up in a blinding light as a shock of noise and heat struck the onlookers, the engines propelling the commodore's starfighter once more into the air. The vessel slowly rose into the night sky, before shooting out of Denera's atmosphere and tracing a bright point of light into the stars.

Afterword

Rowe here. I'd like to thank you for choosing to spend time with my stories. Each of these stories would be a lifeless, inert collection of words without the vivid imagination of the reader to bring them to life. I do hope you've found something meaningful, entertaining, or enriching in the act of enlivening these stories through the act of reading.

If you appreciate the stories in this collection, I'd also humbly ask that you take a few minutes to review this title so that it might find other like-minded readers who might enjoy it as well. Your feedback truly helps to bring other readers to the stories you enjoyed, and it will help to support their author in creating more. Reader feedback is doubly-important for an indie author like me, who doesn't have the PR machine of a big publishing house to direct reader attention toward my work.

Also, if you've enjoyed this title, more fiction like this is available through my website: RoweLit.com. You'll find novels, as well as other short fiction, in Sci-Fi and other genres, both in print and in audiobook form. So please, check in with me there from time to time for more collections of Sci-Fi shorts like these. I hope to catch up with you again soon.

With much gratitude,

Rowe

Made in United States
Troutdale, OR
05/11/2024

19802565R00141